Join Xena as sh
and joins the battle

*All-new, original adventures from
Boulevard Books!*

BE SURE NOT TO MISS
BOULEVARD'S ALL-NEW SERIES STARRING

ON SALE NOW!

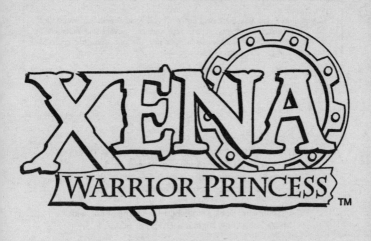

THE EMPTY THRONE

Ru Emerson

BOULEVARD BOOKS, NEW YORK

XENA: WARRIOR PRINCESS: THE EMPTY THRONE
A novel by Ru Emerson. Based on the
Universal television series XENA: WARRIOR PRINCESS,
created by John Schulian and Robert Tapert.

A Boulevard Book / published by arrangement with
MCA Publishing Rights, a Division of MCA, Inc.

PRINTING HISTORY
Boulevard edition / October 1996

The Putnam Berkley World Wide Web site address is
http://www.berkley.com

ISBN: 1-57297-200-9

BOULEVARD
Boulevard Books are published by The Berkley Publishing Group,
200 Madison Avenue, New York, New York 10016.
BOULEVARD and its logo are trademarks
belonging to Berkley Publishing Corporation.

PRINTED IN THE UNITED STATES OF AMERICA

10 9 8 7 6 5 4 3 2 1

Acknowledgments

This is a novel I could never have written without a lot of things happening first: I'm extremely grateful to the Action Pack (which I watched late nights for years when I should probably have been writing instead), to the creators of Hercules who came up with the Xena character—and for the creative types who are responsible for Xena being who and what she is today: a gutsy lady with a deep sense of honor and a truly nifty fighting style as well as a terrific, dry sense of humor. Thanks also to Lucy Lawless and Renee O'Connor for the beautiful on-screen friendship I've done my best to re-create on the printed page—and to the great AOL Xena fans. You know who you are.

To Doug.

For Roberta,
who did her furry darndest to keep me
from getting it done.

And to Lea Day,
who suggested a certain quasi-mortal character
and a certain line.
I'm still laughing, lady.

1

"... I'm not asking for miracles! You know? Just—just a little respect!" Gabrielle shook her head sharply, sending the long, blond hair flying. She glanced sidelong at her companion. "You're not laughing at me, are you?"

Xena shifted her grip on her horse's bridle and caught the corners of her mouth between her teeth to hold back a smile. "Of course not. But even a *little* respect under the circumstances—well, it sounds to me like you want a miracle."

"I—all right." Gabrielle sighed. "Not respect, just a few basic manners! I know we were in a tavern, I *understand* that isn't the same as the Oracle's Grove at Delphi, or the Academy in Athens, and of course I can see that even some of the same men could behave differently in all those places. Still, I was minding my own business, I wasn't even *talking* to any of them, and I certainly wasn't acting like a—like one of *those* women, and I just don't see why being in a tavern means a man doesn't need to behave himself around a woman who isn't behaving like a strumpet, do you?"

1

"Of course not." Xena turned the horse into a narrow, grassy ravine that meandered north. The afternoon was turning hot, and the last water had been left behind at midday. Gabrielle scrambled along the rocky, brushy wall to ease past them and take the lead. "But, Gabrielle, it isn't realistic to expect men like the ones in that tavern to show any kind of manners anywhere—except bad ones. You come from a village, Gabrielle, and you've traveled with me for long enough to know that some men . . ."

Gabrielle sighed as she walked up the slope. "All right, I know how things *are,* I just can't see why they have to *be* that way! And you'll have to admit that for once, I was doing exactly what you said for me to do, I was on the far side of the building with the innkeep's wife!" She cast her companion a dark glance, her hazel eyes stormy.

"And some soldier who just got back from Sparta and was burying the dust of the road in a large mug of mead came over to get another mugful from the innkeep's wife— and pinched you." Xena's ice-blue gaze was briefly not at all amused, though her voice remained light; Gabrielle, her own attention all for the increasingly rough way ahead, didn't notice. "Next time, do the other thing I told you. When someone lays hands on you, yell. Then, even if the damage is done, he won't try anything again, with you or anyone else. Unless he thinks about it first."

The sigh was more exasperated this time. "Oh, Xena, you know how it is—I just hate to feel that you need to take care of me all the time!"

"I know that. I don't take care of you all the time, though; you've talked yourself out of some serious situations all by yourself and you've helped me out of a few. Remember what you said a while back, 'You fight and I'll talk'? You talk just fine, especially when fighting won't work. Everyone has something he or she does best."

2

"And you fight." Gabrielle's voice sounded flat.

Xena tugged at her long skirt. "So? The mannerless clod who pinched you knows how to fight, almost anyone can fight. I'm better at it than he is, but it's still the same thing. Nearly anyone can learn how to kill—that doesn't take talent, skill, or anything really important. You do something a little more unique, Gabrielle. You create."

"I don't really." The girl paused a moment to eye her companion, before turning her attention back to the ground in front of her. "I take the stories everyone knows, that's all—"

"Not true. Not everyone knows them, or maybe they've heard them before, but the stories didn't have much to do with them. You can take a story like that and make it important to people, make them care. You're every bit as good as that boy we left at the Athens Academy. The one who closed his eyes when he chanted."

"Homer," Gabrielle said promptly, and sighed; one hand remained briefly above the branch before she shook her head, grabbed for the hold, and moved upward. "Except he was going to change his name to Orion. I can't think why; Homer's a nice name. You know, I wish he could've seen Ilium—Troy, sorry—and Helen. I think he'd have made a wonderful story of all that. You know, the war, the men who came to fight it—all that."

"Maybe. Maybe you'll do a better story; you could've had his place at the Academy if you'd been more selfish, you know."

"I *was* more selfish," Gabrielle asserted rather breathlessly. "I wanted to stay with you. Besides, I can learn more tales out here—not just the ones you and I live but the ones we hear, doing all this traveling—than I'd ever get in the Academy."

"I suppose."

3

"Sure." She jumped from rock to rock; Xena found a way along the damp, muddy ravine that her horse could manage, and slowly fell a little behind. Gabrielle drew a deep breath and finally went on. "But I wasn't just being selfish that way—I mean, wanting to stay with you. I guess it's all right for some people to get their tales secondhand at the Academy, and then apply their own way of telling to make them fresh. I just like being out in the real world, learning stories from the people who lived them, or living them myself. Besides, Homer will be truly happy there. He'll fit in properly, and he won't have to spend half his life arguing with his father about how he should tell his stories, will he?"

Xena eyed her companion's back thoughtfully. Gabrielle often came across to outsiders as a chattering, silly young girl, but there were unexpected depths to her; she was kind and honest. And perceptive. The warrior shook her head. *Let's not get all weepy-eyed, here. She's a nice kid and also a good cook; you'd have starved on your own by now.* "Well—I'm glad you feel that way about it. It's never a good idea to want something you can't have, especially if you deliberately turned it down."

Gabrielle turned to glance down at her; she was smiling faintly and her eyes seemed amused. "Oh—I know that."

Silence for some moments, except for the jingle of harness, as the two women clambered up the ravine; Xena's horse came placidly at the end of his rein, but all at once he whickered restlessly and nudged her shoulder.

Gabrielle glanced down at him, a frown creasing her brow. "Um—is he trying to tell you there's someone, or a bunch of someones, hiding up there, waiting to jump us?"

"I doubt it; why would anyone hide at the head of a ravine in the middle of nowhere, just in case someone de-

4

cided to drag a horse up it? More likely, he smells water. I've only been in this part of Ithaca once before, but I seem to remember a well not far from here.'' She pressed her companion gently to one side. ''Wait here; we'll check things out first, and I'll let you know.''

''Ah—great! I'll—ah—I'll be right here,'' Gabrielle replied cheerfully, but her hazel eyes were dark with worry.

Xena gave her a reassuring smile, then forged on. The horse was definitely restless; but it wasn't the kind of behavior she'd expect if there were other horses around—or men. He was right behind her, urging her on, butting her shoulder with his head whenever she slowed to check her footing, or the trees and brush ahead. She climbed the increasingly narrow and steep ravine, ears tuned for the least sound that didn't belong in a sleepy summer afternoon in open woodland; both her steps and her mount's were padded by the thick grass, though Xena's footsteps would not have made any sound no matter what was underfoot. Unless she wanted them to.

After one final clamber between enormous boulders, she stepped warily onto level ground, eyes moving swiftly, one hand on the horse's muzzle to keep him quiet. Nothing. Four more long steps brought her out of the brushy tangle and into the open.

There was a small grove to her left—but the young trees were wide-spaced, making it obvious at once that no one could be hiding among the trunks or in the branches. And within the grove itself, she could clearly see the matted, furry-leaved herb that had been planted all around the trees, as well as the narrow, well-tended path that led to a shrine of some sort. She crossed the open ground to the very edge of the rowan saplings. ''Ah. Midwife's shrine to Artemis.'' Such places were unmistakable: here an oak branch supported a small set of stag antlers that had been wrapped with a long garland of pale blue flowers. All around the antlers lay the usual kinds of offerings: a woven grass bowl of young apples, a branch sprouting leaves and tiny, hard green olives, wheat still in bud—anything that represented youth was acceptable to the goddess as thanks for ease in labor. Two small crossed arrows with bright fletchings— Xena frowned at that briefly, gave it up. It made no sense to her, but it wasn't important that she understand it.

The shrine meant the village they were seeking was quite close. Though it required a grove that was not directly in the path of most of the village life—playing children and men with the herds particularly—any midwife worth her salt would make certain the shrine and its grove were near enough to be properly tended. Village women didn't have time to waste in long walks through the woodlands.

Somewhat relieved, Xena turned away. It was most unlikely that any man would attempt to hide anywhere near a grove dedicated to Artemis. Goddess of childbearing, goddess of the hunt—the goddess who seldom showed favor to any man. Her blessing on these trees and this ground would make most males feel uneasy at best.

At worst—if such a man sought to damage the grove or the shrine and its offerings, if he dared hunt *here*—Artemis herself would appear to turn him into a stag and loose her dogs on him, Xena thought; a smile curved her lips as she studied the rest of the flat ground before her. Serve him right, too.

A vast open park ran in all directions for some distance: a lawn of knee-high grass spotted with wildflowers and lightly shaded by a few thin, young rowan trees. To north and west, enormous old olives edged the grassy area, gradually giving way to old and wild woods in the east. Behind her, the ravine, and another tangle of woods, which almost at once dropped sharply downhill.

6

A path went in a straight line from the ravine to the grove and beyond the grove to the west it meandered through the grass before vanishing among the olives—the village must be that way. Another path cut through the grass bearing roughly north, wandering as though wild beasts had worn it down. Just short of a massive olive, she could make out a circle of dressed stones that must be the well. Satisfied, she turned and called out, "It's all right, Gabrielle, he smells the water; come on up."

An hour later, thirst slaked, the two women walked the narrow, winding path that skirted the shrine grove. Gabrielle paused to look at the offerings; she smiled and pointed at the arrows. "Someone's just birthed twin sons—healthy ones, too!"

Xena gazed at them, eyed her companion. "And how did you know that?"

"Because—that's how it's done, at least it was in my mother's village. Arrows because Artemis is the huntress. Two crossed; that's for twins—fletched for boys; for girls, the tips would be painted red. And then, a very bright color like that, the dye they used on the feathers?"

"Good health," Xena finished dryly. They walked on, entering the tangle of aged olive trees that must have once been part of an impressive lord's holding. Now they'd gone wild; what ripe fruit there was unpicked, or pecked by birds, branches broken by winter winds and not properly pruned. It was cooler under the trees, and the light breeze that suddenly ruffled the horse's mane bore the tang of salt water. "I'm not certain I understand why that's all necessary, though; surely the goddess knows who was just born down in that village, doesn't she?"

"Well, of course she does! But anyone who goes by that grove knows about it now, too. And our grove also served

7

a village just across the hills from us. So it was a way to let the women there know. Hardly any of the women my mother's age could write, and nobody had spare time to just go and trade gossip.''

"There never is. I grew up in a village, too, remember?"

"Sure. It's the honor thing, too, though. The offerings."
They walked in silence for some time, the only sound once more the muted clink of the horse's fittings; down a slope and across a dry wash, up the far side. The ground here was dusty, the wind a little stronger, the trees now interspersed with brush, wild rowan, young oak. One ancient olive tree lay across the trail; its inadequate roots still tangled with clods of dirt and its leaves withered. Someone had attempted to cut through the massive trunk to clear the path but had only been partially successful; a new path led around the root ball and past a bramble thicket before rejoining the ancient way.

Gabrielle turned to look at the fallen giant. "It always makes me sad to see an olive tree die," she said wistfully. "They're so important and they're just so—majestic. You can see why the gods have always cared for them. This place needs more men and women to tend it."

"Too many lands are like that just now," Xena reminded her. "Too many men gone to war in the north or the east and not enough of them returning. Too many women with too many duties to manage for themselves and their men, and their families."

"True." Gabrielle looked sad; probably thinking about that farmboy who'd been pledged to her in her home village, so long ago, Xena decided. Not that Gabrielle had wanted the boy then; he'd been a nice, ordinary farmer and she'd wanted—well, just what she'd gotten: adventure, excitement, danger. It was Greek luck at its sardonic finest that had brought her together with that boy at the fall of

Troy. Some god or goddess must have been laughing uproariously over the situation: a boy who'd changed from a green youth grieving for his betrothed into a great warrior who'd helped the two of them salvage what little could be rescued from the wreck of Troy. And now he traveled with the legendary Helen. Gabrielle had been as surprised as anyone, how much she'd come to care for this new man he'd become, how deeply saddened when the boy—the *warrior*—went his own way without her.

"Ithaca . . ." Gabrielle was pursuing her own, vastly different thoughts. "Isn't that where that one Greek captain— I can't remember his name—the Trickster, the Trojans called him? Isn't Ithaca his home territory?"

"King Odysseus," Xena replied promptly. "These are all his lands, though he actually lives on the isle of Ithaca. And Trickster's a good name for him. You'd like the tale about how he almost didn't go with the Greeks to attack Troy."

"D'you know it?"

Xena smiled faintly. "I won't tell it as good as you can, but I know the details. When King Menelaus discovered Helen was gone, he sent word to all the other kings and princes who'd also courted her; they'd all vowed to—"

"—to aid whoever actually won her, if someone kidnapped her," Gabrielle broke in, cheerfully impatient. "I know that part, Helen told me, remember?"

"I didn't know—I should have suspected she'd confide in you, though. Anyway, most of the other kings put together armies, built ships, and headed for Sparta, but Odysseus didn't. And when Menelaus sent someone to find out where he was and why he hadn't answered the summons, Odysseus pretended he was mad. He put on filthy, smelly rags, then went out into his peasants' fields with a team made up of an old lame ox and a wild ass and somehow

9

he managed to till up a few rows with them. But instead of seed, he began sowing them with salt.''

"Oh! Of course! Then King Menelaus' messenger would think he'd lost his mind and go away without him!''

"Exactly.''

"Well, it sounds pretty clever—but it obviously didn't work, because he was there, at Troy, wasn't he?''

"His queen had just presented him with a son, his first child,'' Xena went on after a moment. "He was happy at home, his lands and his people were doing well, everything was peaceful. The last thing he wanted to do was leave all that behind just to fulfill an old vow made to King Menelaus from back when they were both vying for Helen's hand and her dowry. But King Menelaus knew his old friend fairly well, so the messenger he sent was the cleverest man in his household. The man watched this foolishness for a while, then had the Trickster's baby son brought from the palace. He set the child in one of the furrows, just ahead of the plow—''

"Oh, that *is* clever!'' Gabrielle laughed and clapped her hands. "So, of course, the Trickster would have to stop the plow or turn aside, the messenger would know he wasn't mad, and he'd have to go, right?''

"Exactly,'' Xena replied dryly. "Which of course meant that not just King Odysseus went to war, but so did most of the men in his guard, and the men in the villages around his castle and grounds.''

"Oh. Of course.'' Gabrielle's voice was flat, her eyes distant. "Just imagine being a man in one of those villages, a—a farmer or a herder like one of the men from my village—except it's been peaceful for so long, you'd forget there was such a thing as war—and then being dragged off to travel overseas in a ship, to fight in a land you never

10

even heard of. Knowing all along that you might never get home again . . .'' Her voice trailed off.

"And then, being such a peasant, discovering you had done all that so you could reclaim a woman—any woman, let alone the fickle Queen of Sparta?" *Sorry, Helen,* she added to herself.

Gabrielle bristled, very briefly, then sighed. "I know—that's what everyone says about her, don't they? And all she was really trying to do was avoid the destiny the gods wanted for her. Poor Helen."

"Well, yes. Remember to keep that to yourself, though. Wherever she might be, just now, she doesn't need publicity."

"It's just that I get so *angry* when I think about it," Gabrielle began.

"So do I. But I can hide that; your face gives you away every single time."

"I can't help my face," Gabrielle said dryly. "Any more than I can help how I feel about—about that. It's the kind of worth men like that put on women. I don't think any more of the King of Sparta than I do of his soldiers. Have I mentioned just lately that I have a *bruise* on a portion of my anatomy that I—well, I'm sitting with care since that last inn, all right?"

"I'm sorry to hear that. If you ever see your friend with the fast fingers again, yell. All right? Oh—" Xena drew the horse to a halt and pointed toward the west, well downhill of the plateau where they presently walked. "Look. There's the sea, and just this side of it, there's a village. We'll have proper shelter before full dark."

Gabrielle halted suddenly, closed her eyes, and clamped her hands around her temples. Xena gazed at her, her eyes sardonic, and waited for the inevitable "vision."

"Oh," the girl said finally, breathlessly. "I—I can see

11

him! I—wait—'' A long silence; she shook her head finally, opened her eyes. ''He's—he's on an island, partway between the mainland here and Troy, and there's''—her eyes closed, a frown etched her brow—''there's the wreck of a ship on the beach, and a—a little building that's just columns and a roof and a marble floor, and sheer curtains blowing in the warm wind and cushions everywhere, really beautiful ones with gold thread, and—that *must* be him, he's tall and lean and his hair's going gray and so's his beard, and he's got a gold band across his brow with a bird on it, and he's—oh, he's wearing the little pleated skirt that goes under armor, and nothing else that I can tell except sandals, and he's sprawled out on the cushions and there's a lady—oh!'' Her eyes fluttered open briefly and she looked very indignant before they closed again.

Xena cast her own eyes heavenward and waited the girl out. *On an island. What a surprising, remarkable deduction—sorry, vision—isn't it?*

Gabrielle's words tumbled over one another. ''Oh, she's beautiful! Her skin is very pale and she's got cheekbones like I never saw, and hair the color of a raven's wing and it's all piled in curls above a band of pearls and silver and she's—oh *my!*'' She suddenly sounded quite indignant. ''She's wearing the thinnest little chiton I ever did see, she's absolutely indecent, the hussy, I can see right through it! And she's feeding him purple grapes and now she's— oh!'' With a final gasp, her eyes flew open. ''I didn't think *anyone* was constructed like *that*,'' she finished primly, and folded her hands across her own bosom. Her face was rosy with embarrassment.

''If you're done,'' Xena replied dryly, ''the village is that way.'' She pointed; Gabrielle grimaced cheerfully, took the horse's reins. Her color was still high as she set out again.

Another of her usual oraclelike pronouncements, the

warrior thought with some amusement. But it was odd all the same—so much detail, and *that* sort of detail. Curious, if she'd actually seen something for once. Xena brushed the thought aside and followed the horse down the steep, narrow path.

Down a dry creek bed, between enormous slabs of stone; now the path began to crisscross the slope and the angle became more manageable. Gabrielle stopped suddenly; the horse balked and Xena swore under her breath as she slammed into his withers. "Wait," the girl demanded. "You—where did you get all that about Odysseus? The trickster-king? I mean, I know how to find tales and all that's something even *I* haven't heard before." A narrow-eyed suspicious look. "You didn't make all that up, did you? About his infant son, and the mismatched team, and salt in the furrows?"

"I don't make up tales, remember? Besides, I didn't need to," Xena replied cheerfully. She edged around the horse, retrieved reins from Gabrielle's suddenly nerveless fingers. "Can we keep moving, please? I would rather not spend the night in the open if I can help it—not around Ithaca. No," she added as they moved forward, "most of that I got from Odysseus himself, though of course he tried to put a better face on why he didn't want to go."

"You *talked* to him? When? Where?" Gabrielle's voice was a breathy squeak. "And—and you didn't *tell* me?"

Xena shrugged. "I was out on the beach, among the Greek ships; we ran across each other. I—let's say we each know of the other, though we'd never met. We talked." Gabrielle gave her a sidelong, disbelieving look. Obviously, there was more to it; as obviously, she'd probably never hear about it. "We were a little busy at the time, if you recall. After we left Troy, you and I, I forgot. Being here brought it back."

"I'm surprised either of us made it this far," Gabrielle said. "After all, he's under a curse, and if things are going the way they usually do with curses, then everyone around him is just as likely to be struck by lightning. I mean, they say Hera doesn't like him one bit. He's irreverent, supposedly. And the gods who sided with Troy absolutely hate him. And then, he's supposed to be the one who came up with that wooden horse, you know."

"It *was* his idea, which doesn't surprise me at all. He didn't like the way it was used, and he pulled out to sea when Menelaus used it; turned his back on them. Now the gods who favored the Greeks don't like him, either." She paused. "Shall we?" Xena eased down a steep incline, drawing the horse after her. A moment later Gabrielle came plunging down the track behind her, mumbling under her breath. It was probably just as well Xena couldn't make out the words.

This east side of the narrow cart road was largely wild: orchards and groves scarcely tended or left to the brambles and beasts, a few narrow, fallow fields presently high with midsummer weeds. Between the track and the sea, fields rippling with ripe, golden wheat sloped away toward a rocky edge and the sea some distance below. A low, rough hedge separated fields from dusty track.

The road itself was barely wide enough for a small oxcart or pull cart to which the peasant would hitch himself as the beast; it was badly rutted from winter rains, patched here and there with a clod of grass or a handful of pebbles; it ran back south, curving along the edge of the ledge they'd just come down until with a sharp eastward bend it vanished just short of a wild-looking, dark forest. North, it held a nearly straight line, then crossed a rickety-looking bridge before disappearing among a cluster of huts and low buildings. "That must be Isos," Xena murmured. "It's changed since I was here last."

"Oh? When were you here last?"

"Before we met," Xena replied shortly. Before she'd changed, Gabrielle realized she meant, and dropped the subject. Shielding her eyes with her hand, she turned to look over the field.

"I'll bet the wind is nasty in spring, out there," she remarked. "You know," she added slowly, "I don't think I see a single man out there. Even in *my* village, bringing in the harvest was man's work."

"Mmmm." Xena dismissed the harvest and the village men, turned north, and tugged at the reins. Gabrielle fell in beside her, but she glanced back now and again toward the field, a frown puckering her forehead. Something wrong there; she could just *feel* it.

The bridge clattered underfoot; the track broadened just beyond it into a dusty square surrounding the village well and the communal stone trough where the women did the washing. The entire area was deserted; there was no sign of life in the surrounding huts. Xena eyed the huts warily as she led her mount over to the trough. Gabrielle ran to draw water for the horse as the warrior princess stepped into the open, her face tight, her arms away from her body, tense and ready.

The eyes she finally found in a shadowed doorway were very round, and well below the level of her own. A boy of perhaps eight summers, his only clothing a ragged brown tunic, came cautiously into the open; another followed him. Gabrielle remained where she was, her hands wrapped in the horse's reins. "We won't harm you," Xena said gently. "We're looking for someone—an inn, the Bright Foam. It's owned by a man named . . ."

"Eumaeus," the second boy broke in; he was tall, very

thin, his dark green tunic threadbare but clean and neatly mended, and his hair a fall of soft, pale gold that would shine in the sun. When he spoke, he sounded much older than he looked. "He is my father." He turned and pointed to a thatch-roofed building well along the track, beyond the square. "That is our inn, the Bright Foam. The food is quite good and the bedding is clean. My mother Isyphus will take care of your needs." A very small smile tweaked the corners of his mouth. "She's very easy to find, she has hair like mine."

Gabrielle took a step toward them; the boy glanced at her as though seeing her for the first time, glanced at the horse with awe; his friend tugged at the fluttering green tunic and licked his lips, turned to dart across the square, between two sagging huts. Before either woman could say another word, the second boy was gone, after his companion.

Gabrielle shook herself and closed her mouth with a visible effort. "Well! What was that all about?"

Xena pointed. "Bright Foam; if there's anything to learn, we can probably learn it there." She was acutely aware that people surrounded them: hiding in darkened huts, or back in the trees, in the deep stable next to the inn, all gazing at them. She could almost smell the fear in the air.

No visible reason for it, but an obvious one, nonetheless. The lord of the lands had been absent for well over ten years; most of his army was scattered, missing or dead. The villagers and peasants of Ithaca had little or no protection, and by now, every brute and thug in all Greece must know it.

2

The interior of the Bright Foam was light and airy, thanks to an open doorway and several unshuttered windows. Surprisingly clean for a small village inn—but the reason for that stood in the center of the room, arms folded across her body, watching them. Gabrielle's eyes went wide; Xena gave her a small, unobtrusive poke and a sidelong look, though she doubted the girl was likely to say anything. Still—this was one of the most massive women she'd ever seen herself.

Taller than most men, broad everywhere; one of her upper arms was probably as big around as Gabrielle's waist, or her own. A great curly mass of golden hair tumbled across her shoulders and hung in untidy coils over an astonishment of a bosom. She wore a loose gown of the same worn green cloth as covered the boy in the square, and an ample apron over that. A scarf of the green fabric strove to keep the hair off her face and neck; it wasn't succeeding very well. The woman narrowed deep blue eyes and gazed intently at first one, then the other of her visitors. Gabrielle smiled nervously and edged back a pace. "Well?" the woman demanded finally; her voice boomed.

"I'm seeking Isyphus," Xena replied, her own voice low and even, nonthreatening.

The look remained hard, the voice loud. "I'm Isyphus. Why looking for me, eh?"

"Lodging for the night, and food." She drew a pair of coins from the narrow stash inside her belt, flipped them up and caught them. "We're on our way to the isle of Ithaca, to see Queen Penelope."

"Are you, now? And just why, I'm wondering?"

"It's about the king—" Xena began.

Isyphus let her arms drop and she took a step forward. "The King—praise every god from Zeus downward. You mean there's been word of him at last?"

"No. We've come on an errand from the King of Sparta. We were hoping to learn something from the queen."

"King of Sparta," Isyphus said darkly. "He's the one called our king off on a stupid quest to retrieve that hussy Helen!" Xena stepped casually back a pace; one foot came down hard on Gabrielle's, and whatever angry retort the girl would have made went unsaid.

"Please." Gabrielle edged forward nervously, suppressing a yelp. "We've come a long way today, and I'm thirsty and my feet are tired. If we could maybe talk about all this sitting down, and over something cold? And if you have it, I'd prefer cider to wine, myself."

Isyphus gazed at her for a very long moment, then for answer, shrugged massively, turned on her heel, and crossed to the counter, where several jugs had been placed. She pulled three cups from the shelf on the wall behind her, tipped pale amber liquid into one, deep red wine into two more, then brought them to the nearest table. Xena collapsed bonelessly onto the bench and crossed her long legs before her.

18

Gabrielle sat next to her, across from the now expressionless innkeeper and cautiously sipped. "Mmmm. That's quite good. Thank you. Ah—I hope you don't think I'm being rude, or nosy or anything, but maybe if you could tell us why you were trying to drive off paying customers." She glanced up sharply as movement in the back of the large room caught her eye. One young woman with a baby on her hip and a little girl clinging to her skirts hovered near the narrow doorway that led into the stables; a mumbling graybeard hobbled after her.

"Not everyone who comes here pays, or creates custom." The innkeeper turned her head, met the younger woman's eyes, and nodded once, sharply. The young mother took the old man's elbow and led him to a bench in the corner, then settled the children beside him before going behind the counter. She took down a mug, began polishing it.

A clatter of horses, a man's raucous shout; the young woman's mug rattled on the counter; the little girl began to cry. Isyphus got to her feet and drew an enormous club from under the bench, but Xena was already at the doorway, sword loose in its sheath.

Gabrielle gingerly tugged at the innkeeper's apron. "It's okay, honestly. She can deal with whatever's out there."

"This is in case she can't," the woman replied, and hefted the club menacingly.

Gabrielle's smile faded. "Oh. Well, sure, I agree, it certainly can't hurt to have a backup plan, can it?" Her voice faltered to a halt as someone in the street beyond uttered a particularly filthy curse.

Xena had been leaning casually against the sill, arms folded. She shifted her weight slightly, considered the view along the track. Seven rough-looking, heavily armed men had left two others down in the square, where they were watering two spirited horses laden with heavy packs. The others now strode purposefully toward the inn, all shouting and laughing, trying to top each other's stories.

". . . shoulda seen the look on her face when I shoved my way into the bedroom . . ."

"Yah! So while you're back there 'entertaining' the lady, I was talking her papa into handing over the dowry—and I ain't splittin' those coins, either."

"You're both wet! What real coin they had was down at the headman's hovel; they just sold the wheat crop—"

"—so you're buyin' for all of us, right, Kalamos?"

The leader laughed and swore. "Maybe. Maybe we don't gotta buy nuthin here, eh? Just like the last rat hole!" He pulled up just short of the entry; two of his men slammed into his back and began cursing him heartily. "Shaddup!" he snapped, then, with an ineffective attempt at a smile, he added, "Well, bust my head if it ain't Xena!"

"Kalamos," she purred, and raised one eyebrow. "I'd call it luck, you crossing my path. Astounding luck. Wouldn't you?"

Luck, Kalamos thought with a particularly evil curse; his throat was very dry, all at once. Some god or another was snickering at him just now. *Of all the hovels in all the villages in all of Ithaca, she has to be waiting for me in this one.* Behind him, the men were whispering. He half turned, once again snapped, "Shaddup!" Silence. The smile he offered the lounging warrior felt better this time; it must not have notably improved his face, because Xena's smile was all teeth, her eyes chill. "Xena! Princess!" His voice cracked; he cleared his throat, tried once more. "Long time, isn't it? I mean, don't think I've seen you since I left Draco's camp, ah, um, that is, I, ah . . ."

"Since *I* threw you out of Draco's camp, you mean." The smile broadened, revealing more teeth. The eyes were still night-blue circles around steely-blue centers; eaglelike. Hawklike. Kalamos swallowed past a tight throat. *Predatory,* he thought nervously. Xena's voice was a low, throaty, ominous growl. ''Because you stole from Draco, remember, Kalamos? I certainly do.'' The two men down in the square were leading the now unladen horses up the track, coming warily. Xena shifted ever so slightly so she could keep them and the others in view. Behind her a child wailed briefly; the high-pitched howl became sobs, these fainter as a tremulous woman's voice soothed it; Gabrielle's concerned, high voice rode over all, very briefly, before the innkeeper silenced her with a brief, snarled word of warning.

The warrior's eyes flicked toward the leader of the band of lowlifes: Kalamos hadn't missed any of it. Women and babes inside: soft, frightened creatures, easy takings. He licked his lips, glanced quickly at those behind him, cleared his throat. ''Ah—so, listen, what about I buy you some wine, we talk about old times?''

''What about we stay right here?'' Xena countered, her voice deceptively soft. Her teeth-only smile raked the milling group. Kalamos, who had drawn breath to make another would-be cheerful remark, found himself suddenly without voice. ''Until we get the ground rules straight,'' she added.

''Ground—rules.'' Kalamos blinked, shoved greasy hair behind his ears, and tugged at the motley bits of leather and quilted cloth that had been tied together to make up his armor. The men behind him were becoming restless, their whispered remarks increasingly ugly. He couldn't miss the shift in mood. They didn't know what they were up against; all they saw was an attractive, dark-haired woman with sweet lips, bare arms and legs, entirely too much pale throat showing above armor, and weapons that might be nothing more than bravado. Make the wrong

21

move here, and his leadership days were numbered. *Make the other wrong move, and Xena slits me from gullet to gizard,* he thought gloomily. He pulled himself together and made one last effort. "Ah—rules, hey, darlin', who needs rules between old friends? You know, I've heard the most—ah—amazing things about you lately."

"Oh, really?"

"Yeah, but, ya know? I didn't believe 'em, I'm a lot smarter than that, believe me, sweetheart."

"Are you? Smarter than what, Kalamos?"

"Right. Did anyone really think I'd believe that Xena the Warrior Princess gets religion or something, then splits from her army, dumps a treasury that would make a grown man weep—and goes out to protect the peasants! Sounds like one of those pointless songs those stupid bards with their cheap lutes are always wailing out. Never could understand it, letting your backside get numb while some guy who doesn't know a decent drinking song bellows out verse after verse about the names of ships and who's in charge of them. Where's the profit in that kinda thing, hey, Xena?"

Xena laughed throatily. "Wouldn't be much profit in that, would there? Stupid songs or protecting peasants—not much difference, is there?"

"None at all," Kalamos agreed cheerfully. "Now, lookit, we've got this great thing going here in western Ithaca, and I'm gonna show you how big a man I am. I'm gonna forget all about that little incident back in Draco's camp—hey, you men, straighten up and pay attention!" he bellowed as the whispering behind him became an ominous rumble. "You just listen to me! You want this woman on your side, working *with* you, not *on* you! And trust me!— you think I'm good at hauling down a profit? I'm a babe in arms compared to Xena! She *really* knows how to maul a peasant until he squeals!'' He took a step forward, lowered his voice.

Xena's lips quirked as she listened; her companion obviously thought she was amused, and his men accepted that. *Idiots and fools, every one of them. And this is the worst mistake Kalamos has made since he believed he could safely steal Queen Phaedra's pearls from Draco,* she thought coldly.

"Look, Xena! Sweetheart! We are really onto a good thing here," Kalamos urged. His face bore that young-boy-telling-a-lie-but-just-knowing-you'd-believe-him-because-he's-so-darned-cute look she hated most on his class of male. "I suppose you're here because you heard the rumors. Well, guess what!'' He threw his arms wide. "They're all true! The King of Ithaca never made it home from the foreign war for that slut Helen. All the rumors back in Athens say the gods blew the sea and winds up, sent him so far off course he'll never get home. Hey, sure, we're gonna believe that the gods intervene in matters down here, you and me, right? So, anyway, never mind the gods thing, figure that there's a nasty storm, a whole buncha ships sink, and the King of Ithaca's ship goes down. Hey, just because a guy's good with a sword doesn't mean he can fight winds and high waves, right? So kingie-baby's making fish food, and there's this whole this entire god-blasted *kingdom!* And the fish-food-kingie guy was so good at running a kingdom that Ithaca is still pushing out coin and trade goods, even with him years dead! And—and it is all ours! With nobody to even shake a finger and tell us, 'Hey, boys, don't do that kinda things to the nice people, don't rape the women, don't steal the cache pot of coins from the old guys.' Who'd dare? There isn't anyone fool enough to say, 'You fellows go home, let the nice folks keep the profit

23

from the harvest, keep their virgins, keep their craft coin. 'Cause if you don't, the wrath of Zeus will fry you. . . . ' "

He ran a hand through short, greasy curls, swore as his fingers encountered a snarl of hair, rubbed his hands together. "Right. Zeus never cared about for anyone down here but the pretty virgins—like my friend Malmo, back there. Realistically, this place and time, there's no more king, no army, nobody but a buncha scared peasants and a few scattered towns, and everything for the taking. Xena, honey, it's the sweetest party you ever saw, and it runs from northern Ithacan border to southern Ithacan border and right down to the sea. Now, you just listen to me, sweetheart." He paused and quirked the boyish grin that was said to draw the more innocent of the camp followers to his bedroll—once, anyway.

Xena raised one eyebrow, but seemed inclined to hear him out. He glanced at his silent following, tried to warn them with a look to keep quiet, so long as he had control of things. *She's buying it. Always knew she was just another dumb girl, under all that armor. Sweet-talk 'em and even the babes with blades fall for you, Kalamos.* "Rumor has it you're traveling with a cute, mouthy little blond girl in peasant's rags, though no one seems to know why. Hey! I don't care why you want her, maybe she's more your type than I am, whatever. You go ahead, keep the kid if you like her, okay?"

"How kind of you," Xena murmured. Her eyes bored into him, pale blue fires, but he was beyond noticing.

"Well, sure! I'm a nice guy that way, ask anyone." His grin widened, and he suddenly laughed. *Home free. Hey, Draco, wish you were here to see this!* "Xena! Anything for my good friend, right? Whatever you want—well, almost anything, okay? But listen, Xena, with you at my side, we could bleed this kingdom dry, who could stop us? And even if, say, the worst happens and somehow the king shows up one day with his army at his back—well, we're already gone, aren't we? They've been fighting gods and the sea and who knows what-all, they been gone so long that first time someone sees their ships, the gossip flies home faster than they can sail. And us? Well, we hear the rumors, too, and we're halfway to Sparta or Athens before they can shove the ships up onto that island of his." He swung his arms wide; a foolish grin spread across his face. "Besides, you think after being gone so long, those men are gonna want anything but to get home and stay there? Even old Odysseus wouldn't be able to force 'em back into armor after their last experience."

"You amaze me, Kalamos," Xena put in flatly as he paused for breath and looked to his companions for an admiring reaction. They were giving it to him, in loud, enthusiastic, and profane fashion; somebody clomped him across the back so hard he choked and fell, coughing harshly, into the doorjamb. He regained his balance and his breath, offered her a crooked grin. "Kalamos, I sincerely apologize for my previous thoughts about you. I didn't know you were capable of reasoning your way to the latrine and back, let alone remembering why you went there."

His smile wavered but the cheers and rude comments of his followers had put backbone in him. Xena closed the distance between them, ran a finger down his bearded cheek and held it under his chin. "Tell me," she added very softly, "did you think I'd offer you a share of my traveling companion—or did you figure you'd beat me for her, one-on-one?"

Her sarcasm couldn't be mistaken by anyone, this time. His grin vanished; Kalamos fumbled at his belt for his sword; Xena flipped her wrist and brought her fist, thumb first, up under his chin, then fell back a short pace and jabbed an elbow into his throat. He collapsed heavily, twitching and whistling for air. She leaped over him, appraisingly eyed the clutch of suddenly silent and wide-eyed grubby ruffians behind him.

"Well," she said quietly. "What have we here? You!" she added sharply, and leveled a finger at the short, black-haired, heavily bearded fellow who'd spoken so loudly about the young woman he'd assaulted. "Malmo, isn't it? You like pretty girls, do you? There are two inside the inn, cleaner, and prettier than anything you ever laid hands upon." She went to a broad stance, spread her arms, elbows high and hands twitching above her assorted weapons as he swore and took a step forward. "There's no one in there to protect them but a middle-aged innkeeper and an old drooling man. All you have to do is get through *me*."

He swore, took another step, drew his short sword. Xena laughed unpleasantly, drew her own sword, and tossed it into the room behind her. "Sword to sword—against *you*? Did you need such a weapon against the girl with the dowry—the one you assaulted? The one you raped? Big man?" Behind her, Gabrielle shouted something; her voice was urgent and frightened both. Xena chopped a hand that direction for silence and tipped her head to one side. "Big man," she murmured, low in her throat. "I'm really scared—big man."

He roared out something, threw himself at her, sword high and to one side. She blocked his upraised arm with her own, driving her elbow deeply and painfully into muscle and nerves, then caught hold of his ears and slammed her knee up between his legs, hard. His eyes bulged and he fell, huddled around his violated personals. Two enormous brutes behind him drew their swords as one, leaped across him, but Xena was already spinning on one heel.

With a piercing shout, her free foot shot high, slamming into one chin, then a second.

Her eyes focused on sudden, furtive movement out by the horses. One of those tending the beasts had drawn a bow. She ran forward; two of Kalamos' men who were trying to trap her between them stopped short. Xena clamped a hand on the nearest shoulder of each man, launched herself into a tight forward flip; four full, high-speed, open-body handsprings brought her face-to-face with the bowman. His jaw sagged; the bow hung loose and forgotten in his fingers. He cast his eyes sideways; the other horse tender crouched behind one of the beasts and from the sound of things was having difficulty stringing his weapon. She ripped the bow from a nerveless hand, spun it rapidly, and slammed the end into the man's temple. He staggered back, fell full into the nearest horse. It whickered nervously, danced away, exposing the other bowman, his weapon still unstrung. He giggled nervously, dropped the useless stick, and fumbled at his belt for his knife. She gripped his ear, spun him sideways, and planted a booted foot in his backside, sending him sprawling. The horse shrilled, reared high, and came down in a panic, barely missing his head, then bolted. The would-be bowman shrieked in turn, scrambled to his feet, and ran after it. She spared both a brief glance. *Mindless fools, using stolen warhorses as pack beasts.*

She spun around. Several thugs were still on their feet, but she could tell they were no longer in a mood to fight, even if they hadn't figured it out yet. She sauntered back toward the inn; they moved as a pack, backing away from her nervously. She smiled. It wasn't a pleasant smile, and none of them returned it. *Can't let any of them walk out of here; they'd just wait until we left and then come back. Bad idea.* If they wouldn't fight, she'd have to push them.

"Well?" she demanded softly. "One woman, all by herself? And what—let me see. Four—no, five of you!" Silence. "Of course, if the odds scare you that badly . . ."

One of them, who'd been urgently whispering some possible course of action to his companions, turned bright red and launched himself at her with a wordless yell of rage, knife held high in a white-knuckled grip. Xena met him halfway; a sharply placed spin kick caught him midchest and sent him flying; the remaining four men were already on her. Xena laughed, slammed one against the building; the next went down from a knee to the belly and an elbow to the back of his neck; another was trying to circle behind her, but a well-placed, sharply jabbed heel took care of him.

The last of them tried the direct approach, his mouth wide as he drew sword and shouted all the heroic battle cries he knew. Xena mumbled an extremely nasty curse under her breath, grabbed two handsful of filthy shirt, and slammed her forehead into his face. She stared down, once more expressionless, as he went limp.

She stood very still for a long moment, eying first one, then the other of the fallen men. From the sounds of things, Kalamos was still having a hard time getting air. Someone beyond him groaned.

"All right," she said finally. "I know at least one of you can hear me. You pass the message on to the rest of your friends here. This village—this part of Ithaca—all Ithaca—is *mine*. I hear about any trouble in any part of this kingdom, anywhere around here, and I'm going to come find you. And next time I'll be angry. Got it?" She stepped back, waited with folded arms as limping, mumbling, and groaning men helped each other up and staggered north, after the horses. None of them, including Kalamos, would even look at her; none of them made a move toward the fallen packs back in the square.

At the far end of town, Kalamos slowed and cast a wary glance over his shoulder. Xena merely stood where she was, arms folded; the ruffian shuddered, turned, and let one of his companions help him up the road.

When the last of them had vanished around a bend some distance on, Xena brushed her hands together and went back inside.

Back inside, the old man had apparently fallen asleep; his toothless mouth hung open and he snored softly. The little girl sat under a table, peering out warily, and the baby was nowhere in sight. The young woman was still behind the counter, and apparently polishing the same mug; her hands moved automatically and her eyes were fixed on the doorway.

Gabrielle and Isyphus sat at the nearest table, Isyphus listening with a bemused expression on her face as Gabrielle chattered away. As Xena dropped down next to her companion, the girl laughed cheerfully. "Well, I guess *that's* settled, so now maybe we can get back to the long, cool drink and maybe some food?" She glanced at the warrior, laughed again. "See, Isyphus? Told you she'd take care of a few mangy louts, no trouble! Why, I could tell you stories . . . !"

Xena reached for her abandoned cup, cleared her throat quietly and began to drink, her eyes fixed on the far wall. Gabrielle colored, stuttered, and fell momentarily silent.

But it was impossible for her to stay quiet long. She took a small sip from her own cup, set it aside, and planted both elbows on the table. "Well, anyway, if we were to stick around for dinner, what would you be feeding us?"

Isyphus tipped back her head and roared with laughter. When she sat up straight again, her eyes were wet and her shoulders shaking. "By all the gods at once, warrior, how do you keep your ears on your head?" Xena smiled, raised

29

an eyebrow, and drank again. "You're right, though, lass; you predicted just what she'd do, and I'm beholden to you both—the warrior for sending those brutes away empty-handed, and to you for keeping my mind from dwelling on what might happen in here next, if they overcame her."

She turned to the young woman at the counter. "Nionne! Leave the babes here, and the old man, go make certain the stew's not burning, and add some of that dried lamb to it, will you?" Nionne blinked rapidly, gazed at the cup in her hands as though wondering where it had come from, set it down, and went out the rear door. Isyphus watched her go, sighed, and shook her head, then settled her forearms comfortably on the table. All at once her eyes were worried again. "You said before—the trouble—that you wanted an audience with our queen? Because of the king?"

"King Menelaus of Sparta wanted to find out about him. Everyone else has returned home, but the Spartan king just received a message from your queen. He wanted someone to find out what was going on in Ithaca, and his messenger found us."

"Oh." The innkeeper's eyes filled with tears, which she blotted on her apron. "The poor, poor lady: that sweet young lad to care for, and her man gone so long and her not knowing where—and don't I know just how she feels, poor lady—and then, the past year or so, it seems there are all these filthy, unwashed, *evil* men, preying on the villages hereabouts, because they know we haven't a king and his army here to protect us.

"Now, we were all right for the longest time, some of our men learned to fight for the king, last time the pirates came around here raiding the coast, and one or two of 'em were good enough to teach the younger lads the skills— enough they could hide in the trees and hedges and use slings or arrows to shoot down nasty creatures like those

30

just now. But now—" She sighed heavily, blotted her eyes on her apron once more.

Gabrielle, visibly confused, glanced at Xena, who shrugged. "Um—Isyphus? I don't understand what you're saying. I'm sorry, but you know how it is, sometimes when I've been walking all day and breathing a lot of dust or something, I just—" Her eyes went wide as Xena's foot tapped her ankle, hard. She drew a deep breath, let it out in a gust, smiled uncertainly. "Yes! Well! What I'm trying to say, I guess, is where are all the men from this village? The way you're talking—I'm truly sorry, but are you trying to say all your men are—are dead?"

The innkeeper sighed heavily. "If we only knew! But it's harder than that. Except for the lads and the old men like my daughter's wedded father over there, almost every man in this village has vanished without a trace."

Silence for a long moment; it was broken by a raucous snort of a snore from the old man in the corner, who suddenly sat up, arms flailing wildly. The little girl scrambled from beneath the table and ran to him, began talking to him in a soft voice. The ancient grew calm as she talked; he finally patted her cheek with a withered, tremulous hand, his eyes closed, and he seemed to sleep once more. Isyphus smiled fondly. "My granddaughter, Niobe. Resembles her father, mostly. He was the first to disappear."

Another silence. Niobe patted the old man's knee, then came across the room to lean against her grandmother. Isyphus wrapped a protective arm around the child and drew her close. "What happened?" Xena asked.

Isyphus stroked hair from the child's brow and shrugged heavily. "No one knows," she said quietly. "That's the worst of it, not knowing. Or why—that's even worse, because if we knew why, perhaps we could prevent the loss of what few men remain in the village. Or—or what if it spreads to Ilyan, across the hill? Or to Ildros, half a day's walk south of here?''

"Whatever 'it' is," Gabrielle added somberly. "You don't know anything at all?''

"Well—'' Isyphus shrugged widely, then wrapped her arm around Niobe once more. The child eyed Xena in obvious astonishment, shifted her gaze to Gabrielle, who winked at her. A shy smile tugged at Niobe's mouth; she buried her face in her grandmother's ample bosom. "If we do know anything, I don't know what it might be. But I'll tell you all about what's happened hereabouts, and maybe one of you can see something we can't.

"It was late spring, the last seed had gone into the ground, and the oaks were beginning to properly leaf out— they come last, you know. And we women had been gathering young oak branches to begin the ceremony in honor of Athena. Well, you can find any amount of those on the saplings and young trees at the edge of the road, and partway to the women's shrine, but the men needed to bring in several large, dead branches of oak felled by winter storms, to make the fire. Four of them—let me think.'' She leaned back and tugged at one earlobe as she thought. Nionne came back into the large room, and Niobe pulled free of her grandmother's arm to run to her mother. "My Eumaeus, Nionne's Andrache, and the brothers just come of age this year—Hectos and Inyos. Well, they came back all wide-eyed and pale with some confused story about a pale blue light in the midst of the old glade and a curious smell. I think it was Inyos who said he'd heard a woman singing something odd in a low voice. He couldn't catch the words, though.

"Next morning, Andrache and the brothers went back at first light to investigate—and never came home.'' She

32

glanced warily toward her daughter. "When Leander and Olymos went to see if they could find trace of those three, they vanished as well."

"Oh, how—how perfectly awful!" Gabrielle whispered. Isyphus gave her a watery smile and patted her hand.

"You have a good heart, lass. It was bad—and it got worse. The strangeness around the glade vanished that night; I know, because Nionne and I went to see if there was anything we could sense—"

"Was that wise?" Xena asked dryly.

"Well—it had only taken men, and full-grown ones. And we both bathed in sacred warding herbs before we went, of course. There's no wisewoman in this village but some of us know a thing or two. Still—after all that, there was nothing to be seen, sensed, heard, or felt. And since that day, men have vanished, one or two at a time, from almost anywhere except out in that square at bright midday, though I'd not be surprised if someone did."

Nionne came to the table with a jug, from which she refilled cups. Gabrielle smiled up at her and held a hand over her cup. "I'm drinking your cider, if you don't mind, it's awfully good." Nionne nodded, went back to the counter, and returned with another, smaller jug.

"My poor Andrache," she said; her voice was low and throaty, and it gave her a sudden beauty. "If I knew where he'd gone, what evil chance overtook him—" She shook her head, poured cider into Gabrielle's mug. "It's been hard for us, this year. Not just these brutes coming through the village whenever they wish and taking whatever they can find. Women's work is hard enough in a land like ours, there's little or no rest, spring, summer, and fall, and not much more in winter, and now we've our own work and that of our men to accomplish. There are children—frightened children—to soothe and protect and raise; we've got

33

to do what we can to protect all of us from the likes of those you just ran off, warrior.''

''I know about life in a village,'' Xena said quietly.

Gabrielle shook her head, sending straight golden hair flying. ''This—oh, that's awful! How terribly sad and not even knowing what's become of anyone!'' She spun partway around to gaze into her companion's eyes. ''We have to *do* something!''

''It would be wonderful if you *could* do something,'' Nionne said wistfully. ''But I don't know what it would be. Mama,'' she added as Isyphus drained her cup and got to her feet. ''I've got the stew nearly ready, but you'd better season it, you've got a surer hand.'' She paused as Xena held up a hand.

''There are packs in the square. Someone should bring them so we can find who those men stole from and return things to them. The rest—well, I'm sure you can use it here.''

Isyphus nodded and turned to her daughter. ''We'll get them in. Daughter, you come with me. You'll never learn how to season if you don't watch. Warrior, you and your young friend are welcome at my inn for as long as you wish to remain.'' She went out, followed by Niobe and Nionne, who retrieved her sleeping baby from somewhere behind the counter.

Xena waited until they were out of hearing. ''Gabrielle— it's a sad tale, but don't raise these women's hopes without good cause.'' Gabrielle stared at her, visibly confused. ''Most likely those men are dead. There are beasts—''

The girl was already shaking her head. ''It couldn't be beasts, not with all that other stuff going on. Lights and sounds, and a woman singing . . .''

''Imagination, or too much wine, or not enough sleep— there are plenty of reasons for seeing and hearing something that isn't there. And here, where the villagers are too busy with daily life to keep the wilds in check, where there are no king's armsmen to oversee problems? Never mind that; the fact is, a large number of men are missing, and not one of them has returned.''

Silence. Gabrielle gazed anxiously and unhappily at her friend. Xena gave her a brief, would-be reassuring smile in response. ''I understand how you feel. But most likely something killed them all. Dead is dead, and there's nothing I can do about that.'' A short, miserable silence. ''I'm sorry. I'm not happy about it, either. But there's no reason we can't remain here a few days, at least take a look at this place. Maybe there's a clue they didn't see. And this is the peak of the harvest; we can probably help them a little with that, ease the burden. At least watch out for more of the likes of Kalamos.''

Gabrielle nodded finally. ''It's just that—well, it seems so unfair!''

''Life's unfair. You know that.''

They went out to the glade early the next morning, with Isyphus in a small oxcart to guide them.

''Here it was, or so Eumaeus told me,'' she said, and dabbed her face with her apron.

Gabrielle watched Xena slowly begin to explore the glade. ''What happened to Eumaeus—I mean, not what but when?''

''Well, he—he went north on the road not a week ago, he and two other of our men, to drive the best cart to the shore south of the palace island; they were taking the annual two kegs of new wine for the palace. There'd been no sign of problem along the road, we didn't think that there might be trouble. And it takes a full day each direction, you don't want the wine slopping in the kegs and ruining

35

the fermentation, of course. So no one was surprised when they didn't return early the third day, or even on the fourth. Everyone loves Eumaeus, he often goes with the ship to transport the kegs and talk with the palace servants, then comes back . . . but when five days came and went, and there was no sign of any of them . . .'' She sniffed loudly, blotted her eyes once more.

Gabrielle patted her broad back and tried to think of something soothing to say. Nothing occurred to her, so she patted the woman's shoulder once more, and turned to watch her companion. Xena squatted in the center of the glade, shifting grass back and forth a few narrow blades at a time, her eyes intent on the ground. She got to her feet, studied the area, then moved from broad-trunked oak to tall and graceful rowan, to ancient and half-dead oak, all the way around the glade.

The sun was near peak when she finally gave it up. ''I'm sorry, Isyphus,'' she said as she climbed back onto her horse. ''If there was something here to give anyone a hint of what happened, it's long gone. I can't tell a thing.''

The next day dawned bright, cloudless, and already hot. A
dozen village women, skirts hiked high for ease of movement and sheltered under broad-brimmed woven straw hats,
worked their way down long furrows, one hand bunching
wheat stalks while the other hand deftly wielded a curved,
long-bladed knife to cut them. The bundles were laid down
next to the row, the bent-over cutters backed a pace down
the row, another bundle was gathered in and cut. Behind
them came other women who swiftly separated one stalk
from the rest, wrapped it twice around the bundle, tied it,
and dropped it to the ground. Girls and young boys followed them, the girls gathering up bundles and dropping
them across outstretched, spindly young male arms. Once
a boy's arms were full, he'd turn and stagger over to one
of the sideless carts waiting in the track, drop his bundle
on the growing stacks, and return for more.

Xena was only partly aware of all this as she stood near
the end of one completed row. Her eyes moved constantly,
checking the track, the paths leading from it into woods or
rock or brush; the several cuts that dropped from the fields

down to the sea. Anyplace and everyplace where someone might hide.

At first light she'd been backing along one row with the cutters, but shortly before sunrise, the first filled cart had been jumped by five grubby swordsmen. She'd dropped her harvest knife and drawn the dagger, sprinted across the open before any of them could get the frightened mule that pulled the cart under control, and flattened three men with her fists and elbows. The fourth threw himself from the back of the cart, dagger high, ready to strike; she side-stepped, caught hold of his ankles, and threw him two man lengths down the road. Unfortunately for him, the knife was underneath when he landed. The last man eyed her glassily, backed slowly away, the knife sliding from a shaking hand; she smiled. He caught his breath on a whimper, turned, and hared down the road.

She let him go. *Leave one of them free to spread the word that this village is no easy mark from now on, because there's someone here to protect the innocents. Bah. Hardly worth the bother, most of his kind would scoff and call him coward or incapable, and come anyway to test their own luck. This becomes boring,* she thought sourly, and wiped her hands—and her knife—on the grass. One of the men at her feet groaned and tried to sit up; a small, deadly booted foot shoved against his chest and held him flat.

"A suggestion," she said evenly. "Leave the knives and all the rest in a pile, right here. Back away, go quietly. You might live to find another knife, somewhere far from here."

Silence. One of the other men let his eyes drop; he pulled several knives, a long dagger, and a short sword from various hidden sheaths and threw them at her feet, backed cautiously away from her on all fours, and waited.

"You heard," he snarled finally. "Get yourselves killed

38

if you like. That's my bundle and I'm going. Now." One of them was grumbling to himself; Xena cleared her throat, eyed him inquiringly as he glanced up. The silence this time was very uncomfortable. Several more knives, a short bow, a sling, and a bag of stones completed the pile before the other two men stood, arms well away from their sides, and warily backed off. She folded her arms, gazed back expressionlessly, waited. All three backed some distance down the road, turned as if loath to break eye contact, and began walking down the road after their long-departed comrade. Once they were beyond the normal range of a thrown knife, they took to their heels. Xena gathered up the weapons, tossed them into the cart in front of the bundled wheat, and returned to help with the crop.

The women had stopped work and were watching her warily. Isyphus finally laughed, breaking an uneasy silence. "Well! That was quick." Xena shrugged, smiled briefly, and bent over the knee-high wheat.

That night several men snuck into the village and stole one of the carts, but they didn't get far with it; instead of the expected open track south, they found a still, shadowy figure awaiting them on the rickety bridge. Two of the village boys waited in tree shadow until the bridge was clear and the last of the ruffians had been plucked from the dry creek bed by the least injured of his companions. Xena eyed them dispassionately, gestured sharply with her thumb for them to back away. Someone groaned unhappily as she whistled; the boys emerged from shadow to gather up fallen weapons before taking hold of the cart shaft and turning it back toward the village.

"The harvest is intact?" she asked. A confused and rather shy mumble was her only response; her brief smile was hidden by shadow. "Good. Get it into the stable, and stay in yourselves. Go now." She waited until the boys were gone, the cart lurching unsteadily across the bridge, the swords, daggers, and small shields within it clanking against one another. Her eye moved to the huddled, subdued men on the narrow track.

"I know at least two of you—and I recognize you," she added, leveling a finger at a ragged brute who nursed an aching head and groaned loudly. Someone else was cursing inventively in a low, flat voice. "Be quiet," she ordered. Silence she got. "Be grateful you can feel the bruises. Next time you won't." She waited. Then: "Get moving while you still can." Two of them helped the injured leader to his feet; the others staggered up and followed slowly down the track south. Xena remained on the bridge, arms folded, watching until they were long out of sight.

She spent most of the next morning and midday watching over the women or pacing along the road to make sure the lads taking the carts back to the village were all right. "It's quiet enough," Nionne said as she brought the warrior bread and crumbly cheese, a few soft grapes, and a deep wooden mug of cool wine. "Maybe you've chased them all away."

No point in alarming the woman, Xena thought. She drank, set the cup aside, and smeared cheese over the bread with her fingers, bit into it. "Maybe," she mumbled. Nionne seemed reassured; she moved into the shade to share food with her babes.

Gabrielle patted little Niobe's cheek and got to her feet. "It's awfully quiet, isn't it? Do you suppose that whatever he is, that Kalamos, called off his brutes?"

Xena tucked bread and cheese into her cheek. "What do you think?"

"Mmmm." Hazel eyes searched the road, the cliff beyond it, the abandoned olive grove and the tangle of brush and trees. "I think that even if he did, there are probably

40

a lot of other brutes out there who don't even know Kalamos, and wouldn't care what he said. That's supposing he listened to you, of course; he didn't look too bright.''

"He's not bright. Just cunning. That's why he's so dangerous.''

"Oh?'' Gabrielle considered this, finally shrugged. "Well, I'm not going to worry about any of that. I just think I'm a lot happier with you out here watching over things. So are the kids. Do you know they were actually listening to my stories this morning, instead of looking around to see where the next trouble was going to come from.'' Silence for some moments. "They've only got about another day to finish this field; it's going pretty well, actually. Did you know that a couple carts of this crop is going on to the palace, along with two tuns of wine?''

"We're going on the boat to the palace with it,'' Xena said. She finished her wine, handed the cup to Gabrielle, and stood. "Take this. I'm going to look around some more.''

Nionne sat cross-legged in tree shade, nursing her infant, one arm around Niobe, who appeared half-asleep. Several of the other children lay dozing on a sheepskin rug. Gabrielle went back over to join them; she and two little girls resumed a game that involved piles of small sticks and plenty of giggling.

Most of the women sat in shade, their backs to the pyramid of rocks that had been hauled from the field and piled along the cliff edge. Xena crossed the field, clambered up a massive boulder, and shielding her eyes against the brightness of sun and sea, slowly turned, searching the shore below, the jumble of rocks, the brushy, boulder-strewn cliffs, then the broad, sloping fields, the empty track. No one in sight at the moment. That didn't mean anything; there was no shortage of riffraff around here. *No shortage of stupid riffraff,* she thought disgustedly. These people weren't impoverished but they didn't have much. Men like Kalamos would have to be desperate or dumber than the average thug to go after a small village.

Of course, they weren't all looking for wealth; there were plenty such men who got more enjoyment out of terrifying the helpless than they ever would from bags of gold and gems.

Just below her, sharp movement. She spun, glanced down at Isyphus, who was staggering to her feet, her face utterly white, staring with wide eyes. Across the track, something or someone was moving into the shadow of vine-entangled young oaks from an open, sunny ledge. Xena leaped from the rocks, ignored the woman's outstretched hand, her wordless shout, and sped across the half-cleared field, leaped the low hedge, skirted the cart, cleared the ditch beyond it—and stopped short, astonished.

A man in a faded green shirt and neatly patched, worn brown britches was crawling slowly and painfully, his immediate goal the ditch. A ring of graying hair stood up wildly around a sunburned, freckled bald patch. He stopped short as he took in the booted feet planted in front of him, swayed back and forth weakly, then simply fell over. His breath came in harsh, loud snorts. *No threat here,* Xena decided, kneeling beside him.

Hurrying feet behind her, a murmur of women's voices; she turned partway around to shout, ''Stay back until I'm certain he's safe!'' The man looked up at her; brown, hurt eyes met hers. Xena stared; the rest of his face was so ordinary she'd not have known him from another such middle-aged villager—but his nose was a pig's snout.

Isyphus halted next to her and emitted a faint squawk before dropping to both knees and gathering the man to her bosom. ''Eumaeus! It's my Eumaeus! Where've you been

42

all these days?'' His arms pressed feebly against her; she leaned back to look at him and seemed to see him clearly for the first time. Her mouth sagged open. ''Who's done this to you, husband?'' she whispered. He shook his head, closed his eyes, and nestled into her. Xena laid a light hand against his throat and, when Isyphus whimpered, touched the woman's arm and shook her head minutely.

''He's alive; just exhausted. Let's get him to the cart, take him back to the village. He'll need food and water before he can tell us anything.''

An hour later most of the village women were crowded onto the dusty track before the inn, murmuring worriedly. Xena stood motionless near the back door, watching for Nionne or Isyphus—both women were sitting with Eumaeus in the one-room family hut, waiting for him to recover enough that he could speak. Gabrielle paced back and forth, gazing out the main door, then out the narrow window slit in the south wall, then into the stable, where Xena's horse dozed in the farthest stall and boys packed the bundled wheat into large straw baskets for transport to the palace.

Gabrielle sighed finally. ''What do you think could *do* that to a man?'' she asked quietly.

Xena shrugged. ''That's more a question for you to answer, isn't it? A god, a wizard? I don't deal with those any more than I have to, and I don't know much about any of them. Sit and think about it while we're waiting, why don't you?''

''I've thought,'' Gabrielle said, ''and I can't think of anything, and I honestly don't feel much like sitting.''

''Sit anyway,'' Xena growled. ''You're making me dizzy.''

''Oh. Sorry!'' Gabrielle dropped onto the end of the

bench. ''You're right, it could be either, or something else. Still,'' she added, but turned as Isyphus clomped into the room.

''Warrior, he wants to talk, if you'll come?'' For answer, Xena rose swiftly and strode across the chamber to follow the woman, Gabrielle on her heels.

The poor innkeeper looked even more odd and out of place freshly washed and brushed and tucked into bed in a clean nightshirt. Nionne held his head while he sipped from the cup in her other hand. Isyphus took her daughter's place and cuddled him briefly against her bosom. After a moment she touched his face, gestured toward the silent, still Xena. ''Husband, this is the warrior who protected us from ruffians the past days. She's trying to help us still, if you can tell her what happened to you?''

''Ahhhh.'' He blinked, swallowed, and burrowed against Isyphus, much as little Niobe had. ''That's—so good, Issy. I've thought of little else these past days, just to get back to you. I didn't even think about how you'd see me, what you'd think. . . .'' His voice trailed off.

The woman's arms tightened around him and he squeaked faintly. ''Eumaeus, no one ever called you a handsome man,'' she said in a mock-severe voice, ''even when you were a lad, and the village headman's son. You're something much better; even with a pig's snout, you're *my* man, and a good one. No one here, including little Niobe, will consider you less a good man because you've—you've changed. But, Eumaeus—the other men, all the others—'' She gave him a gentle little shake before clasping him to her bosom once more. ''The women out in the street, they'd like to know where their men are, what's happened to them.''

''Some of them,'' he murmured faintly. With an effort, he pushed away from her and sat up straight; one hand rubbed thoughtfully against the bridge of his snout. Gabrielle eyed him sympathetically, then eased away to sit with her back to the far wall. "We'd gone to deliver the wine to the boat, the special shipment for Queen Penelope. Now, a man daren't push the oxen at such a time, road isn't much good, the kegs'll stir up, and the stuff won't be drinkable until it settles again. Affects the price, but that isn't the main thing. It's never been said of village Isos that we sent the queen dregs-tainted wine, have we, wife?" Isyphus shook her head, then whispered against his ear. "Oh. I'm sorry, warrior; my mind's still wandering. Well, we couldn't go fast, so we drove long hours to make up for that, and so it was well past dark, the moon a mere sliver, and that nearly sunk into the sea when we heard it." He licked his lips nervously. Isyphus held the cup for him, but he pressed it aside.

"At first, I thought it must be the wind, though young Aleppis has keener ears than I and he named it a voice—woman's voice, high and with odd words in it. Foreign, maybe. Though maybe just with an odd accent. Well, wife, with so many of our men gone who knows where, I slowed the team even more—and was about to turn the cart and come back here, fast as the oxen could manage it, and be damned to the wine as well. But—but somehow, I couldn't do it." His eyes flickered across Gabrielle, mildly curious, fixed on Xena. "Was the strangest thing, altogether. The cart went on as if someone or something had a stronger hand on the oxen than I did, and then all at once, we stopped. I could hear it now, clearly: a high, thin woman's voice but not irritating somehow the way a screechy girl's voice can get to you, though it hackled the hair on my arms, I can tell you. Well, young Aleppis and his friend Hesper were off the cart and gone, striding into the woods before I could so much as snatch at 'em!"

He drew a shuddering breath; his eyes were wide and all pupil as he relived the moment. "And then, imagine it, I could truly not stop myself, I was following after the young fools! Now, wife, I had no urge whatever to discover what or who was singing, but my feet weren't mine to direct anymore. I slid from the cart and started into the woods, but there was a dry rill just inside the trees; my ankle turned—the bad one, you know? And I went down, the leather strap on my sandle snapped and the heel flapping. So I clutched at my ankle with one hand and cursed under my breath and tried at the same time to either fix the strap or shed the sandal because that voice kept telling me somehow, even though I couldn't make out a word—well, I just had to go, didn't I? And I could hear the lads crashing through the brush blindly, falling down, and one of them went nose first into a tree and swore—why, I didn't know any man of us knew curses like those! But all at once the sandal came free, and I threw it aside, got to my feet somehow, and went after them, hands in front of me so I wouldn't flatten *my* nose. So for all my years and their lack of them, I wasn't far behind when they moved into an open place. All at once there was light—nasty, green light it was—and I could see Hesper quite clearly, and then I could see *her,* too."

"What did she look like?" Xena asked quietly as he paused for breath.

"Well . . ." He considered this, one finger rubbing his snout in what must be an habitual gesture, though at the moment it looked quite odd. "Well, not very tall, and very slender, not a genuine curve to her, so as I could tell." He smiled, leaned into his wife with a happy sigh. "Not like some," he murmured, and with a visible effort brought himself back to the moment. "She was pale, and her hair— why, I've never seen anything quite the like. It was redder than bronze armor or a new copper coin and it shone with flecks of gold. And it hung straight as a waterfall, nearly to her feet. She wore something so white it hurt my eyes, and her own eyes were the color of the sea on a cool, cloudy morning—or the green of new wheat.

"Odd you could see so much at a distance," Xena put in.

Eumaeus considered this. "So it is. And I saw truly— you'll hear in a moment. At the time it didn't seem odd, though it does now. Well, I wasn't far behind them, but still within the trees when she raised her hands and said *something* that made my bones ache. And then she laughed. My legs went weak and my head spun, and I fell down. But even though I was almost too afraid to breathe, I had to see what had happened to those two lads. Well, do you believe me if I tell you there was that woman still, and she was still laughing nastily—but instead of our lads, there were two pigs—pretty, plump pigs, one brown with a darker spot along his back, the other black as Aleppis' hair, and why, I don't know but I could all at once understand what she said."

Silence. Isyphus gave him a little more wine and murmured something against his ear. The innkeeper patted her arm and managed a smile for her and for his daughter. Nionne smiled back, but Gabrielle noticed she wasn't looking at him directly.

"And what did the woman say?" Xena asked finally.

"Say? Oh . . . Was such odd things." He blotted his brow, swallowed hard. "I'm—I'm sorry, warrior, my head felt so strange, and everything was confusing, nothing like anything I'd ever seen before in my life. . . ." His voice trailed off, he closed his eyes.

Xena glanced at Gabrielle, who raised her eyebrows and shrugged. *No god or wizard I know,* the shrug said.

But after a moment Eumaeus spoke again, eyes still closed, obviously quoting as best he could recall. " 'My, what handsome pigs. You are handsome, aren't you, my sweet little pigs?' There—was a lot more like that," he added in a small voice. "Didn't think she'd ever be done, cooing love words at them, though she didn't look the type to fuss over pigs, and she didn't sound as though she meant a word of it. All at once, though, she turned and stared out through the trees, and she sounded so angry, I couldn't look at her anymore." His voice changed, hardened. " 'So King Odysseus wouldn't accept my hospitality? Good enough for his men, but for him—oh, no! Sweet little piggies, wouldn't you like some cold, hard, raw acorns?' And then she laughed." He shuddered; Isyphus wrapped her arms around him and murmured soothing words. "And she said, 'Of course you wouldn't. You'd like nice, dull peasant fare, vegetables in broth and roast vegetables, and common, dull, ordinary dirty peasant fodder! Because you know who you really are, still, don't you? However you look to outside eyes?' " He drew a sharp breath, was quiet for a moment. "The way she laughed made all my bones ache, I couldn't watch another moment. I felt so weak, so ill. When I looked again, she was gliding across the open ground with all the grace of a snake and the pigs trotted along behind her. But—but the oddest thing," he added in a small voice. "Do you know, the black-marked pig slowed and looked back and I would swear he looked at me with Aleppis' eyes?"

"No!" Gabrielle sat up very straight indeed. "It must be . . ." Xena cast her a warning glance and a shushing gesture, not to break the innkeeper's concentration, but he hadn't even heard her, so intent was he on his tale.

"Well, of course, I was light-headed, wife," he went on after a moment. "And how could a pig have Aleppis' eyes?

But where had two pigs come from in the first place, out there in the woods? And proper, fat, well-tended pigs they were, too. But those pig's eyes made me feel so strange, the world spun all around me and went away, and when I woke next, it was dark and damp, the moon gone, and no sound but owls in the distant trees and a snap and snort nearby from a grazing stag. I felt my head because it ached so curiously, and all was well until my hands came upon my nose—and," he finished in a small voice, "it wasn't mine at all!"

Isyphus held him close and cooed at him softly for some moments. He finally sighed and sat up once again. "Well, warrior, your pardon for a waste of your time with such a mad tale, and I doubt you'll believe a word of it. But my nose wasn't so before I stepped down from that cart, and look at it now!" Gabrielle started, but Xena cast her another warning glance.

Isyphus patted his shoulder, ruffled his hair affectionately. "But, husband, how is it you made it home?"

To her visible surprise, he chuckled, though the sound had a definite snort to it that clearly embarrassed him, and he fell momentarily silent. "Well, wife, I had a long day and a night to think about it while I found enough strength to return to the road—and then once there I discovered the cart wrecked, the oxen gone, and the kegs vanished, not much to my surprise. So I had more time to think while I found my slow and unhappy way back home, and even so I'd given up when I saw this honored warrior and then your face. No, wife—lay it to my years and my ankle and my sandal; if I'd been on the heels of those two lads and in the open, no doubt I'd be a pig as well, yoked to her will. And I don't doubt it that every man missing from Isos has gone the way of Aleppis and Hesper." He spread his arms wide, sighed faintly, and fell back against his wife's bosom, a smile curving his lips. Xena got to her feet, gesturing for Gabrielle to join her.

"Innkeeper, you're exhausted and no wonder. Rest now. I'll do what I can to aid your village—though I don't know exactly what I *can* do. My friend here will tell the other women what's happened, then we'll try to think how best to mend matters. Rest if you can, and eat." She touched his arm, turned, and left. Gabrielle, her face solemn, patted the woman's shoulder, smiled at a very worried-looking Nionne, and followed her friend.

Gabrielle remained silent and thoughtful while Xena talked to the village women and watched them disperse; she was still quiet when Xena tapped her arm to get her attention and gestured toward the inn. Once within the large room, she crossed to the counter, filled one cup with wine and the other with cider, brought them to the table, and dropped into a chair. Gabrielle took the cup and drank, her eyes fixed vacantly on the far wall. Xena moved a hand across her line of vision, back again. The girl blinked.

"So. You're the teller of tales, Gabrielle. What ideas did you get from that story?"

"Ideas," Gabrielle echoed vaguely. She shook herself, blinked rapidly. "It's awful! That poor man! Imagine—did you see the look on his daughter's face? I mean, Isyphus didn't even seem to *care* that he's got that—that nose," she finished in a small voice. "But Nionne—"

"Nionne should be glad she has a father, whatever he looks like at the moment," Xena said firmly.

"All right, I know that. But ordinary people don't always see things that clearly, do they?"

"Maybe not. But you might be surprised how quickly people accept what's put before them, whatever it was like previously," Xena said evenly. "That isn't our problem, that's for Nionne to sort out. What did that to him?" And

50

as Gabrielle gazed at her blankly, Xena tapped the back of her hand with one hard finger and added, "God, goddess, enchantress—what?"

"Oh. I thought I had something back in there, but—well, all right, a god could do that, of course, but most of them stick with plain old straightforward violence. That kind of subtle thing might be more the tool of a goddess, but . . ." She buried her face in her hands, mumbled to herself for some moments. "Only Artemis does much of that magic— shapeshifting, you know?—and she usually goes after specific men who've violated her rules and then she turns him into a stag, not a pig. The shrine way back up on the plateau—it hadn't been violated. I could've told if it was, but it wasn't. So probably not Artemis. But—" She rubbed her eyes, shoved hair behind her ears, drummed fingers on her cheekbone and then her shoulders.

Xena waited her out patiently; Gabrielle could talk a lot of nonsense, and at times it seemed she rambled on like this on purpose. Maddening at worst, irritating at best. But she really did know such things. One just had to be quiet, and let her sort through her stock of knowledge in her own, confused, loquacious fashion.

It worked. Gabrielle suddenly sat up, snapped her fingers. "Got it! At least—" The gaze she turned on her friend was extremely confused. "It can't really be anyone else, but what is she doing *here*?"

"Tell me," Xena said evenly. "I'll find a motive." She drained her cup, got up to refill it, and dropped back onto the bench.

"Well—shapeshifter. And with a fondness for pigs," Gabrielle said. "Circe. It's the only possibility."

"All right. Who's Circe?"

"You don't—?" Gabrielle began, astonished. Xena cast her a dark look; the girl smiled uncertainly, shrugged, and

51

said, "All right, she's not that well known. Mostly because she lives on an island . . . um, sorry, can't recall the name of it . . ."

"Not important." Xena waved that aside. "Circe. Who, what, and why?"

Gabrielle grinned crookedly, held up fingers, and made a visible effort to be direct. "Who." She turned down one finger. "Powerful sorceress, said to be half-immortal, but they say that about all magic users, don't they? What: she's a shapeshifter, but not an ordinary one because she doesn't change her own shape, she changes others. Why." she ticked off the third finger, paused a moment, then sagged. "Why, I simply don't know."

"All right. Good enough." The warrior sipped her wine, leaned back to stare at the smoke-darkened ceiling for some moments. "If I recall correctly, Eumaeus said something about this female talking to the pigs, saying Odysseus wouldn't accept her hospitality?"

"Oh!" Gabrielle was halfway to her feet in her excitement. "Oh, I got it! Yes! All right, this is a bit complex but I think it works, give me a moment." She got to her feet, turned away, and after a very still moment, began to pace. "All right. Circe can turn any human into any kind of beast—but it's almost always men, and she usually sticks with snakes or pigs. And they say her spell changes their bodies, but nothing else; so a man she caught would look like a beast but he'd know what he really was." She spun around, looked at her companion anxiously.

"Makes as much sense as sorcery ever makes," Xena allowed. "But what about the king? You mean, he's back on some island running around on all fours and eating acorns? But then, why is she here?"

"Wherever he is, in whatever shape, that isn't it," Gabrielle said excitedly. "The spell didn't work on him. Nothing else makes enough sense!"

"Somehow, it didn't take on the king, and that made her angry?"

"Sorcerous types usually have low boiling points, don't they?" Gabrielle retorted. "Maybe he was behind the others, like poor Eumaeus, except none of the spell reached him, or maybe—wait. There's supposed to be a way to keep shapeshifting magic from working. . . ." She considered this for some moments, finally sighed. "Sometimes— I heard about it, I think it's an herb you eat or drink because only another sorcerer would know. So what if the trickster king had warning about what was happening to his men and found a way to avoid being caught in the trap?"

"Circe might be angry," Xena allowed.

She didn't look convinced about any of this, Gabrielle thought in mild exasperation. "Angry! People—beings like that aren't used to being thwarted, you know; she'd be furious, I'll wager you anything."

"Mmmm." Xena considered this for a long, thoughtful moment, finally shook her head. "It's possible she'd be angry enough to come to Ithaca and take vengeance on his people, especially since he's away." A smile quirked her mouth. "I don't suppose she's the thin-clad hussy from your—ah—vision?"

"I don't know." Gabrielle was pacing again. "But I doubt it. Would *you* play smooch games with someone who turned your soldiers into pigs?"

"Maybe if I had been enchanted in another way." Xena swung her legs down from the table and turned so she could watch her companion pace.

"Well—but she's only supposed to have this one kind of magic." She was quiet for some time, pacing the length of the room, her eyes unfocused; now and again she mumbled something under her breath. Finally she sighed, came over, and sat once more. "I'm sorry. None of that is for sure, and I know I heard once about the herb that counters such magic, but I just don't remember what it is."

"Never mind, Gabrielle, you've done just fine so far." Xena drank the last of her wine, shoved the cup aside. "Maybe you were right after all. It might just be possible to restore those men to their village." She held up a warning hand as Gabrielle turned an eager smile her way. "I'm not saying for certain. Just maybe. It's worth the try." She grinned crookedly. "Better to go against a sorceress than a goddess, don't you think?"

"Um—well, sure. Maybe." The girl's smile was fading fast. She made a visible effort to rally her sagging spirits. "Besides, according to Eumaeus, this copper-haired creature *did* mention the king. So maybe if we can get close enough to her and find a way to talk to her, we can learn where he is, and at least have something useful to pass on when we finally get to Queen Penelope, right?"

Xena's smile broadened; her eyes were wicked. "Talking's what you do, remember? You figure out what to say to a sorceress to keep her entertained."

"Oh. Right," Gabrielle managed. "And while I'm doing that, where will you be?"

"Working out everything else, of course." She rose to her feet in one lithe motion and set the drained cup aside. "I want to go back and talk to Eumaeus again. Maybe he's remembered something else. Anything at all could be useful."

"Useful," Gabrielle mumbled darkly, but when the warrior turned and raised a questioning eyebrow at her, she merely shook her head.

4

Nionne met them in the doorway, and held up a hand. "The healer's with them. She won't be long, though." She blotted red-rimmed eyes on her sleeve. "My poor Andrache, wandering in the woods on all fours! And—and what can the healer do with something like *that*?"

Gabrielle drew a deep breath, hesitated only a moment. "Nionne, honestly, your father's not really that bad."

"Did you get a *good* look at him?" Nionne demanded bitterly.

"I did," Xena said evenly. "It's no worse than the kind of bad scars you can pick up in battle. It'll draw stares for a while, then no one will notice. At least he's alive."

Nionne snorted and blotted her eyes again. "Maybe that's how things are among soldiers and warriors," she said. "In a village—well, I guess you don't realize how things are in a village, once you warriors have moved on. Nothing big ever happens, so anything small is talked about and talked about—just now my mother's saying the same thing, at least he's alive. Once the gratitude for that wears off, and people have to look at him and—and that—that—"

"That snout," Xena said deliberately. Nionne and Gabrielle both winced. "I know more about village life than you'd think. People might gossip and stare, but in a small community like this, they aren't deliberately unkind."

Gabrielle rallied at that, and squared her shoulders. "You know, she's absolutely right, Nionne. I mean, I grew up in a village myself—a little bigger than this but they're all really the same, aren't they? I mean, the same crops to plant, weed, harvest—animals to deal with, goats to milk, babies born, people die, a fever comes in and half the town gets ill, the weather goes bad or soldiers come, and everyone's afraid. . . . So whenever someone changed a lot, like my uncle who had a tree fall on him and after that he didn't really walk, he just kinda scrambled and crawled around—" She blinked rapidly, remembered where the thought was supposed to be headed, and picked up the thread. "Sure, it got talked into the ground, and some people were really gossipy, just like you'd suppose. But no one actually came out and said rude things where my uncle or his people could hear it. Because they knew they'd still be living together in the same village next year and the year after that, and honestly, where's the sense in alienating your neighbor so much that you split the whole town in half? Over something like that?"

Nionne merely looked at her, her mouth twitching unhappily. Gabrielle blinked, shrugged, and tried to smile. "Well, all right, that's maybe just how I see it, but if you can't change anything, what's the point of being unhappy about it? Weeping won't make your father's nose normal again, will it?"

Nionne sighed heavily, then turned as the healer came out of the hut.

She was young, with a girl's reedlike figure, her plaited hair tied together with a simple leather thong at the base of her neck. Shaking her head, she said, "I did what I could to cheer your mother, Nionne, but there's nothing I can do to heal an enchantment—and that's exactly what this is."

"Oh—wonderful," Nionne said flatly.

"Go home," the healer ordered, as flatly. "Take the babies and go home, Nionne, until you can look at your father and smile and possibly even mean it. Go on, shoo." Nionne grumbled under her breath, swept past them all, and stomped into the inn. The healer glanced at Gabrielle, fixed her attention on Xena.

"You're certain it's enchantment?" the warrior asked. "Or was that a guess?"

"It's as good as any diagnosis, isn't it?" Sarcasm edged the healer's voice. "It's not a reaction you'd get from eating the wrong mushrooms, or shellfish out of season." Her gaze shifted to Gabrielle, who was looking at her in surprise. "Well?"

"Um—I'm sorry, didn't mean to stare," Gabrielle replied with a brief smile. "It's just that—if you're the healer and midwife, you seem so—ah—well, so young."

"The infants prefer someone nearer their own age," the healer replied dryly. Gabrielle considered this as if uncertain whether to laugh or be offended; she finally laughed. After a moment the healer's lips twitched and she smiled. "I'm touchy on the subject, sorry. My grandmother was the last healer for the villages around here. She properly trained me, though, as well as she'd have trained my mother, if Mother'd had any trace of the gift." She held out a hand. "I'm Epicaste, glad to meet you."

Gabrielle met the hand halfway. "Pleasure."

"I know who both of you are, of course; I've been over in Ilyan, tending a difficult first pregnancy, only just got back this morning. Kind of you to chase off some of our less pleasant guests, warrior."

57

"*My* pleasure," Xena said dryly. "Did he talk to you, about what happened?"

"Some." Epicaste shook her head. "It's all new to me, men into swine, but there's always something new to come along."

"I need to talk to him," Xena said. "That all right?"

"Can't hurt him any, that I can tell."

"Good. Gabrielle, why don't you and the healer go talk about herbs while I'm here?"

"Herbs . . ." Gabrielle said vaguely, her brow crinkled; it cleared as she remembered. "Oh. Those herbs. Gotcha. Healer—Epicaste, you have a few minutes, share a little cider, maybe?" She was already talking rapidly, waving her arms as they crossed to the inn. The young healer looked a little glassy-eyed; plenty of people did, their first conversation with Gabrielle, Xena thought. She smiled after her young friend, then went into the innkeeper's hut.

Isyphus had fallen asleep, her head at an uncomfortable-looking angle against the wall. Eumaeus lay with his head against her shoulder, but as Xena stopped at the foot of the bed, he carefully eased away from his wife and sat up, then swung his feet to the floor.

"It's all right, innkeeper, I can come back—"

"No." He pushed himself upright, walked slowly across the room, and dropped onto a low bench against the far wall. "She needs the sleep, poor lass," he added, with a fond glance at his sleeping wife. "But she won't hear us over here. Poor Issy. It's not been easy here of late. But she tells me we have you to thank for ridding us of the ruffians."

"Some of them. They're not all gone, you know." At his gesture, she sat down on the end of the bench, turning so she could watch his face and the only door at the same time.

"I know. We won't be free of 'em until we get our king back, if we ever do. But this other thing—" He grimaced, touched his snout. "What can we do about that female, about our men?"

"We're working on that," Xena said. "My young friend has an idea or two. If we can decide who the woman is and how to repair matters, will you show us where she was the night you saw her?" He went pale under sun-darkened skin and there was fear in his eyes. She'd have to push him. "Once she has all the grown men from around here, what's to stop her from taking the boys—or the women and girls? Your son deserves a better future than that, doesn't he? And your granddaughter?"

He was quiet for so long, she wondered if she'd offended him. Not that she could let it matter, someone would have to give them a place to start, and there was only Eumaeus at the moment. But after a long silence broken only by a gentle, whuffling snore from the bed and the distant cries of boys playing a game, he sighed and nodded. "You're right; I don't like it. Who would? And I don't believe she'll still be in that place, warrior—"

"She might not be," Xena agreed. "She probably won't leave any trace of her passing, either; not if she's a sorceress. But I can track a pig," she added flatly. He looked curious but merely nodded again as she got up and left him. She was muttering to herself as she strode off behind the inn, across the dry creek bed, and into the nearest field. "Tracked pigs for my mother when I was still in plaits. Can't stand pigs." She considered this. "Hate pigs."

The field was empty at this hour; the ugly rows of stubble would eventually be chewed down when they loosed the goats and oxen here, and after that the villagers would replant. If there were enough of them left to replant. She strode through the cut stalks, leaped onto high-piled rocks, and stared down at the sea and an ever-narrowing crescent of wet sand.

Three days in this village already. But she couldn't turn her back on people in such need. King Menelaus would simply have to wait for an answer to his message. "Old brute," she growled, and turned back to study the track, the rock and woods beyond it; the back side of the village. Four boys sprinted briefly into sight, vanished beyond the inn, and distant cheers greeted the footrace.

Too bad the Trickster hadn't made it home yet. Be too bad, of course, if he didn't make it home at all; his people needed him desperately. "Too bad he couldn't have found a better way to trick that messenger in the first place. I can't remain here forever, though." Get the men of Isos back, get them restored to man shape, if possible. Then she could teach them basic weapon skill and, more important, how to use stealth and tricks to overwhelm trained soldiers and skilled thugs. They'd be as able to care for themselves as any villagers in times like these. "And King Odysseus will owe me one." She smiled faintly. She'd liked the wily Odysseus despite herself; unlike his friend and fellow king Menelaus, he didn't take himself seriously and didn't lord it over others. And he used his head for something besides a place to pour ale.

The sun was low in the sky, casting a golden sheen over the sea, when she finally climbed down from her perch and sauntered back to the inn.

Nionne was in the yard behind the inn, stirring a large pot that hung over a spluttering fire. Fragrant steam wafted on the evening breeze: herbs and garlic, some kind of soup or stew. The woman gave her a sidelong, rather nervous glance, then went back to her stirring. *Embarrassed about her earlier outburst.* Nothing she could do about that; the woman would either get over it, or not. And that only mattered to Eumaeus, in the long run.

Gabrielle and Epicaste were hunched over a pair of empty cups, Gabrielle listening intently as the healer and midwife named herb after herb, pausing at each; each time Gabrielle shook her head wearily. "Thyme—not the common but the red-flowered—"

"No. None of them, actually."

"Self heal, hypericum, scutelary?" Gabrielle merely shook her head. "Valerian—no, no, wouldn't be that. Yarrow—wait, I've left something out." Xena poured herself a mug of ale, then leaned against the counter to watch them. The healer was muttering to herself, ticking off the fingers of one hand then the other, back again. "Got it. Absinthe—you might know it as wormwood?"

"Wormwood!" Gabrielle shouted, and slapped both hands on the table, then yelped and shook her right hand. "Ow! I hate splinters!" She began working it free with her teeth.

Epicaste laughed and grabbed her hand. "Stop that, you'll make a mess of it. Let me." She squinted at the girl's outstretched fingers, scratched gently with a nail. "You think absinthe, really?"

Gabrielle nodded. "Ouch!"

"Hold still, then! I can't retrieve a tiny bit of wood if you're twitching like that! Wormwood . . . hmm. I don't use it much, there's too much can go wrong if it's not prepared properly. And it's not good for much of anything—"

"My mother and her sister dosed the village children every spring, for—ah—parasites. Ouch!" She yelped as the healer's fingers jerked; Epicaste dropped something tiny and dark on the table between them. "You got it? Thanks!"

"You *can* use wormwood for that," Epicaste allowed cautiously. "I wouldn't. But—"

61

"They added *lots* of water," Gabrielle said. She wet the tip of one finger, touched it to the table, squinted at the splinter. "But someone—I remember someone saying something one of those times when they were steeping the stuff about how else you could use it, something about strong enough and it would prevent a shape change."

"Mmmm. Maybe."

Xena set her cup aside, crossed the room, and dropped onto the bench, settling her shoulders against the wall and crossing her ankles on a corner of the table. "Do you two really have something, or is this all speculation?"

Gabrielle shrugged. "It's the thing I was trying to remember—wormwood. And the one tale I heard about Circe, there was something said—let me think." She closed her eyes briefly, suddenly smiled. "Got it. 'The bitterness of silver Artemis spread so within his body that even Circe's spell could not bear to taste it, and so was turned aside.' "

Xena eyed her sidelong, her face expressionless. "That's it? But you called it wormwood, and *you* said absinthe?"

Gabrielle's smile turned apologetic; she spread her arms wide. "It's got at least three names; tell me about an herb that doesn't. Artemis is the really old name for wormwood, which is what the people around my village called it; they apparently call it absinthe here, and I've heard that name, too. But—yeah. Unless you have a better idea, that's it."

"That's not half it," Epicaste said darkly. "The stuff is as difficult to work with as poppy or valerian—one tiny mistake in the preparation and you've killed the person you're trying to heal."

"It's not *that* hard," Gabrielle protested. "I used to watch my mother do it all the time."

"Impasse," Xena put in neatly as she paused for breath,

62

before the argument could heat up. "Maybe if one of you explained the problem to me?"

Gabrielle glanced at Epicaste—who looked from her to the warrior—finally shrugged. "All right," she said. "It's a plant you can find on the edge of the woods, pretty thing, silver gray, tough as those rocks out next to the wheat fields. You harvest the leaves and sometimes the stems or the tough branches, though I don't recommend that last; make a tea with the leaves, or shred the stems, break up the branches and let them soak for a few days. Then, if you're at all a kind healer, you have to find something neutral in usage and strong in taste and scent to conceal the flavor, the stuff is absolutely awful." She held up a hand and began ticking off points. "You don't want to oversteep the tea, or use boiling water on the leaves, or leave any of the leaves *in* the tea, or—" She paused, frowning. "You certainly don't want to distill it, though a few fools have."

"Why?" Gabrielle demanded. "I mean, why not?"

"Makes a liquor a hundred times stronger than ale; you see monsters and purple spots and you want nothing else to eat or drink but that—and it finally kills you. Rots your insides completely away."

"Messy," Xena put in. "But with a little care . . . ?"

"Look," Epicaste said earnestly. "I can't tell you from personal experience, and *her* experience is from the days she was still playing with dolls. A 'little care' can get your patient very dead." Xena merely looked at her, and waited. The healer sighed heavily. "All right. I can send word to my grandmother over in Ilyan, see if she has any *real* knowledge of it. If there's a use like you say, Gabrielle, she'll know about it—her mind's still good, it's her legs that won't carry her back and forth anymore."

• • •

Four days later Gabrielle and Epicaste found a place to build a fire north of the village, so the seldom-shifting west ocean winds would blow the odor of steeping wormwood away from the houses and fields. Eumaeus' son and several of the other boys spent the morning bringing in bundles of wood—logs and kindling, enough to complete the task—and Nionne and several of the other young women came near midday with baskets full of feathery, silver-leaved branches. They left quickly; the word had already spread about the smell involved in steeping the stuff. Gabrielle looked at the piles of things at her feet.

"All right. Now what?"

Epicaste dropped down to the ground, cross-legged, and unrolled the scroll her grandmother had sent. "You get the fire going and start separating the leaves into a pile; I'm going to read this out loud one more time."

"Then we'll make half as many mistakes," Gabrielle agreed cheerfully, and reached for the nearest basket; the healer gripped her wrist and eyed her somberly.

"It had better do more than that. I already told you—"

"Hey." Gabrielle knelt and dropped her hand over Epicaste's. "I'm just trying to lighten the mood here, I'm not making light of what we're doing. I know how dangerous the stuff is, and believe me, I'm going to be more careful than even *I* think I can be. It's just that—well, it's easier for me if I'm not so tense when I'm doing things, I make fewer mistakes."

"I'm sorry—"

"No, don't be sorry. You just read, and I'll get started stripping leaves."

Back in the village, Eumaeus sat behind the counter, dispensing wine, ale, and cider to women and the few remaining older boys who'd all been out in the square, threshing the first wheat. Isyphus ladled the last of the soup into Xena's bowl, then carried the pot back to the kitchen. She was quiet until only Xena remained, then snorted inelegantly. "Never saw such mannerly people!"

"Now, wife," Eumacus began, but Isyphus cut him off. "Did even *one* of 'em look properly at you?"

He shrugged. "I'd rather they didn't, just now. Don't worry it, wife; I don't mind much. Except for Nionne, of course."

"Shame to her!" Isyphus sounded very near tears. Eumaeus slid from the tall stool and came around the counter to clasp her close.

"There's no shame," he said. "She's just—she's not strong that way, and you are, Issy. You can't blame her for that; she's always minded when things were different, even when she was a babe. I don't expect her to change now."

"Her own father!"

"Well," Eumaeus said thoughtfully, "it's still a shock to *me,* and I don't need to look at myself, do I?" He looked past her as Xena finished her soup and got to her feet. "Warrior, you really believe those little girls? That this stuff'll make things well again, somehow?"

"I'm working on the somehow," Xena replied as she set the bowl down and resettled her sword belt. "And it may not work, but at least there's a chance. If you do nothing— what then, innkeeper?" She gave him a brief smile. "For what it's worth, I think we'll win out." He really had a nice smile, she thought as she stepped into the street; it warmed his whole face, odd nose and all.

A rather subdued crowd in the square; they were busily threshing the grain heads, the boys pouring the separated kernels of wheat into loose-woven bags or enormous baskets, the little girls carting the cloths full of chaff over to the inn stable where older girls poured the oddments into feed bins; still other children and one or two of the old women gathered up the straw, which would be dried for now, softened in water, and woven into baskets over the wet, dark winter months. Out the other direction, she could just make out a tall column of smoke bending eastward: the healer and her helper busy preparing wormwood.

"If this works . . ." Xena muttered as she crossed the bridge to make a wide circuit of the town. It had to work; an angry and powerful sorceress wouldn't give them a second chance.

The same thing was visibly on Eumaeus' mind four days later, as he, Isyphus, Xena, and Gabrielle rode and walked north along the track that led to the boat landing where the queen's wine should have gone. The innkeeper and his wife rode in the small village cart behind a tired and aging donkey. Gabrielle now and again rode in the back of the cart, facing the way they'd come, more often walked ahead with the warrior, who stalked quietly along the road, her eyes moving constantly, watching for any hint of movement among the trees or ahead on the road.

Behind her, she could hear the man talking in a low voice but couldn't make out the words. He sounded worried—no real surprise there. When she'd laid out the plan he'd been extremely skeptical; the healer's reassurances hadn't noticeably helped. What little courage he'd shown earlier was clearly failing. When Gabrielle joined her a little while later, she confirmed this.

"I guess he forgot I was back there," she said quietly. "He's sweating, he's scared half-silly, he keeps saying things like, 'They're both younger than Nionne and we both know how clever *she* isn't, wife.' I wanted to shake him, but I understand what he's going through. I guess it didn't help any, just the four of us coming."

It was a familiar argument. Xena sighed and ran down the other side of it yet again. "Why would we be any safer bringing Epicaste? She doesn't know the first thing about magic and she's the only midwife and healer for three villages. If we've done everything so far right, then four of us will be more than enough—and if not, why waste more lives than four?"

"Oh. Thanks," Gabrielle replied dryly. "I agreed to that, remember? I just don't really think I want to hear about it all the way out here."

"Whatever makes you happy," Xena muttered, and fell quiet. The only sound for some time was the harsh breathing of the donkey and the creak of the cart.

She could hear Eumaeus mumbling again all at once: "Just about—no, we'd passed that oak, the one with the funny growth by that fat root—and then there was—now, were we already beyond the small grove of plane trees, or not?" He went on in this fashion for some time. Isyphus might have been nodding or shaking her head; she wasn't making any sound, though. Finally, he cleared his throat and announced, "This place—well, I think so, warrior."

"You *think*," she replied evenly.

"This or another just a ways up," he replied unhappily. "It was dark, I told you that, and there are several places look just like where we stopped; I can't recall which of them we might've passed that night. And—if this is where we were, the cart's completely gone."

"No surprise there, husband," Isyphus grumbled. "Someone's got new firewood, that's all." She fell quiet as Xena held up a hand and Eumaeus drew the donkey to a halt. Both they and Gabrielle watched as the warrior, bent nearly double, walked back and forth along the track, now and again going to one knee to study something none of them could make out. She finally stood and shook her head.

"No sign of anything here." There was no sign of a splintered cart at the next place Eumaeus thought he recognized, but at the third, even Gabrielle could make out the scattered chips of wood along the right-hand side of the track, a dribbling trail of them crossing to the seaward side and vanishing into the trees.

"No villages hereabouts," Isyphus volunteered. "Could be anyone."

"Not so important at the moment," her husband reminded her. He sounded nervous. She patted his hands and both looked at Xena, who sent her eyes toward the thick woods east of the track. Eumaeus sighed and got down from the cart, took his wife's hands, and kissed them. "Remember what *is* important," he urged her quietly. "No cart and beast is worth your life, woman."

"Don't fuss over me," Isyphus replied gruffly. "I'm not going to challenge a pack of ruffians for it. I'm just making sure none of my fellow Ithacans see the opportunity for free transport; carts like this don't grow on trees and neither do donkeys! Mind you take care yourself!" she added tartly. Her eyes were very bright as Xena fished a large water bag on a heavy strap from the back of the cart and settled it across her shoulder, then led the innkeeper and her young friend off the track, around heavy, thorny brush, and across an area only marginally less impassable than the brush. Once in the clear, she stopped.

"You're certain this is the place?" Xena asked in a low voice. Eumaeus, his eyes wide and all pupil, nodded. Gabrielle glanced behind them, then cautiously to both sides. "Which way next?" He thought a moment, then pointed due east. Xena resettled the strap, shifted the large bag against her hip, and eased her way through a thicket of sapling oak trees and tall, furry-leaved berry bushes. A deep-cut streambed barred their way a short distance beyond this; she scrambled down to damp ground and smoothed stones, turned only long enough to make certain her companions were still with her, then clambered up the far bank to watch and listen. Aside from a distant bird or two, the woods were very quiet. *Watchful,* she thought. Not particularly a good thought. She shrugged it aside, waited for Eumaeus to point the way, and set out again.

A few paces on, she found a narrow deer path and, in its midst, a broken sandal, which she scooped up and passed back to Eumaeus. He nodded once, dangled it by the broken strap, then stuffed it into his belt. His face was damp, the hair clinging to his brow, even though it wasn't particularly warm at the moment. Gabrielle kept glancing warily across her shoulder, as if she sensed or feared some-one might have crept up on her. Xena gave her a brief, reassuring smile, looked to the innkeeper for direction, started walking once more.

It seemed an hour, probably it was only half that long, by the angle of shadows, when they came to a small meadow. Eumaeus caught at Xena's wrist, pointed at the clearing, nodded vigorously. She held up a hand, pointed down: *Sit and wait,* the gesture said. Eumaeus did so im-mediately; Gabrielle looked briefly rebellious, but the warrior glared at her and she dropped down cross-legged at once. She smiled up; a corner of Xena's mouth quirked as she pressed an open palm the girl's direction: *Stay put.* Gabrielle nodded, leaned over to whisper against the inn-keeper's ear. He nodded vigorously, but the warrior was already on her way around the meadow, moving silently from shadow to shadow, gazing into the open, back into the trees. She'd made over half the circuit when bent grass drew her attention, and she went to one knee, a hand out to gently touch the stalks. They were dry, but not com-pletely dry—whoever had passed here, going generally north, had done so in the past one to three days. Any wetter, the grass would stay completely flat for a week or more; too dry and it would either be broken off at the base or back upright again. Either way, much more difficult to gauge time. Or numbers, or even direction. *Just the right amount of moisture,* she thought with a smile, and gazed in the direction the bent grasses pointed. *One to our side.*

Several paces beyond the meadow, among the trees, a depression in the ground had held just enough water for two prints to form in the damp dirt: a pig's unmistakable, two-toed mark, and a small, narrow, dainty sandal. The smile broadened, became a momentary flash of white teeth; she remained where she was for a long moment, listening and watching, but there was no further sign and the prints themselves were at least a day old. Finally, she got to her feet and went back to her companions. A gesture brought both to their feet; a few whispered words explained the situation. Eumaeus was, if anything, even paler than he'd been, the ruddy-brown snout and the deep red hairs sticking out of it a stark contrast to his pallid face. There were freckles across the bridge of Gabrielle's nose; something seldom visible.

"It's all right," Xena whispered. "No one close by. Save the worry for when we find them."

"Right," Gabrielle said dryly. Eumaeus merely nodded, and even then, his head wobbled, but his hands were steady as they started across the meadow.

5

The wild animal track went on for some distance, then crossed another track, and another; the going was slow here, since the ground was very dry, and what few tracks remained were faint, crisscrossed with stag, rabbit, and wild boar prints. Late in the afternoon, the path began to climb. Xena sighed, shifted the bag on her shoulder, then thought better, slung it to the ground, and gestured to her companions to drop and stay put. Eumaeus seemed too tired even to be afraid at this point. Gabrielle merely nodded, gathered the bag close, and leaned back against a tree trunk so she could pull off one supple brown boot and massage her foot. The warrior caught her eye, glanced meaningfully at Eu maeus, and took off up the hill, moving swiftly and in utter silence.

Wants me to make certain he doesn't panic and run, Gabrielle realized. She bit back a sigh. *As if I could do anything to stop him, if he wanted to take off, or yell.* She looked in his direction, realized he was watching her through exhaustion-dulled eyes, and smiled reassuringly. His expression didn't change. She set the boot aside, scooted closer to him, and whispered, "She'll be back. But you know what, I think we're pretty close if she wanted to scout." He nodded once, licked his lips; his eyelids sagged closed and he rubbed the bridge of his snout. Gabrielle felt a deep surge of pity that left her eyelashes damp. *Poor man. If he has to live like that forever* . . . Well, he'd just have to manage if that was the case. And villagers really did accept things when they had to. But Nionne still couldn't bear to look at him. *Her attitude is bound to affect how little Niobe looks at her grandfather. How awful.* She couldn't think of anything to say; finally she sat back, removed her other boot, and flexed a very overheated and sore foot.

She could hear the cry of a distant hawk high above their heads; a scurrying in the brush nearby that meant something like a mouse had heard it, too. The cry repeated directly overhead, shrill and wild, then faded, and was gone. The mouse or whatever had gone to ground. Somewhere a breeze soughed through high branches, though none of it reached the people on the ground; somewhere behind them and to one side, she could faintly hear the tinkling of water over stones.

Between one breath and another, Xena was with them again, crouching to settle the bag across her shoulder. She beckoned; Eumaeus blinked at her sleepily, and Gabrielle leaned close so the warrior could whisper against her ear. "She's up there, on the plateau; there's a nice little grove and pigs everywhere, at least fifty of them."

"That's too many," Gabrielle protested softly.

"Mmm. More than one village." Xena shook her head. "Not important. We go, now." She touched the innkeeper's chin, caught hold of his ear, and drew it close to her mouth. "Eumaeus, you had better stay here for now. One of us will come for you." If they prevailed against Circe, and could coerce or persuade the sorceress to remove the spell from him.

"Zzzznnnnrrk!" He started, eyes wide, and clapped a hand across mouth and snout. Gabrielle bit back a grin. "Sorry," he whispered. "Tired. I'll stay—here."

"Good. Under the brush there, wait for us. If we aren't back by the time shadow's here"—she drew a line in the dust—"then go back to the track, take your wife, and go home."

"You?" he murmured.

Xena smiled faintly, shook her head. "Nothing you can do for us then," she whispered. "But it won't come to that."

Gabrielle forced tired, hot feet back into her boots, leaned close to the innkeeper's ear. "It's all right, honestly; she'll fix things, she always does." His lips twitched, but he didn't say anything. Xena was already on her feet, eyes searching the vicinity. Gabrielle got up slowly and cautiously, groaned faintly as her feet took her weight once more. Xena met her eyes, laid a finger across her lips; Gabrielle cast her eyes up and grimaced, but nodded, and was utterly quiet after that. The warrior put her lips against the girl's ear.

"Ready to talk?" she murmured. Gabrielle grimaced cheerfully, though her eyes were worried. After a moment she nodded cautiously. "Good. I'll dispense this stuff as quickly as I can. You talk fast." She turned and led the way up the narrow, winding path. Gabrielle squared her shoulders, swallowed hard, and followed.

The last of the climb was a hard one. Dry dirt dribbled from around plenteous stone; the least wrong move would bring down a deafening fall of rock. *Not a good idea,* Gabrielle thought dryly as she tucked a corner of her skirt into her belt and wrapped one hand around a sapling. All at once, instead of nothing but tree branches, limbs, and leaves, she could see sky, and then, as suddenly, the slope leveled out, became something comfortably climbable. Xena dropped to her hands and knees. Gabrielle bit her lip, tucked the other side of her skirt up, and went down almost flat. Moments later she came up beside her friend and slowly raised her head.

Xena tugged at her hair; Gabrielle allowed herself to be yanked down until she could barely see across level ground. There was grass—tall grass, mostly trampled flat here. A few wildflowers dotted the grass; mostly she could see stems or stalks, leaves, and bitten-off heads. There, the little jagged-edged, round leaves that marked spring red-berries, but many of them were gone as well, and there wasn't one faded berry to be seen anywhere. Beyond the edge here, perhaps worth twenty of Xena's long-legged steps and twenty-five of her own, stood a grove of slender young trees not much more than a tall man's height. In the very midst of these someone had piled gorgeous cushions: richly woven, embroidered, tassled. Gold thread glinted in the late-afternoon sun. It took a moment for her to spot the woman reclining among the cushions; from this angle, mostly, she could see pigs.

There were red pigs, pale pink ones with glistening snouts, black ones with pale spots. One gray-skinned, skinny-flanked old boar with heavy white bristles sprouting from the tips of his floppy ears tottered across open ground, cutting off her view for a long moment while it pushed its snout through the grass, searching for something it could eat. It finally snorted and moved on to collapse in the sparse shade of a low rowan. A black-spotted, sleek brute chased after another solidly black pig, who squealed sharply as the chaser bit his tail. A pack of them, at least fifteen pigs in a solid mass, stood at the north end of the grove, swaying slightly back and forth, their beady little eyes fixed on the pile of cushions.

Xena tapped Gabrielle's hand to get her attention, pointed to the center of the grove. Gabrielle squinted, stared, finally lowered her head to a point below ground level, and nodded. "I see her," she breathed. Xena's eyes were pale, sardonic fires; she pointed at her companion, made rapid open-and-shut gestures with her hand. Gabrielle wrinkled her nose and grinned ruefully. *Yeah, right, I talk.* She pointed to the large water bottle, jerked a thumb in the direction of the pigs and then toward her open mouth. Xena grinned wryly, gave her shoulder a hard pat, then slid away. Gabrielle counted under her breath. *Three minotaurs, four minotaurs, five minotaurs . . .* Time. She drew a deep breath, expelled it in a rush, and got to her feet, forcing a cheery grin. Across the meadow, beyond more pigs than she'd ever seen in one place, a pale-faced, red-haired, utterly gorgeous woman scrambled to her feet, scattering cushions everywhere. Pigs squealed and ran in all directions, but those coming Gabrielle's way squealed again and veered around her. The woman was staring, her eyes wide, her lips parted in visible shock.

"Hi, there!" Gabrielle called out cheerfully as she gained level ground and started forward. "I'm Gabrielle, and you know what? I'd know you anywhere, you just have to be Circe! Ah—can we talk?"

Dead silence; the few remaining pigs edged away as she came across the meadow. The red-haired woman stood very still, her bearing almost regal, arms at her side, her chin high. The effect would have been even more majestic, Gabrielle thought critically, if her hands weren't bunched into fists.

The woman's eyes were banked green fires. *All right, keep the smile where it is, keep the chatter light, keep it friendly, be pleasant. Set her at ease; strange woman, foreign country, who knows if the old boyfriend's gonna show up to fix things or not? Who knows, she could be nursing a broken heart and just waiting around here to see if Odysseus might ride by.* Stranger things had happened, on the earth, above and below it. *And remember,* she told herself cautiously, some magic wielders could read the thoughts of those who confronted them. . . .

She smiled very widely, waved again, and came on, cheerfully determined.

Circe hadn't moved yet, except to flex one tiny, white-fingered fist. Gosh, Gabrielle thought, her own eyes wide. She's the tiniest woman I ever did see! Hair fell from a gold-and-pearl band, a red-gold waterfall that stopped just short of her ankles; her gown was an eye-dazzling blue white edged in a gold-threaded, embroidered key pattern, the corners touched with pearls or little gold wire arabesques.

The face beneath the band and under all that wonderful hair was rather plain, actually: her mouth was quite small and dissatisfied looking; her eyebrows heavy and dark, and drawn together so they almost formed one bushy line; her chin receded, and it was spotty. But her eyes would be nice, Gabrielle decided judiciously—that wonderful, rich green—if they weren't so angry looking.

She suddenly couldn't think of another thing to say. When Circe finally spoke, she'd covered most of the ground to the edge of the grove; the sorceress's voice was a low, throaty purr. *Like Xena at her most dangerous. Ouch, not a good thought.* "How do you know my name, mortal?"

"Well, I didn't at first," Gabrielle confessed. "But it was just so obvious after a while, especially once someone described you. There can't be two women in all the world with such hair, or such wonderfully tiny feet, or such a little waist . . . and of course, I've heard so much about you!''

''Oh. What have you heard?'' Circe wasn't used to talking to women, Gabrielle thought; the realization steadied her, all at once. *I can do this!*

''Well—I've heard all about your island, and all the men you've captured and turned into beasts. . . .'' She very carefully didn't look anywhere but at Circe. The sorceress spat out a word; the remaining few pigs squealed and scattered. ''Well—ah, yes! Sure! And then, you know what I heard? Most recently they say you offered lodging and food to some of the Argives and they acted just like—'' She faltered, searching for a word. Circe smiled coldly; Gabrielle felt the hair on her neck hackling.

The sorceress's smile broadened, but her eyes were as cold as a midwinter sea. ''—like pigs,'' she said softly. ''They drank my wine, and ate my fruit, and drank more wine, and spewed everything upon the carpets and the sand; they accosted my servants, pummeled the men and the women—well, you have the look of a virgin, girl, so I won't go into detail about that.''

Gabrielle primmed her lips and rubbed a certain bruised portion of her anatomy. ''I know more than you might think. But I'd rather not hear about it anyway.'' Circe caught the gesture and laughed; the few pigs inside the grove squealed and scattered, and Gabrielle held her ground only with a strong effort. ''And, um, I'd really rather you didn't use the V-word quite so loudly, okay? It's not exactly my finest accomplishment, it's just something that's happened—okay, something that *hasn't* happened! Whatever! I just—''

''Save yourself,'' the sorceress broke in wearily. ''*Men* aren't worth it.''

• • •

A distance away, Xena moved slowly, cautiously, and in utter silence through the bushes north of the sorceress's meadow and glade. Finally satisfied with her position, she glanced warily around, listened intently, then knelt and slipped the strap of the heavy bottle over her head, settled it on the ground, and scratched softly against a tree trunk. Moments later she scratched again, a little louder. A pig came warily into sight, eyed her with visible doubt. She smiled, lips together, nodded, and uncapped the bottle. The pig's snout quivered as steam from Isyphus' soup wafted into the air.

"That's right," Xena whispered. "Come here, I have something for you." The pig quivered all over, launched himself at her. She poured a capful of soup on the ground, watched as the little beast lapped it all up—along with a generous mouthful of mud and dead leaf bits—then eased slowly to her knees.

"All right, my friend," she murmured in a noncarrying voice. "I know you're a man under that exterior; go out there and tell your comrades to come and have a mouthful of Isyphus' soup." She caught hold of an ear, bent to speak against it. "And prove to me you're really intelligent. Remember, there's a sorceress out there who'd probably kill you all, if she knew what I was doing here. Don't let her know." She released the ear, swatted his ample backside. "Go!" The pig eyed her wildly, turned, and scrambled out of the brush.

For a long moment she wondered if he'd had the least clue of what was going on here, but a moment after, she could see him, rubbing against a pig with very similar markings, his snout moving rapidly. For one moment she wondered how—and if—they were communicating; a breath later she dismissed it with a hard and silent oath. Her nose wrinkled as she suddenly became aware of the faint but unpleasant odor of unwashed pig. *I loathed pigs back in my father's village; I have no reason to like them now.* Pigs who'd been men—but these weren't just any men, were they? They were villagers, honest husbands, sons, and grandfathers, men who protected their wives and families from men like Kalamos, at whatever cost to themselves. Who worked the plows or cut wood, doing the physical work beyond the strength of most women and children. She set her jaw and her eyes were chill blue fires. *Next time pick men like Kalamos for your toys, Circe,* she thought blackly. Half a dozen pigs threw themselves into the thicket, panting, their eyes wide, frightened and imploring, all at once.

Gabrielle shoved hair off her forehead and tried again. "Look, the virgin thing isn't an issue for me, it's not that important. But, you know? I'd really like to try to understand why you turned all those men into—well, why pigs? I mean, why not butterflies? They'd take up less room, they'd only go after your flowers, drink the nectar.... Well, it's an idea, don't you think?"

Circe laughed sourly. "They'd find a way to wreak havoc among the blossoms. Don't you understand, girl? The shape doesn't matter! You can make them snakes or bugs, bats or leopards, lions or rabbits, it still—does—not—matter!" Her voice rose querulously. After a moment she regained control and the timbre dropped sharply to that throaty purr Gabrielle found most unnerving. *Seductive!* she realized all at once. *That's what it is! She doesn't know any other way to deal with something two-footed, except to seduce it—* She swallowed, hard. *Or turn it into a pig.*

"I'm sorry." She did a little nervous dance, flung her arms wide, and smiled deprecatingly. "I really don't un-

79

derstand why pigs. I—don't get me wrong, it's not you, it's me, I'm just dense that way, I guess!''

Circe laughed shortly, ran her hands through long, brilliantly red hair. ''Silly little girl. All men are swine. Ask any woman, she'll tell you the same thing.''

But Perdicas wasn't a brute—even if he did find his own life without me! Gabrielle thought suddenly. *And that boy, Agranon, he was so sweet. And just think of big, bosomy Isyphus and cute little Eumaeus, even if he does have a snout instead of a nose!* She drew herself up straight, squared her shoulders, raised her chin, and smiled proudly. ''Listen, I'm not half as little as you are. And you know what? You might have been around the island a time or two more than I have, but you're *wrong*.''

Circe's eyes narrowed to tiny slits and her mouth was ugly. ''Are you trying to start an argument with me, mortal child?''

Gabrielle sighed, shook her head. There was a long, uncomfortable silence. ''Look, I'm going about this all the wrong way,'' she said winningly. ''I don't want to argue with a neat person like you. I wouldn't want to even if you didn't have such an—ah—*unusual* talent. But I think I know what your problem is, Circe. You just don't get out enough.'' The sorceress cast her a wild-eyed look, as though the conversation had just turned on its head. ''No, honestly! Because you're meeting all the wrong kinds of guys. Now, personally, I think you've done the right thing, coming to the mainland and getting away from that island of yours. Out there, you're stuck with whatever the waves toss up, right? But you have all the choices you'd ever want now, you can find yourself a nice-sized town or a city, check out some fellows who aren't sailors or fighting men. I mean, look at why you're doing all this.'' She flung her arms wide to include the meadow; there wasn't a single

80

pig in sight. Circe frowned slightly, but a moment later sank to her cushions, fascinated by the flow of words from the girl before her. "Let's see if I got it right; you're angry and making pigs out of Ithacan peasants because a middle-aged, married man with gray hair turned you down, is that it?"

"Well, but, I *wanted*—" Circe began sharply. She stopped as Gabrielle shook her head.

"Well, sure you wanted him—he was probably the best-looking man on the whole ship, or at least he was the captain, right? Did you know he'd just come from another island where he was—well, he was lying in an open pavilion and this—this floozy in a tiny little sheer chiton was feeding him grapes, and—"

"How do you know *that*?" Circe demanded.

"Oh," Gabrielle said airily, "I had a vision; saw it all. Shocking, I call it, I mean, if his poor wife ever found out!"

"Calypso!" the sorceress growled.

Gabrielle blinked at her. "Oh—oh, you mean *that* Calypso? That's the floozy? Ah—you mind if I sit down?" she added, and plopped down on the grass. "My feet hurt," she confided. "It's a long walk from Isos, you know. Calypso!" she went on thoughtfully, and tried not to notice that the little flame-haired creature was grinding her teeth. "Well, that explains it, then! I guess you probably think he was cozying up with *her* but you weren't good enough—"

"I didn't know he'd been *with* her until you told me just now," Circe gritted out.

"Oh. Right! Well, all the time he was with her, Odysseus didn't know who he was, she does that to men—"

"She—what does she do?" Circe felt blindly for a cushion and drew it under her elbow.

"Didn't you know? It's her one magical talent, she makes them forget, that's all. I'll just bet you that's the only reason he had his head in her lap so she could drop grapes on him. But by the time he got away from her some-how—"

"How?" Circe demanded sharply.

Gabrielle shrugged. "Probably one of the gods coming to his rescue. There are plenty of gods interested in that man just now, and not all of them in a friendly way." She shifted uncomfortably. "Sorry, I have a—a bruise; some-one pinched me."

Circe snorted and primmed her lips angrily, but after a moment the corners of her mouth twitched in something suspiciously like a smile. She fished a cushion from the stack and tossed it over.

Gabrielle caught it. "Thanks! Well, you know, I'll bet it's just as well you didn't keep that man around. I know Poseidon doesn't like him at all, and unless your island's all mountains . . ." She paused meaningfully. Circe seemed to be considering this; her eyes were very wide. "I think you're much better off without him," Gabrielle added per-suasively. "I mean—gosh, just look at you!" Circe did, as best she could, then stared at her companion. "You're one of the most gorgeous women I've ever seen!"

Circe blinked. "You think I'm—pretty?" She shook her head. "It's the gown, the hair, the gems—"

"Oh, nonsense! Your eyes are wonderful and that hair—! Wow!"

The sorceress caught hold of a length warily, between thumb and forefinger, and looked at it. A corner of her mouth twisted. "Really?"

"Trust me," Gabrielle urged. "You don't need magic to find yourself a really nice boy." She leaned forward and

82

smiled. "I think you just don't have enough self-confidence."

Down in the brush, Xena poured out the last of the stew, hung the bottle from a nearby branch, and gazed into worried pig eyes. There must have been thirty in the little clearing; her nose twitched. "That all of you?" she asked very softly. The first to drink the stuff lowered his head awkwardly, slowly brought it back up. "Didn't miss anyone?" The gesture for "no" seemed to be beyond him. She held out a hand, fingers splayed. "Stay here. I'll call." She backed away from them, watching; they stayed put. She turned, eased her way back toward the grove.

Once away from the pack, she paused and took a deep breath. A breeze would've been nice; one preferably blowing from her across them. She set out once more, finally eased two heavily leafed branches apart, peered cautiously into the open. Gabrielle was talking, her hands waving, the hair swaying across her back. Good. She was sitting cross-legged in the grove, near enough that the sorceress could probably grab her—not so good. But Circe looked utterly stunned. *Buried under an avalanche of words. Better yet.* Xena grinned, then settled down to study the terrain across the meadow. Some place where she could jump into the open, no more than a few paces from that grove . . .

It took a moment to locate something suitable, several long moments to backtrack so she could reach it without being seen.

"Self . . . confidence . . ." Circe repeated blankly. With an effort, she shook herself. "You said you knew about me! It doesn't sound like you do at all!"

Gabrielle waved a dismissive hand. "Oh, I know all that

stuff. Like that you live on an island where you don't have any competition for whatever men show up, and where anyone who washes ashore hasn't got much option for leaving.'' She smiled and leaned closer. ''I think you owe yourself better than that, honestly, Circe. I mean, *Calypso* does that—you know, picks up whatever washes onto *her* island—and we've already decided what *she* is, haven't we?''

''Shameless hussy,'' Circe muttered.

''Well, but you're not. You're—you've got lovely skin, and those green eyes and that wonderful hair. And you look really nice in that fancy chiton, but I'll bet you'd be even prettier if you wore just a plain blue one. And just think about it—instead of a gray-haired, set-in-his-ways old stump like Odysseus, you could find yourself a handsome young man who likes the same things you do.''

Silence, as Circe considered this. She shook her head finally. ''My face—''

''There's nothing at all wrong with your face,'' Gabrielle said firmly. ''We can't all be the beautiful Helen, after all—'' She hesitated, but Circe merely shrugged and waved Helen aside. ''And you know, most men I've talked to are put off by that much prettiness. They think, 'Well, she's so beautiful, why is she here with *me*?' You've got wonderful eyes, you know, and''—she gathered her courage in one deep breath—''and I know an herb or two that would take care of your—ah''—she touched her own chin—''those,'' she finished lamely. ''But I'm telling you, any man gets to know and love his woman, and he won't care what she looks like.'' *Or the other way around,* she thought wistfully. *Poor little Eumaeus.*

''Really?'' Circe sounded wistful, and her eyes were very wide.

''I swear it. No, you need a man who deserves you, and who will have something in common with you. And, you know what? I would wager right now, it won't be pigs you have things in common with. Right?''

"You know," the sorceress replied thoughtfully, "I really *don't* like pigs very much. Odd—never thought of that before."

Gabrielle laughed. "Of course not! You never had a reason to. But imagine a boy you could do things with, talk to, play with—somebody who'd listen to you. A friend, maybe?" She stopped, raised her eyebrows.

Circe was laughing sourly. "A man as a friend? You're mad, girl!"

Gabrielle shrugged. "It's not common, but that's only because men and women don't often try to be friends, they just—well, they just manage, that's all. *I* have men who are very good friends."

There was a long silence. Circe eyed her sidelong, clearly uncertain whether to believe all this; she let her gaze shift to her hands then. Gabrielle glanced quickly around the grove, and was rewarded with a quick flash of a hand not many paces away, and directly behind the sorceress. Xena there, letting her know everything was ready.

It's not right, she thought suddenly. *I've been gaining her trust all this time, the poor lonely girl, and I just know I'm right about her, and then—if we do it this way, trick her, it won't change anything, except then she'll really be angry.* She eyed the brush where the long fingered hand had just shown, rubbed the side of her nose cautiously, and sent wide, rather wild eyes toward the sorceress, who was still quietly contemplating her fingers. *Hope she understood that—that she'll let me handle this my way.*

Xena freed a long blade of grass that had found its way into her boot, eased down onto her haunches, and considered the strange look that had greeted her signal. She sighed then, very quietly. *She's up to something,* Well—maybe it was just a "I'm not ready yet, give me a little time." Who knew? she thought gloomily, then eased forward so she could at least keep an eye on things.

Circe stirred. "You aren't just making that up, are you?" she asked suspiciously. "Men as friends?"

"Cross my heart," Gabrielle said, and suited gesture to words. "I—well, see, I'm a bard; not an official one, of course, but I know a lot of the tales and the myths and I tell them, and, well, a lot of people like to listen when I do tell them. And a couple of my very dearest friends are bards—they're at the Academy in Athens, actually—and *they're* men."

"I—I see. How odd!"

"It's not so odd, you're just not used to the idea yet. Once you try it, though, trust me, you won't want to go back to coercion again. Although—I suppose if you really wanted to, you could, of course."

"Of course I could," Circe replied, but she no longer sounded threatening. The silence was a friendly one this time, and when the sorceress met Gabrielle's eyes, she smiled, rather shyly. It transformed her from a rather menacing little presence into a very attractive one.

"Um—listen," Gabrielle said suddenly. "You know what, Circe? I like you. And just to show you how much, and how I think this little talk has gotten to you, I'm going to trust you with something."

Back in the woods, Xena clenched her teeth to keep from swearing aloud and glared in an ice-eyed fury at her companion. *Blue Hades, she'll ruin everything! And I'm going to have to sit here and let her; if I jump in now, it won't help one single thing. Gabrielle, I'm going to . . . to . . .* Even a usually vivid and murderous imagination failed her

86

at the moment. She clutched branches with white-knuckled hands and listened.

"We had a plan," Gabrielle began; Circe held up a hand.
"We? Plan?"

"Um—well, let me explain, it's complicated."

"Oh?" The suspicion was back in her voice, Gabrielle thought nervously. *Oh well, too late to change back now.*

"You know all the villagers you lured away and—and changed? To get even with Odysseus? Well, we—okay, my friend and I—we had this plan to help those poor women get their husbands and fathers back home and on two feet again. We were going to feed them wormwood and—I wish you wouldn't glare at me like that," she added in a quiet little voice, "it's making me nervous."

"It's supposed to make you nervous," Circe growled. "Wormwood!"

"Ah—sure! They call it hyssop around here—"

"I know what else it's called. *What plan?*"

"Well—ah—oh, right. Feed the pigs wormwood and then trick you into changing them back to men. You know, 'I bet they aren't really men, you're just saying that'—so you'd make them men once more and then you couldn't shift them back. . . ." Her voice trailed away. Circe's eyes were narrow slits, her mouth tight. "Look," Gabrielle began again, "I'm telling you about it, aren't I? Because once I came over here and started talking to you, Circe, I realized you weren't an evil sorceress, or a bad person: you just— you just didn't know what you really wanted. I realized that I could like you, as a friend. Well, cheating you that way isn't what friends do to each other."

Silence. Circe's eyes slowly opened a little more. She tipped her head to one side, studied the girl from under a single brow. "It's not?"

"That's what I've been telling you, isn't it? Maybe the trickster king does things that way, but I don't. I'd *like* to be your friend, Circe, maybe help you break free of your old life, if I can."

The sorceress gave her a crooked grin that transformed her entire face. "I see. And all *I* have to do is change all my nice little pigs back to men—is that it?"

"It would be nice, if you did," Gabrielle said.

For answer, Circe flowed to her feet, put two fingers in her mouth, and let out a piercing whistle. Pigs came flying from across the meadow to mill nervously before the grove. She looked at the pigs, frowned down at Gabrielle. "Nice?"

"Nice. I know some women who'd be really happy, if you did."

"They don't know any better, that's all," Circe snapped, but the fire had gone out of her. She raised her hands and murmured quietly for some moments. One of the pigs squealed shrilly, another snorted. Gabrielle slewed around just as Eumaeus dragged himself into open ground, moaning and clutching his snout. A breath later he let his hands fall. The nose wasn't in great shape; it was thick, oddly upturned at the tip, and had visibly been broken and healed wrong at least once in the past. He ran a trembling hand over it, then smiled and sat down on the grass rather as though his legs had given out.

Gabrielle sighed happily; when she looked away from him, scores of men were sitting up feeling their arms and shoulders gingerly, or staring at other men in astonishment. One of them suddenly caught sight of Circe and her blond companion and shouted a wordless alarm. Men scrambled weakly to their feet, ready to run, but Gabrielle jumped up and hurried toward them.

"It's all right!" she yelled. "Ask Eumaeus, I'm a friend, and so is this lady!"

A black-haired, beardless young man pointed a trembling finger. "All right? Are you mad? She turned me into a pig!"

"Oh, that wasn't anything personal, and she's not going to do that again. In fact, if you want to leave right now, feel free. Eumaeus can get you back to the road." She didn't need to issue a second invitation; most of the men were out of sight, yelling and swearing, before she finished speaking.

Behind her, Circe sighed. "I don't know. As pigs, they were at least *quiet*." A faint sound behind her, someone clearing her throat. Gabrielle turned, and the sorceress spun around.

Xena stood very still at the edge of the grove, arms folded, a corner of her mouth twisted into a sardonic half smile. *Oops,* Gabrielle thought. But she couldn't be too angry; it had worked. She took a step forward and wrapped an arm around the tiny redhead's shoulders. "Circe—meet Xena."

Circe's head tipped back; her eyes were enormous. "That's your friend?"

Xena's smile broadened; it wasn't noticeably much warmer. "Fortunately for her," she said quietly.

Gabrielle laughed and patted Circe's shoulder. "She's such a kidder!"

6

Early evening, the following night, the single dusty track of Isos was brilliantly lit. Smoky torches smudged the air between the trees, blocking early starlight. To the west, a ruddy line marked the last hint of sunset, while just above the shoulder of the eastern hills, a new moon rose, casting faint shadow across stubble-covered fields. The inn was brilliantly lit, and from the open entry came the sound of music—a slightly out-of-tune lute nearly overwhelmed by exuberantly pounded drums, and a wavery young male voice occasionally smothered by both.

Gabrielle and Xena wandered slowly down the track and, at the far end of the village, paused and turned to listen. "That's great," Gabrielle finally said softly. "Listen—they've made a song in your honor, for saving them all."

Xena sighed very softly; her eyes were fixed on the horned moon. "I thumped a few stupid thugs. You're the one who convinced Circe to change the villagers back to men."

"Well—sure. But if you hadn't thumped the thugs, I wouldn't have been around to talk to Circe. Remember?

90

You fought, I talked, and hey! It all worked out just fine, didn't it? You know," Gabrielle went on thoughtfully as they slowly ambled back toward the inn, "it's a shame Circe couldn't have seen this—" Xena stopped short, and the girl glanced back at her. "Oh, I know she couldn't have, they probably wouldn't have wanted her around, after all that."

"Probably not," Xena replied dryly.

"But she could've learned a lot, just watching all those happy reunions."

"I just hope everything works out the way you think, Gabrielle."

"Works—oh. That. Well, I can't think of any reason she'd be happy around this part of the world; no one particularly likes what she did and there aren't any decent-sized towns. And, you know how it is, things are easier when you have a goal, right?" Gabrielle glanced at her friend and smiled cheerfully. "So all I did was put those things together, and it was obvious she should go to Athens, find the Academy, and look up Homer."

"And if she encounters someone halfway there, like, say, your friend the Spartan?"

Gabrielle shrugged. "Well, she can take care of herself, obviously. But we talked about that before she left this afternoon. It's a matter of degree, really. One guy like that Spartan—*poof!*—he's a pig or something, she explains the ground rules to him, and changes him back. You'd have to be stupider than any thug I've seen lately to try *that* twice."

"They're pretty stupid in packs," Xena reminded her. "In fact, the larger the pack—"

"Sure, the dumber the average thug. But even someone like your old buddy Kalamos would understand one of his men suddenly walking around on four feet and squealing, wouldn't he?"

"Maybe—"

"So she turns one of them and warns 'em to back off or they all go the same way. But I also explained to her what you tell me all the time. You avoid them when you can, it's easier on everyone. I think she liked the sound of that."

"I wish I had *your* confidence in her."

Gabrielle grinned impudently. "Oh, I really wouldn't worry about her. Everything I told her about Athens, she's *really* excited about getting there, seeing all the sights, checking out the shops, maybe finding herself a nice, plain blue chiton before she goes in search of Homer." They walked in companionable silence for a few paces, weaving a way through happy villagers, who stopped singing and dancing to call out, "Xena!" or "Gabrielle!" or "Here come the heroes!" Xena greeted this with a faint smile and a wave of her hand, Gabrielle with a wide smile. "You know," she said as they stepped beyond the pool of torch-light and walked past the stable, "I would just love to see Homer's face when he gets a good look at Circe. And when he hears her story—wow!"

"Maybe."

"Oh—I think so. Once she stopped scowling so fero-ciously, she really was rather pretty, you know. And she has beautiful eyes. And that hair—imagine having hair like that!" She sighed wistfully.

Xena snorted. "Imagine having to comb it every day."

"Ah—yes. That's a point." Gabrielle ran a hand through her hair. "Good one, too. But I can see her with a friend or maybe a lover or a husband who'll want to comb it for her, it's so beautiful."

"I'll take your word for it."

"Well, *I* would. And you know, I just have a feeling, Circe isn't going to see that island of hers again for a very long time." She sighed happily. "But you know, I certainly hope Nionne learns something from all this. I mean—who'd've thought her father had a nose like that normally, and then she was upset about . . . ?''

"Yeah. It isn't a pretty nose, but it's all she'd ever known. Remember what you told Circe about looks, why don't you? Besides, you know villagers; most of them don't care for change of any kind. Especially since change usually means something bad's just happened.''

Gabrielle nodded and cast her companion an impudent grin. "I never forget it—why do you think I'm here with you, instead of back home, married to Perdicas? Dealing with flood or drought, or more thugs—and probably already the mother of three or four howling babies?'' She shuddered. "Not that I have anything against babies, they're adorable! Like little Gabriel. Did I mention I think that's a really sweet name for him? But—no babies for me, not just yet, I guess.''

"Mmmm.''

They passed the inn, edged through a mob of villagers crowded around the well, clapping time for three men who had linked arms and were dancing something extremely athletic. Gabrielle's eyes were wide. "Gosh! How do they do that?''

Xena glanced that way, shrugged. "Hard work and practice, like most things.'' They finally broke free of well-wishers and celebrants, walked slowly up the rickety bridge, and gazed toward the distant, smudgy purple line where sea and sky met.

Gabrielle, as usual, broke the silence. "Do you think the trickster king will *ever* get home?''

"Don't know. He has a lot against him.'' Xena considered this, raised one shoulder. "He might already be dead, and who'd ever know?''

"Oh.'' Gabrielle sounded so unhappy, the warrior turned

93

and laid a hand on her shoulder, gave her a smile.

"He's good, though, very good at surviving." Her smile broadened. "I notice you haven't mentioned it, but I owe you an apology. About Calypso."

"Oh. Well, it's not really important. Except that now we know he *was* alive not that long ago, and he was at least as far from Troy as Circe's island." She sighed. "But there's so much ocean between there and here, and we *know* Poseidon's really angry with him. And—well, almost everyone but Hermes, and he's just a messenger!"

"Hermes isn't the only one," Xena assured her. "If you recall, Athena's said to be quite fond of him, even if she can't always protect him. But I don't think he needs that much protection, he can take care of himself. And if I believed in wagering, I'd put the odds on Odysseus."

"Good," Gabrielle said. "I think. Um—when do we leave for the palace?"

"The new wine won't be ready for nine more days; that gives me a little time to teach these people how to protect their village. When the cart leaves for the north coast, we'll go with it." She drew a deep breath, let it out, flexed her hands. "I wish we could go now; Odysseus' island is pretty much unprotected, and that includes his queen and his son."

Gabrielle snorted angrily. "Hmmph! You'd think since old King Menelaus was so eager to have his friends drop everything to go grab his *property* that he'd offer to pay for a guard to take care of his friends' palaces!"

"You'd think that way," Xena reminded her. "I would. Menelaus wouldn't."

By the time the cart started north, the day had turned hot and muggy. Gabrielle rode in the back, next to the rectangular baskets of wheat, her back against the enormous, padded basket that held the thick clay jugs of wine. Progress was necessarily slow so as not to jostle the wine and render it undrinkable. Xena strode alongside the cart, constantly checking the track ahead and the woods enclosing it on either side. By midmorning, even she had relaxed—a little; there was no sign of trouble anywhere. Any trouble that did jump them would still be extremely sorry. "How much further to the sea?" she asked finally.

Hesper started nervously; it was the first thing anyone had said almost since leaving the village in the blue-gray hour before dawn.

His friend Aleppis cuffed him across the ear, good-naturedly. Gabrielle smiled. *They picked on each other the same way back in Circe's meadow, when they had four feet and tails.* The kind of friends who couldn't express friendship in any other fashion. "She asked a question, you dolt! Princess—"

"Just Xena," the warrior replied flatly.

Aleppis cast her a nervous, sidelong glance, then nodded, and cuffed his friend's shoulder. "Xena. It's—well, we'll be there just after midday, even as slow as this."

"Ah. Good. Any sign of trouble there?"

"Trouble?" Hesper snorted, very piglike. "There's been nothing *but* trouble in all Ithaca since our king left his wife and baby son, *and* his responsibilities, to go chase after that strumpet Helen!"

Xena cast her young companion a warning glance; Gabrielle cast her eyes up and grimaced, but kept quiet. "Trouble," the warrior prompted after a moment. "Recent. Any?"

"Not that we've seen, Xena," Aleppis replied. "But we don't go out to the palace. We deliver goods to the ship, make certain they're loaded correctly, instruct the sailors if

95

there's anything like the wine that requires special care, then we turn the cart and go home."

"Might be nice to see that palace," his friend said wistfully as he shoved a thatch of blue-black hair out of his eyes. "They say it's a wonder, all spread out across the hillside, white marble and columns, fine statues, and a grotto dedicated to Athena, and the queen's tapestries—"

"Ahhhh, and what does a peasant like *you* know about fine tapestries?" Aleppis demanded.

"Just enough to know I'd like to see one," Hesper replied, and punched his friend's arm.

Gabrielle chuckled; both young men cast her a slightly startled glance, as though they'd forgotten she was there.

The road began to slope up as the trees came to an end. Here, gray-green, scraggly brush lined the track; as they climbed, it was gradually replaced by rock—boulders, slabs of stone, precariously balanced rockpiles. The donkey slowed, and slowed again as the track narrowed and became even steeper; the brush grew very tall here, and finally grew so thick most of the rock could no longer be seen. A hawk's piercing cry rent the air, and Gabrielle started.

Other than the hawk, there was no sound for some distance, except the creak of harness and wheels, the twig-against-twig noises made by the basket of grain, the donkey's labored breathing. As they neared the summit, Xena held up a hand for the cart to slow even more, then bounded up the track, easing into brush shadow along the western edge of the path. Gabrielle twisted around to watch her, one hand shading her eyes. The warrior's hair blew wildly, streamed briefly straight out behind her; she then dropped below the crest of the hill, shoved the dark strands behind her ears with an impatient hand, and gestured them on.

Aleppis urged the donkey on; it didn't want to go. Hesper

finally jumped down and hauled at the headstall, his feet firmly planted. When the beast finally decided to move on, Hesper's feet went out from under him and he fell flat on his back; only a quick roll to one side kept him from being run down. He staggered to his feet, swore, and jumped onto the back of the cart, next to Gabrielle, who grinned at him crookedly.

"Nice work," she said.

"Stupid beast," he replied darkly, but after a moment he glanced at her from under his brows and an answering grin tugged at his lips. A moment later the cart crested the hill; a swirl of strong, cool wind blew Gabrielle's hair in all directions, and when she drew a startled breath, one strand went into her mouth. Hesper retrieved it neatly. "I'd hold on to the stuff, or find a way to tie it," he shouted over the sudden roar of wind. "It's usually strong out here, but this is worse than usual, straight up the coast from the south. Could mean a storm."

"Wonderful!" she shouted back, dragging her hair behind her ears and wrapping it around one hand; the other hand clung to the side of the cart as it began jolting downhill. Xena suddenly appeared at her side.

"There's a boat waiting on shore," she said. "We seem to be in luck."

"I think that's Socran down there, waving," Aleppis called out over his shoulder. "He looks excited."

"Socran —excited?" Hesper slewed around and crawled forward to look. "Socran was never excited a day in his life. He's half-asleep most of the time. I think something is wrong."

The boat pulled up on shore was one of the new, squat types, a partial deck at her bow and another across the broad stern, and narrow benches at the rear for the tillerman and at the fore for a watchman. Midships, three steps down from deck height, benches on both sides for two or three oarsmen flanked the central single mast and the large central opening. At the bottom of this opening, planks had been wedged into place just above the piled ballast stones, forming a platform to hold cargo. The ship was small, maneuverable, reasonably fast, good in a rough sea, operable by only a few men, cheap to build, and eminently practical. At the moment it had been drawn up on the sand, and three men moved around topside, two of them attending to the sail and oarlocks, while the third kept watch, gazing up the hill or out to sea or along what could be seen of the narrow beachline. The fourth man came striding rapidly across the sand as the cart drew to a halt.

Aleppis held the suddenly excitable beast in check as Hesper jumped down. "Socran, what's wrong? You're as pale as your shirt!"

The gray-haired but still sturdy Socran was nearly stuttering in his haste to get the message out; his eyes were wild. "Men—men on the island! They came out of the sea, a dozen small boats, swarmed over the palace, we had no chance against them! They've taken control of everything!" Hesper clapped him on the back; the shipman clutched his arm so hard the boy winced and tried to free himself. "Ugly, crude men, they are! Why—they've threatened the queen herself, and ever since the prince tried to escape, they've been—who's that?" he gasped as Xena came from behind the cart, Gabrielle right at her heels.

"She's a friend, Socran," Aleppis said. "Helped us—well, never mind that. We owe her our lives—"

Socran eyed the two women with visible disbelief, then shook his head. "You'd joke at your mother's funeral, boy, I know you. This is serious—this is *real*! It'll be *our* lives, and those of our families, if we don't load this ship immediately and return to the palace. They said so, and I for one believe them!''

"Believe who?" Xena asked quietly. For a moment she thought Socran might try to ignore her, and it seemed that was his intention, but Hesper freed one hand and caught hold of his shoulder.

"*This* is serious and real, too, Socran," he said flatly. "Tell her."

"It's—they haven't said his name, most of us haven't even seen him, and they don't call his captain by name, either. He's an ugly brute, twenty men or more under him, and all of them ready with their fists, or their knives. They said—''

"You already told us that," Xena said quietly. "What does this captain look like?" Socran's eyes were enormous, pale gray and they protruded rather like a frog's. The warrior bit back a sigh and suggested, "Tall?" He nodded. "Taller than I am?" A shake.

The sailor finally found his voice again. "About so high." He measured with one hand, not much above his own head. "And so"—he spread both well apart—"in the shoulders. He wears black leather and—and dirty bronze plates sticking out from his shoulders, so they look even broader. And—and wait," he added excitedly. "His hands! This"—he held up his right, shook his head rapidly—"no, this one!" He folded down the index finger, eyed Xena warily.

"Missing one, left hand," she murmured, and smiled. It wasn't a pleasant smile.

Gabrielle wrapped both hands in flying hair and squinted against the sun. "Let me just guess," she said resignedly. "You know him, right?"

Xena's smile broadened, but her eyes were chill slits. Socran swallowed and backed a pace away, nearly falling in the thick, soft sand. "I know him," Xena replied. "He's Draco's man."

"Draco—oh, right. Great," Gabrielle said. "Ah—let me guess again, this means Draco himself is probably—"

"Draco!" Socran staggered forward and caught hold of the warrior's arm with a white-knuckled grip; she freed it easily, transferred his hands to Gabrielle, who winced as he held on. "That's—everyone knows who Draco is, he's— he's a—"

"Exactly," Gabrielle said. "Um—if you don't mind, that hurts," she added. Socran blinked, confused, then with a muffled oath, released her. She smiled. "Thanks. But your worries are over, okay? This is Xena, you probably didn't know that, but she's a warrior and she can fix everything." Xena cast her eyes up slightly, and met the man's wide-eyed, obviously frightened gaze with a smile that was meant to be reassuring.

Her own gaze shifted, out to sea, fixed thoughtfully on the slight darkness well to the northwest that might have been Ithaca. "Draco," she murmured. "Well, well."

Gabrielle eyed her unhappily, wondering if she hadn't spoken too quickly. But Socran looked so scared. . . .

Hesper caught his attention and nodded once sharply. "She saved the men of Isos—well, it's too long a story to tell you now. One day, when all this is over. But believe both of us, you can trust her, Socran."

Aleppis came up beside his friend, one hand still restraining the mule, and nodded. "Truly, Socran."

"Truly, Socran," the islander mumbled under his breath, then glanced sidelong at the warrior to see if she'd caught that. He managed a shaky smile. "Sorry. I mean—"

"Sure," Gabrielle broke in cheerfully. But her face darkened as she turned to look at Xena, no less anxiously than Socran had, but for a different reason. "Ah—can we talk, for just a moment?'' She glanced at Aleppis, who still had a death grip on the reins, though the ass no longer seemed likely to bolt. "Maybe if you three started getting the baskets out to the ship, there wouldn't be any time wasted while we're discussing a few matters?''

Xena nodded once. "Load the ship. We won't be long." She led the way back from the sand onto sparse, wind-bent grass. "Well?''

Gabrielle was quiet for a moment, her eyes distant and a frown etching her brow. "Don't tell me what you have in mind, I could see it in your eyes back there.''

"Oh?''

"You're gonna walk up to Draco and his goons and you're gonna tell them you're the same bad, old Xena they knew and loved, right? Just like with that louse Mezentius, and all the other times . . .''

"You have a better idea?'' Xena asked softly as Gabrielle's voice faded.

"I might, if you let me think for a bit.''

"We don't have that kind of time, Gabrielle. You heard the man. Draco wouldn't lie about a little thing like killing hostages.''

Gabrielle spread her arms in an exasperated shrug; hair blew wildly in all directions. With an oath that raised her companion's eyebrows, she recaptured it and firmly wound it around one hand. "Yeah. I guess he wouldn't. But, you know, if you ask me, one of these days, you're going to try that trick once too often, and—''

"Maybe," Xena broke in. "This isn't that time. Draco will be suspicious; that's his nature. Polyces won't—he's gullible.'' She held up a left hand, index finger tucked against her palm and smiled unpleasantly. "He'll believe anything I tell him.''

"But—''

"Gabrielle, I appreciate your concern. Truly." Xena laid a hand on her arm. "But there are innocents out there—women, children, servants who've never needed to use weapons, who wouldn't know how. Any armed men Odysseus might have left behind to protect the queen wouldn't be a match for Draco. We're all they have—unless you want to send a messenger to King Menelaus, and wait for him to send us an army."

Gabrielle snorted. "Oh, right; he'd be sure to do that for his old friend, wouldn't he?"

"He might. King Nestor might. It would take weeks; those people might not have weeks." She stalked across the sand. Socran's attention was divided between the crate of wine, the ship, the two women, and what he visibly imagined on the distant palace island. He was all but wringing his hands as Xena came up and nodded to Hesper.

"Set that down; we need to talk," she told him. Socran began to stutter. "I'll be quick; stay quiet and it'll be that much sooner we can leave. Better yet—go get your shipmates on deck and we'll all talk." She gave him a small shove that sent him scrabbling for balance; he righted himself and ran. Xena took his place between the two villagers, balancing the wine basket while they hefted it by the woven straps at each end; Gabrielle cast her eyes heavenward and followed.

Two of the shipmen were barely adolescents; the tillerman was older than Socran—a frail little white-haired fellow with a very strong right arm from steering vessels most of his life. To his credit, he silenced the others with a gesture and a low word as the warrior came aboard, and another sharp word against Socran's ear silenced him as well. Hesper and Aleppis struggled to stow and fasten the basket on the hold planks; Xena spared them a quick glance, then eyed each of the sailors in turn.

"Are there any of you who don't have family back on the island?" The boys glanced at each other and timidly raised their hands.

"My father went with the king, my mother died last autumn. My only family is my cousin—" He indicated the other boy with a sidelong jerk of his head.

"Rozenos' mother raised me; my father went with the king, too. My mother died birthing me."

Gabrielle blinked rapidly, turned away to quietly blot tears.

Xena nodded. "That's good. You two will remain here." She indicated Gabrielle. "We'll take your places." Before either boy could protest, she turned her attention to the tillerman. "What happens when you go back? Is there a guard on shore?"

He gazed beyond her for a moment, nodded. "They told us two men would be waiting—one on foot where we draw up, a horseman behind him on solid ground. The one on foot would come aboard and check the ship thoroughly; the one mounted is to ride to the palace or their camp if there's anything wrong."

"Wrong. Like, say, he finds half an army with the cargo?"

"Or any of us missing, or the cargo not what it's supposed to be. Anything at all, they said."

"Mmm. What's your name, tillerman?"

"Melaeus, warrior." He pointed into the hold where a black-haired, black-bearded bear of a man wrestled ropes around the wine basket. "And that's Xoran."

"Well, then, Melaeus. Let's set these two lads ashore and get this ship back in the water. Wait—we'll need what cloaks and hoods you two have. You can keep ours for now."

"You can return to Isos with us," Hesper said as he clambered back onto the deck.

"Return to Isos as quickly as you can," Xena told them. "And send a message out to the south, to Pylos. Use my name when you reach King Nestor's palace, tell him what's happening in Ithaca. Tell them Xena strongly suggests he send messages to the other kings that the alliance owes aid to the house of King Odysseus." She took one of the proffered tightly woven and lanolined blue cloaks, fastened it around her shoulders, and handed the other to Gabrielle. "Go," she said. Hesper looked as though he wanted to say something, but let Aleppis tug him away without further word. The two island boys were already down on the sand, shoulders against the bow of the ship, ready to shove it back into the sea.

Gabrielle stuffed her hair into the blue hood, snugged it down, and gazed around her with a sour look. "Gods, but I hate boats!"

Xena cast her a sardonic smile. "You can walk, if you prefer."

The girl laughed, though she didn't sound wildly amused; she flailed for balance, caught hold of the rail as the ship slid backward through the sand with a series of bone-rattling jerks. "Well, all right, here we are. Wonderful travel accommodations, which oar's mine?" Socran snorted with laughter but clapped one hand over his mouth as both women turned to look at him.

Xoran pointed to the port side. "The front oar. Warrior, you can take that—" He indicated the back starboard place.

She was already shaking her head. "I'll stay port, help Gabrielle."

"Mmm—ah—of course," he murmured. Melaeus shouted as the ship wallowed across low waves; Xoran ran to free the sail and Socran for his oar. Gabrielle was staggering, wildly off balance. Xena caught hold of her arm and walked her across to the low port-side bench and settled her under the long oar, then eased under the oar just behind her. Melaeus nodded sharply, glanced over at the starboard oars where Xoran was just taking his seat, and began to turn the boat to sea. It fell into the wave trough, sloshed awkwardly across the crest of the next, rocked alarmingly back and forth. Spray wet the small deck and the benches.

"Oooooh. We're facing the stern," Gabrielle moaned. "We're riding backward, and I can't see anything except sky!"

"It's how you do this kind of thing," Xena said easily. "Row on my count, you'll forget all about it." She eyed the two men across the open cargo area, braced her right foot against the block, and tapped against Gabrielle's seat with her left, setting the beat.

It wasn't going to work for long, she knew. Gabrielle's face had been bright green most of the way to Troy, and she'd been sick twice during the very calm return journey. To the girl's credit, she held out for at least an hour before she groaned again and fell across the oar.

Xena laughed mirthlessly, and increased her pull on her own oar, to compensate. "If you're gonna be sick, do it over the side."

"Sick! I think I'm dying." She managed a breathy little laugh. "Maybe I'll walk after all."

"Even *you* aren't pure enough to manage that," Xena countered cheerfully. "You just need some air. Go on up on deck, breathe deeply. It'll help. If it doesn't, you'll be close enough to the rail you won't throw up on me."

Gabrielle moaned again, but finally slid from the bench, nearly cracking her head as a wave lifted the oar blade outside and lowered the inner portion. She gave the hold one wild-eyed look, dropped to all fours, and crawled slowly toward the stairs. Xena glanced at the starboard side; both men were watching Gabrielle with amusement, but as they caught the warrior's cool gaze they went immediately back to close concentration on their work.

"Oooooh." Gabrielle dragged her skirt from under her knees and swarmed shakily up the steps, edged out onto the deck. "It's even worse up here, the deck is moving like a—ohhhh, I'm gonna die." The wind picked up her hair and sent it swirling around her face as she neared the rail; she caught hold of as much of it as she could and, one-handed, edged the rest of the way over to the railing, slewing around to sit with her face against the wood. "Hey," she announced brightly after a moment, "it's not so bad up here; really, I feel a *lot* better. The air's nice and cool and it's—oh, gods," she added in a sudden change of mood. "That's disgusting! The water's *white* on top!"

"Don't look at it, then!" Xena shouted. "And don't forget to stay out of sight once we get close to land. That hood and cloak won't fool anyone once they can see what's under it!"

"Gotcha," Gabrielle moaned; she caught hold of her hair firmly in both hands, shoved it back under the hood, and snugged the hood down tight around her face. The ship lurched into a trough as Melaeus brought it around to stay with the wind; she groaned deeply and fell back flat on the boards. Xena bit back a smile and dug her oar more deeply into the rough water.

7

It was very late afternoon by the time they came near enough to the palace island, and Gabrielle soon gave up. Keeping out of sight, she crawled back down to the rowing level. "I can just make out someone on the sand," she said quietly. "There's a buncha tents back a ways, and smoke from a fire. I could see the palace but not anyone around it. The sun's right at the edge of the sea."

Xena flexed her hands, gripped the oar again, and nodded. Gabrielle eyed her nervously, looked momentarily as if she intended to say something—probably start the argument about Draco again, from the look of her—but she finally shrugged and dropped down onto the rower's bench. She took hold of the oar rather gingerly.

"Save your hands," Xena muttered. "I've got it." But she freed one hand to gesture urgently at the rowers on the opposite benches. Socran braced the inside end of his oar beneath the lip of the hatch and scurried around to crouch at her side. Gabrielle eyed the arrangement, tugged at her own oar, and managed to get it out of the water and shoved down to match Socran's.

The graybeard was utterly white, his eyes all pupil. Xena gave his shoulder a rough pat before gripping the oar two-handed once more. "You remember the plan?" He nodded. "All of it?" He nodded again. She kept reservations behind her teeth, smiled at him. "Good. Stick to it. Exactly. Understand?"

"Or we're—" He licked dry lips, swallowed.

"Dead. Right. Don't worry; you'll do fine, all of you."

Socran nodded one last time, glanced forward nervously, and scuttled toward the bow to watch as they neared shore.

Gabrielle muttered something under her breath as the ship rode up a wave and slogged awkwardly down the inland side. Several sloppy shifts in direction later, it nosed onto the sand with a faint scraping noise. Melaeus called out orders from his place at the tiller; Xoran ran to secure the wildly flapping sail. A moment later, he swore, and Socran ran back to help.

Gabrielle shifted her weight and turned to face her companion, but as she opened her mouth, Xena tapped her lips and shook her head. Half a breath later a deep bellow came from shore.

"That the shipment of wine from the mainland?"

Melaeus turned back from fastening the tiller to one side and crossed the deck to lean over the bow. "Yes!"

"I see two of the men who went with you. Where's the other two?"

"Down below, making certain the basket didn't shift just now." He looked back across his shoulder; Xena was letting Gabrielle down onto the wine basket. A moment later she followed.

"All right!" Another voice, higher and a little more distant. "You remember the rules here, tillerman? We know each of you, where your families are, what would hurt you most if you've done anything you shouldn't, this trip!"

"No one's done anything against orders! None of us would dare!" Mclaeus shouted back.

"Good. We understand each other! Metrikas is coming aboard to check the hold, the decks—each of you. If he doesn't like any little thing he sees, he tells me, and I ride to the palace. And we know what happens after that, right, tillerman?"

"We know!" Xeros shouted after it became obvious the man was awaiting an answer.

"Good. Metrikas?" Down in the hold, Gabrielle flailed wildly for something to hold on to as a very heavy object landed on the ship's port deck. Xena grabbed her arm, held her up until she regained her balance, then with another warning touch to her lips, let her go, and gestured urgently toward the shadows behind the large grain basket. Gabrielle closed her eyes briefly, shook her head, and moved. Xena risked a quick glance overhead, then eased quietly back into the shadow cast by the deck.

"All right, tillerman—there's three of you here, where's the other two?"

"Down there, I told you." Heavy footsteps rattled the planks and stopped directly above her.

The loud, deep voice echoed through the hold. "I don't see them. If you're tricking me, tillerman, you'll pay—and so will they."

"They're shifting stone back where it belongs; some of the ballast broke free as we came in. You don't want this ship holed as well, do you?" A moment's silence. "Does me no good to call them, before you ask; they're both deaf."

"Deaf?" Metrikas laughed harshly. "What's the good of a deaf sailor?"

"They know what to do, and when. I don't ask anything else."

Xena let her gaze move across the open port; it was starting to get dark out there. A faint, grim smile curved her lips, and she flexed her hands. Melaeus and his friends were doing just fine; much better than she'd expected. Any moment now . . .

"By Hades, they'll hear *me*!" The entire ship shook as a great red-haired brute leaped into the hold, barely missing the wine basket. "Where?" he demanded. "I don't see them, tillerman!"

"Right here," Xena murmured against his ear; he squawked in surprise, spun on one heel. Her elbow cracked immediately into his windpipe—no point having him yell for help—then she buried both fists in his vast belly. He clutched at his throat, whooping for air, but the second punch didn't even seem to faze him—unless the narrowing of small, piglike black eyes meant anything. The warrior cast her eyes briefly heavenward, muttered a curse, and leaped. Someone his size probably wouldn't be quick in the best of circumstances, and caught by surprise in a small space while trying to remember how to breathe was among the worst. Her hands clamped onto the opposite lip of the hold, and she spun around, caught it backhanded, and used the momentum to swing back and then forward, booted feet tucked close as he staggered after her, ready to flatten her with one enormous fist. She slammed both legs out, hard; this time the blow doubled him over and swung her back once more.

She dropped free, leaped across the distance between them, and brought her arms down across the back of his neck. He staggered and fell to his knees, still clutching his throat. Xena swore, slammed a boot heel into the side of his head. He fell over on his side. She drew a deep breath, expelled it in an exasperated gust, signed to Gabrielle to remain where she was. She glanced up; the lower sky was a sullen red from this angle, the sun well down by now. Xoran was staring down from the rower's platform, wringing his hands; just behind him, she could barely make out the other two. She gestured urgently in the direction of the bow—and the shore.

Xoran shook himself and ran to obey, as Socran shouted into the hold. "Hey! You down there! Are you all right! Hey! Oh, gods, what a mess!"

Xena smiled briefly, took a pace away from the fallen brute, and listened; Xoran certainly sounded urgent. "Hey! Your friend just tripped and fell into the hold! He's unconscious, and he's bleeding from a cut on his head!"

"If this is a trick . . . !" came the reply from shore.

"Why would it be a trick?" Xoran shouted back desperately. "He's bigger than all five of us together, and besides, we know the penalty for trickery! He's hurt, I tell you; he got his big feet tangled up in one of the oars and fell, headfirst, didn't you hear him land?"

The rider sounded uncertain. "I—I'm going back to the palace!"

"Not without your friend you're not! We can't get him out of the hold, he's too big! And he's going to bleed to death, so you might at least toss up a clean length of cloth so we can bind his brow, if you're going to leave him here!"

Momentary silence. Finally: "All right! I'm coming aboard. You back away, right back to the tiller, every mother's son of you. Otherwise—"

"We have no reason to trick you, aren't you listening?" Xoran shouted frantically. "No reason at all! I don't want my wife and sons murdered because you were afraid to come see to your friend!"

"Back away from the bow, all the way back—" The guard sounded nervous.

From below, Xena watched all three men retreat warily. Silence. Then a thump, footsteps in the bow. They stopped. Xena eased back into shadow and drew the hood over her head.

"There's only three of you up here." The guard again.

"The boys were down there when he fell, shifting ballast. They're still down there, trying to see if they can help him." Silence. "They're *boys,* Krinos! You looked them over before we left, what threat could they possibly be?" Another silence, broken by slow, cautious footsteps coming down the deck. They stopped, just short of the rowing deck and the hold.

"Hey, you down there. Step away from Metrikas, let me see him."

"The boy's deaf, weren't you listening to what I told your friend?"

"He's not *my* friend, he's Captain Meronias' brother," Krinos replied sourly. "So the boy's deaf, is he?" He bent to set one hand on the edge of the hold. "We'll see about that," he added grimly as he leaped down next to the large wine basket and just behind the supposed boy. A swift glance up reassured him; the fool sailors were almost too scared to blink. They wouldn't dare try anything, even with both of them down here and one of them injured. Krinos swaggered forward, squared his shoulders, and tapped the boy's arm with a hard finger.

The boy turned; pale, oddly familiar eyes met his. "You—you aren't—who are you?" he demanded. A positively wicked grin was his only answer. "I *know* you!"

"Oh?" The voice, a deep, throaty, dangerous purr—that was familiar, too. He blinked; she suddenly wasn't there. He swung his head wildly, searching; a faint creak overhead, and he looked up just in time to see her launch from

112

the lip of the hold, straight at him. It was the last thing he saw for quite a while.

Xena brushed her hands together, eyed Krinos with satisfaction, then softly called out, "Melaeus, one of you: get rope, lots of it. And cloth to gag them!" At her feet, Metrikas moaned; she cast her eyes up, swore under her breath, and kicked him once more, as hard as she could. Silence. A moment later the sailors dropped into the hold with a quantity of rope and two rags torn from Socran's long, grubby shirt. She nodded, pointed to the enormous mound of Metrikas. "Twice as much rope on that."

Gabrielle emerged from shadow as they finished gagging him. "Oh, my—he's really big, isn't he?" Xena nodded shortly. "So now what?"

Xena glanced at what sky was visible. The last red had faded; nearly dark. "We wait. You—Socran. These two actually know where your families are?"

"No. I don't think so. They threatened—we couldn't take the chance."

"They didn't call any of you by name, which means they probably didn't know you from anyone else on the island, and they didn't know the boys were orphans, did they? But we won't take any chances. Is there anywhere you can hide?"

"Um—there's the Nymph's Cavern—it's on the western shore, the entrance is hidden during all but low tide. We can't stay there forever, though, warrior."

"You won't have to. Get your people, take what food and water you can. I'll send someone to let you know as soon as it's safe. Now, how many men did Draco actually bring?"

"Um—" Xoran shook his head but after a moment began counting on his fingers as he muttered under his breath. "There were twenty-two ships the size of—a little larger

113

than this one. Each carried enough men that they all rode low in the water.''

"Just men—not horses?"

"Men. A few tents, a few bags of supplies, but not many. After they had the palace, they sank every boat but this one and two small fishing boats—so supplies could be brought in, you know.''

Gabrielle was busy working things out on her fingers; what Xena could see of her face in the gathering gloom was anxious indeed. She held up a hand. "Save it, Gabrielle. Let's get these men away to their families first.'' The girl bit her lip and nodded. In turn, Xoran and Socran took Melaeus' strong tiller arm up; Xena caught hold of the lip and swung lightly to the deck after them, then turned to help Gabrielle.

"Ah—the wine?'' Socran asked.

"Leave it," Xena replied tersely. "Go home." The three men moved quickly down the deck, slid over the side, and moved across the narrow sward of sand. Gabrielle waited until she could no longer see them, then drew a deep breath and let it out in a gust.

"Do you have any idea how many men we're talking about here?'' she asked crisply, and held up a hand. "Twenty-seven ships, this size, filled with enough men that they'd ride low in the water means—''

"It means a lot of them," Xena said. "We aren't playing rope tug with them, you and I against all of them. So numbers don't matter.''

"Right." Gabrielle's voice dripped with sarcasm. "So what next?''

For answer, the warrior held up a hand, then melted into the shadows near the bow. Gabrielle dropped to her knees and edged up against the rail. Silence, then a faint, scrabbling sound, as though someone were trying to haul himself

114

onto the boat using the dangling anchor line. She could barely make out a flash of pale face, a quickly upraised hand as Xena warned her silently to stay put. She huddled hard against the wood, hands tucked in her armpits for warmth as a sudden gust of cool wind blew in from the sea, and waited.

Another scrabble of noise. Xena held her breath, listened carefully. One person, not too handy with climbing ropes, trying to be quiet but not very good at that, either. She flexed her hands, waited. A muffled oath, then the stealthy sound of leather on wood. Whoever it was had managed to get his body braced against the ship's hull and was climbing the anchor line hand over hand while his sandaled feet edged up the side. Moments later heavy breathing, and then a cloak-shrouded body clawed at the rail, scrabbled with both feet wildly, and fell to the deck. Xena got to her feet and tapped at the gasping bundle with one boot.

A faint, airless squawk; the bundle quivered, then drew itself upright. "All right, you have me again. I *told* your filthy captain I wasn't giving up." It was a boy's voice: mostly deep and very sullen, except on the last words, when it broke and sailed into soprano. The boy clapped a hand across his mouth and gazed at his feet.

He barely came to her shoulder, Xena realized. She reached, caught hold of his chin, raised it so she could look into his face. It was so dark now she had to lean close, but the features were unmistakable—even without a graying beard. "Prince Telemachus, isn't it?" she asked softly.

For a long moment she thought he wasn't going to answer; then he squared his shoulders and stared directly into her eyes. "Who wants to know?" He peered more closely at her, then eyed what he could see of Gabrielle in the deepening gloom. "You're—you're women!"

"Very good!" Xena applauded quietly, then stepped past him to gaze along the beach in both directions. "Would you mind if we continued this conversation down by the oars? We stand out where we are."

She turned, started down the deck; turned back when she realized he wasn't moving.

The young prince glared at her. "What of it? Who are you, to come sneaking onto my father's lands?"

"I'm the person who didn't break your neck just now," Xena replied softly. "I think that makes me a friend."

"Friend," he said bitterly. Xena gave him a long, chill look, tapped Gabrielle's shoulder, and murmured against her ear.

"Talk to him; if he's not down there ready to listen in short order, I'm coming back to dump him in the tide."

"Got it," Gabrielle said flatly, and stalked over to join the boy, who stood irresolute in the middle of the deck. "She's right about one thing; anyone coming along shore could see us both. How about sitting down here and listening for a moment?" He hesitated; she dropped down cross-legged and patted the deck in front of her knees. "Don't tell me you're afraid?"

"Of *you*?" he demanded rudely, and settled down where she indicated. "So who are you, and who's *she,* and why are you here?"

"I'm Gabrielle, and that's Xena—you've never heard of me, but I'd wager her name is familiar."

He shrugged, apparently bored, but his eyes were suddenly bright. "Sure. She's that woman warrior, I guess. So?"

"She came on behalf of King Menelaus—"

"Him," Telemachus growled. "If it wasn't for him and that—that—"

"Never mind," Gabrielle said hastily. "He sent us to

116

find out how things were going here. Obviously, they aren't going too well.''

''Oh, everything's great,'' he replied sarcastically. ''There's a big party going on and—''

Gabrielle leaned forward and tapped his knee. ''Did anyone ever tell you that you have a bad attitude? We already figured out there was trouble here. Xena's here to take care of it.''

''Oh. One, or maybe two of you against—you know how many men are out there?'' He waved an arm.

Gabrielle grabbed it and brought it down to deck level. ''We were going to stay out of sight, remember? Matter of fact, I have a good idea how many. Not my kind of odds, but then, I'm not Xena.'' Silence.

Telemachus sat back and gathered his feet under him. ''Look, if you two aren't going to let me have the ship, do you mind if I just go now?''

''You were gonna sail this all by yourself? Where?''

He sighed, but stayed where he was. ''I was watching; I saw the older men get off but not the boys. They don't have family here to worry about. I was pretty sure I could convince them to help me sail her. She's not so big. I thought we could make it across to the long bay and get her as far east as—well, almost to Corinth. There's only a little land to cross then, and hardly any distance to Athens. They'd expect us to head for Pylos, if they thought we had the ship—but they'd never catch us in those little open fishing caïques.''

''Not such a bad plan.'' Xena had come up behind them, unnoticed. She eased down beside the boy. ''All right, I can see you have brains, and you're brave and clever both. Obviously Odysseus' son, even if you didn't resemble him.''

''My—my father.'' The boy's mouth twisted. ''He

117

should be here; he should never have gone to Troy.'' His voice cracked again; emotion, this time, Gabrielle thought. *Poor kid.*

''He didn't really want to,'' she said.

''How do you know that?''

Xena shrugged. ''He told me. I have a message for your mother also.''

His shoulders sagged. ''You aren't going to let us have the ship, are you?''

''Your friends are back on the mainland, partway to Pylos, to ask King Nestor for help for you. We could use you here,'' Gabrielle said. Xena gave her a sidelong, dubious look but said nothing.

Telemachus gazed from one to the other of them in silence for a very long moment. ''You—you could?''

''Well.'' Gabrielle shrugged. ''For starters, if you could get us into the queen's apartments, that would be real useful.''

''My mother.'' The boy sighed. ''If she'd let the guards teach me how to use a sword—but all I have is this knife, and I had to sneak that from father's old panoply and keep it hidden.'' He brandished a broad-bladed dagger, the handle curved to form a snake.

Gabrielle leaned away from it and smiled nervously. ''Ah—really nice! Um—if you'd kind of stow it again; daggers make me nervous. Not just yours, any of them . . .''

Xena leaned back and folded her arms. The boy might actually have potential under all that sullen, stubborn, irritating demeanor. She didn't really owe the Trickster anything—but anyone coming home after such a long absence deserved a better greeting than he'd get right now from this son. ''A deal,'' she said softly. ''You help us out. You do what I tell you, when I tell you. And once those men are off this island, I teach you how to fight.''

"You would—" he began eagerly, but the pleasure left him almost at once. "My mother would never allow it."

"I can deal with her," Xena promised.

"She can't protect you forever," Gabrielle added. "We'll just have to explain that to her." She glanced at the sky. "I don't think it's going to get much darker than this. How do we get to the queen?"

"I—well, I can get in to see her whenever I want," he said doubtfully. "They don't take me very seriously."

"That's good," Xena told him. "It's that much more of a surprise when you prove yourself."

He eyed her with patent disbelief, finally shook his head. "There was a passage to the outside from her apartments, but *they* caught her trying to sneak out, and they've broken the wall, closed the corridor. There's a balcony, but it's on the second story. The only other way—that warlord has a man of his on duty in the main passage, all the time. *He* says, to make sure no one bothers her. They won't let her come out at all, and only two of her women can move around, for food and water."

"Mmm. We'll get in," Xena said after a moment.

"We'll find a way," Gabrielle assured him quietly. He gazed at them, eyes narrowed in the gloom. Finally, he shook his head. Dark curls bounced around his ears. "There are only two of you," he said finally. "And you are both— well—"

"Women," Gabrielle said as he hesitated. "Don't let that fool you, Prince." She indicated her companion with a nod. "She's very good at this rescue thing." She glanced up. "Besides, now there's three of us, right?"

"Right," Xena whispered. She looked out across the island. Most of it was dark, and in the distance, she could just make out a line of sharp, low peaks against sea and sky. To the right, a few lamps burned on the ledges of deep

119

stone windows—clearly the palace. Not far from it, almost directly ahead, fires dotted the landscape, flickering red against pale tents and casting black male shadows over tents and trees alike. "We'd better go, this isn't any place to be. Gabrielle, go with the prince."

"Sure. Fine. And you?"

"I'll be right behind you."

Once they were off the ship, Prince Telemachus pulled Gabrielle back against the bow. "Out there—see all those fires? That's where most of them are, especially this time of night." He made a face. "Drinking, mostly. By the time the moon is up tonight, at least half of them will be snoring."

"Where are the guards posted?" Xena murmured close to his ear.

"Besides the one to make sure my mother doesn't get away again?" He shook his head. "There's two at the fishing caïques, someone sleeping in them all the time, or sitting in them, so no one can steal them. There aren't any other guards."

"You're kidding!" Gabrielle protested.

Xena laughed, very quietly. "They don't need guards. Against women and servants and a boy?" The prince stiffened; Xena touched his arm. "That's how *they* see you, remember? It's what you want them to see."

"Oh. Right." He nodded once, then pointed eastward, along the sand. "The road to the palace goes that way, and up into those trees, but there are some tents there. I stay down here, on the hard sand; they can't hear you moving around over the waves, but none of them watch this way anyway—not after dark, because everyone knows ships don't sail after dark."

"Good thinking," Xena whispered. "You lead the way,

Prince.'' He nodded briefly and set off, crouching low and moving fast along the very edge of the receding waves. Gabrielle followed, slowing as she passed the warrior to murmur, ''See? He's all right, really.''

''Really,'' Xena replied dryly, and gestured for her to keep moving. She waited until she could no longer hear their footsteps, held her breath to listen as she gazed all around the vicinity. Nothing moving. Behind her, in the hold of the boat, she could just hear someone moaning, very faintly. She sighed. But they wouldn't stay unconscious forever, and unless she killed both men and dumped the bodies at sea, eventually someone would know what had happened to them. She wouldn't kill them, though; even bodies dumped well out to sea were known to float back to shore. ''Leave it,'' she mumbled. She'd deal with the situation when it arose. She came up from her low crouch, started after Gabrielle and the Trickster's son.

They were waiting in the deeper shadow of a hedge of shaped laurels; Telemachus' mouth twisted as she slid into the darkness between them, but he kept the words behind his teeth. Just as well, the warrior thought; the urge to smack him one was almost overpowering. *Leave it.* He pointed toward a dark corner of the long, low, whitewashed two-story building, nodded once, then, with a quick glance all around, slipped the sandals from his feet, tucked them into his belt, and ran barefoot along the hedge. Gabrielle tucked up her skirts and followed, Xena right behind her, her eyes moving constantly, making sure no one had seen them.

So far as she could tell, the boy was right. She could hear drunken singing, someone bellowing abuse at someone else, men laughing—but all the sound was distant, off by the fires and the tents. It was very quiet around this end of the palace.

Prince Telemachus gained the low steps, then the covered porch, and finally a darkened hallway before he stopped, drew Gabrielle close, and tugged at her sleeve. "Servants' quarters, and the kitchens," he whispered against her ear.

"No one here?" Xena whispered.

"No—home at this hour." He gestured toward the northwest—the direction Socran and the other sailors had taken when they left the ship. Xena nodded. The prince pointed up a narrow flight of steps, then led the way, taking them by twos. But instead of following the barren, empty corridor at the top, he kept going, across a deserted chamber filled with stacks of huge baskets and open crates of clay jugs, onto a long, narrow balcony. He tugged at Gabrielle's sleeve, pointed again, but this time said nothing. Xena nodded; there was another balcony a distance beyond the end of this one—not unreachable by a halfway decent jump. Beyond that was another, as dark as this one, and then another, wrapped around the building's northeast corner. It was there that light spilled through sheer, pale pink curtains onto the white plaster rail. She indicated the distant balcony; Telemachus nodded, then pointed down and tapped his lips. She listened, then looked. No one down there at present; apparently there was, now and again.

"Guard?" she breathed against his ear.

He nodded, then stood on tiptoe to place his mouth close to hers. "At moonrise, and every hour after until dawn."

Xena smiled. Moonrise wouldn't be for hours yet; by the time a guard began pacing around down in the king's shrubbery, she'd have reached the queen's apartments, talked to her, and be long gone.

Gone where, though? She glanced up, smiled again,

touched the prince's arm to get his attention, and pointed. "Safe there?" she murmured. He nodded once. Gabrielle looked up.

"The roof?" she breathed.

"Best view," Xena assured her. It earned her one of those sidelong, rather exasperated looks; she bit back a smile and climbed onto the broad, plastered railing of the narrow balcony.

8

Xena could tell Gabrielle wasn't pleased with acrobatics high above the ground on a dark night; no doubt she'd hear about it later, and at length. For now, the girl gritted her teeth, tucked up her skirts again, and with the prince's help managed to scramble from balcony to balcony without making too much noise. This entire end of the palace was dark, only the queen's windows showing any hint of habitation, though Xena could hear male voices somewhere below and behind them—reasonably sober men's voices. Kitchens, probably; Draco's men or the palace servants getting a meal for him. He didn't keep much of a rein on his army in a situation like this one, but food—his own food—was another matter; he was notoriously fussy about what he ate, and how it was prepared—*when he's not fighting, that is.* In a place like this, with a king's pantries to raid, he'd be indulging a supposedly refined palate.

That was good, though; at an hour like this, he'd be drinking fine wine, sampling the best and most exotic sweetmeats and delicacies available, probably explaining minute differences in taste and texture to some poor underling who was bored half to tears and desperately trying to look both interested and knowledgeable, and all the time longing merely to get out and guzzle the strong, sour ale his raucous friends were swilling down. The last thing Draco would be thinking about just now would be an invasion of any size—unless a full army came roaring up from the beach, trebuckets, siege machines, catapults, and all.

She smiled grimly at the picture it all made—including Draco leaping up and splattering rare wine everywhere—but it wouldn't do, even if she had an army. Not with so many unarmed, helpless people on the palace island and the grounds; it would be slaughter—Draco's slaughter of the servants, the queen, and her son—before he ever turned to fight the outsiders. *Another way. It's there,* she assured herself. *You'll find it.*

One final leap; the queen's balcony and this last were a little farther apart. Xena went first this time, landing in a silent crouch; she turned partway, waited for Prince Telemachus to come next. He easily made the jump, then turned to face the last ledge. Setting himself a long stride back from the railing, he braced his feet and held out his arms. Gabrielle cast an imploring glance toward the starlit heavens, squared her shoulders, and jumped; she teetered on the edge of the railing, then fell forward, taking the prince with her. It was Xena's turn to cast her eyes heavenward as their feet shuffled loudly on the rough surface.

A startled, resonant cry from within, followed by a high-pitched voice. " 'Twas nothing, lady, I'm sure on it. I'll go and just see, though."

Xena dragged Telemachus upright and propelled him across to the billowing curtain, then reached down a hand to Gabrielle. The girl slewed around, winced as her backside made full contact with the floor, and gave her companion a cross look from under lowered eyebrows before she grasped the proffered fingers and let herself be hauled to her feet.

"I didn't need another bruise right *there*," Gabrielle hissed. Xena laid a finger against her lips, then turned to close the short distance between herself and the prince as a woman in servant's practical dark blue peered cautiously around the edge of the length of sheer pink. She caught her breath as Telemachus gave her a wry grin and wiggled fingers at her, but then her eyes had fixed, wide and frightened, on the warrior-clad woman at his back. The prince nodded, as if to assure the servant everything was all right, then stepped forward and gave her a gentle shove, propelling her back into the chamber.

The room was light and airy; pale walls painted top and bottom with exotic blossoms, pale carpets on pale tile floors, the only large furniture a bed swathed in the same sheer pink fabric as curtained the windows, though chairs and piled cushions had been drawn near the open, circular fire pit. It was swept clean at the moment; a cool breeze drifted down through the smoke opening in the ceiling, high above. A small table with beautifully carved legs stood against one windowless wall; it held a gold-framed mirror and bottles of cosmetics. A loom obviously carved by the same craftsman stood near the opposite wall, between two large windows and beneath two strategically placed torches and an oil lamp that lit the stretched work. Seated at this loom was a slender woman clad in loose, sleeveless red. Her skin was an unexpected deep bronze, her blue-black hair untouched by silver. As Telemachus came into the room, followed by Gabrielle and then Xena, she dropped her shuttles and combs and rose gracefully to her feet, arms outstretched.

"My son, you gave me such a fright! Have they finally forbade you to come here, that you must chance the balconies?" Her eyes moved beyond him, then. "Son—who are these women?"

"Mother, no." Telemachus smiled at her, then gave her a gentle hug, a son clearly proud of the still-young and still-beautiful Penelope. Though, so close now to the fabled queen, Gabrielle could make out faint lines between her brows and at the corners of her brown eyes. "It's all right, I just didn't want any of *them* to see us. They're—these women say they're friends, Mother."

"Friends?"

"I believe it. But I brought them to you mostly because they said they had word—from Father."

Penelope felt for the frame of her loom with a suddenly trembling hand and lowered herself to the cushioned chair. Troubled, dark eyes searched Gabrielle's face, then rested on Xena's. "You—you have seen him? My husband? Odysseus?"

"We both did, in different ways," Xena said quietly.

"He's—he's alive?"

"He was. Very alive, when I saw him last."

"Where—?" The queen couldn't manage any more; her hands went to her throat. Telemachus knelt beside her and captured her near hand between both of his.

He really was beautiful, Gabrielle thought judiciously. All that crisply curled hair, dark as his mother's—he didn't resemble her much, except possibly that straight, fine nose, and he was dark, though his eyes were the gray of a winter-storm-tossed sea. He had lovely shoulders and good cheekbones, long, well-shaped legs. Young, but without the usual awkwardness of a young male just come into his first chest hairs and the deepening voice. Without the sullen tone to his voice, or that spoiled twist to his mouth . . . *But be fair,* she ordered herself as Xena told the queen about her meeting with the Ithacan Trickster, on the sands of Troy. *He's had so little chance, no father to raise him, a mother who wants to protect him from anything that might hurt him—a boy would hate that. I'd have hated that. And then, Draco . . .* Besides, he'd just been caught trying to pull off the first stage of a very well-thought-out plan of escape; since those first few minutes aboard ship—when he'd been furious over his capture by what he saw as a pair of girls— he hadn't pouted, whined, or snarled. Well, not much. Just as well, too; Xena wouldn't put up with much of *that* kind of behavior from a mere kid, no matter what his rank. Not with so much at stake here.

It was suddenly quiet in the room, except for the muffled sound of weeping; Xena had finished speaking, the queen had buried her face in her hands, and Telemachus hovered over her, visibly unsure of what to say or do. Xena glanced at Gabrielle, sent her eyes toward the loom and the two huddled together there, and the warning was clear in her face: *Tell her about the vision—but not all of it.* As if I would do that to such a sweet lady, Gabrielle thought indignantly. She frowned slightly, considering how best to present her story.

Xena passed by the loom, patted the Queen's shoulder gently. "My friend can tell you the rest of it. I'll be on your balconies, looking things over."

Penelope drew a shuddering breath and sat up a little straighter; her dark eyes were red-rimmed, and her lips trembled as she tried to smile. "I already knew he'd survived the battles, that he'd left with the others. King Nestor sent a message once he arrived home—and there was a short message from my old friend Agamemnon, just that he'd sailed long after my husband, and that he looked forward to seeing us once again, after he'd settled his own

128

household. I knew his queen wasn't happy with him for going to Troy in the first place, but she's foreign, we never corresponded. When I didn't hear from any of them but Nestor . . .'' She blotted her eyes, blinked rapidly, and gave her son a watery smile. "It's all right, Telemachus.''

"Mother," he said softly, and touched her cheek; she captured his hand and held it against her face while Gabrielle marshaled her thoughts. *All right. Circe, yes; anything about Calypso—forget that.*

"It probably won't sound like much," Gabrielle began with an apologetic smile. "But I'm bard-trained, and you know how it is, you go where someone once walked and sometimes when your footsteps cross his, you have a vision.'' It didn't sound wildly probable to her ears, but the queen hung on her least word, and as she listened, her eyes dried and a faint smile touched the corners of her full, bow-shaped mouth.

"Oh," she whispered finally. "How wonderful, to have a vision like that! I—well, but the gods haven't blessed me that way, only with patience, and a determination to endure until my Odysseus comes home.'' She released Telemachus' hand. "Son, why don't you go help the warrior make certain all's quiet outside?'' He nodded and went. Penelope watched him slide past the thin curtain, lowered her voice, and beckoned Gabrielle closer. "That—that warlord, calls himself Draco. He told me I had no choice but to wed *him*, name him king and my son's guardian. He said there was proof he could give me, that my Odysseus had died not far from Troy.''

"That's a lie," Gabrielle murmured indignantly. "And it's wise of you not to let the boy know what Draco wants.''

Penelope uttered an unhappy little sound meant to be a laugh. "I protect him as best as I can. It's— well, it's nearly impossible now. He's so—so *angry!* Telling me what he'll do to—but it's an entire *army* out there!'' She swallowed hard, blotted her eyes once more. "He's so far from manhood, I know it's difficult for him to stay with me—but it's safest. *I* know.''

Gabrielle smiled, glanced over her shoulder to make certain they were quite alone, then said, ''Ah—Queen Penelope. You know, if I were you, hard as it might be, I'd go ahead and let Xena take charge of him while this crisis is going on—'' She held up a hand as the other woman stared at her, and began shaking her head. "No, I understand how you feel! I don't have a son yet, but I can tell he's very precious to you, with the king gone so long and anyway, your only child, and you remember him when he was just a baby, and barely able to walk. . . . But he's old enough to want to protect you—''

"He can't do that! They'd—they'd murder him!''

''Well, they might,'' Gabrielle conceded. ''Especially if he goes about it his own way, without anyone to restrain him, or point out a better way. Boys feel protective of beautiful mothers; I could see it from clear across the room, when we came in here.''

The queen sighed. "I know he wants to protect me.'' She ran a hand down her cheek. "Beauty, though—my poor Odysseus, if he ever *does* come home. To see this.''

"He'll be very proud,'' Gabrielle said softly. "You might not look like the young girl he married, but you're a very beautiful woman. And—well, from my vision, what I could see of your husband, I don't think he would be even a little bit interested in a gorgeous young woman without a trace of character in her face, or a thought in her head.'' Penelope smiled rather sadly, began to shake her head; Gabrielle took her hand. "No, honestly. I'll bet you two used to talk—I mean, *really talk*—about things you both liked.''

Her gaze went across the girl's head, to fix on the distant

bed rather absently; the smile that curved her mouth erased fully twenty years from her face. "Music," she said dreamily. "We both liked the comic tales the bards brought, but not the tragedies. Much too sad. And we'd walk out to the peak. You can't see it at this hour; but it's grassy and you can see the mainland from there. We'd take a picnic and argue jokingly about—oh, about anything: the flowers, where they came from and why, or clouds, or fish. We both liked a good, silly argument where I could explain to him what god protected what thing, and how it had been created, and he'd just pooh-pooh that and point out lineage and so on, how you could have all the gods you wanted but a flower still needed dirt, and rain and bees to make it grow and fruit, and what else would gods have time for if they did all that personally? He really was the most irreverent man. And—ah, well." She sighed again, but it was a happy sigh this time. The eyes she brought back to Gabrielle were warm this time. "Thank you, my dear. You've done me a world of good, given me something I haven't felt in a long time."

"I—but I didn't do anything," she protested.

"You listened. That's a wonderful gift, you know; there aren't many who can listen the way you do." She looked up; Gabrielle turned as Xena strode across the room and went to one knee by the loom so she could speak quietly.

"No guards around the palace, not on these two sides, at least." She gestured. "Most of the men seem to be out with the tents and the fires."

The queen nodded. "The warlord—Draco—he told me so long as I warned my people to cooperate, he'd keep his army under control, and my women and I would be left alone. He sometimes has a man patrol out there late at night, but he says that's to make certain no one forces his way in." Her shoulders trembled.

The warrior laid a hand on her arm. "There's a way out of this. I'll find it." She stood as Telemachus came up; his eyes were bright and his shoulders squared. They sagged a little as Xena turned to him and shook her head minutely. "Wait here. I'll need you later; your mother needs you just now."

"You won't—" he began.

"I gave my word. But I need to see Draco alone." Her eyes moved, met Gabrielle's. "You stay here, too."

"I don't like it—"

"Gabrielle—you wouldn't like Draco's men, either. Stay here." She strode silently across the shining tile floor, listened intently at the heavy, carved door. Her eyebrows went up as she glanced down; a thick bar effectively locked the door against anyone from the hall—a bar as old as the door itself, from the look of it. She shrugged, slipped the bar, glanced over her shoulder at the three watching her, at the servant who still stood where Telemachus had left her when they first came in from the balcony, gestured meaningfully at the length of wood. The prince came across, waited until the warrior had slipped into the hall, and replaced it.

"My Odysseus had it put on the door when he first brought me home to Ithaca," Penelope murmured. "At the time it reassured me so much; a very young girl brought three days by sea from her family, a young king she barely knew. We used to joke about it, even after Telemachus was born. I kept it there—just as a reminder. I never thought I might need it one day."

It wouldn't hold against a real attack, Gabrielle knew. But to keep some drunken lout from gaining entry . . . Telemachus came back from the barred door, his shoulders squared and arms away from his sides, ready to grasp a weapon. Gasbrielle bit the corners of her mouth to hold back the laugh that would only offend him; he was so clearly trying to move like Xena. "Mother," he said very quietly. "You stay here; I'll be on the balconies—watching."

The queen nodded silently and was very quiet for a long moment, but as soon as her son stepped onto the dark balcony, she bent down to muffle laughter. "Oh, dear. What shall I do with him?"

"Don't worry too much," Gabrielle said. "Xena would never, ever put him into real danger, if she could help it. That isn't how she does things. She'll make him feel good about himself and she'll do what she can to teach him how to protect himself. She won't let him go up against Draco's army all by himself. And, you know, he just might do that, if no one redirects the way he's thinking. An angry, untrained boy in a situtation like this—well, it's pretty dangerous."

"Oh—dear goddess," Penelope moaned, and twisted anxiously at her hair.

"No, honestly, listen," Gabrielle urged. "Sometime he's gonna have to learn how to fight. If the king hadn't gone to war, he'd have trained the boy in some of the combat skills already, wouldn't he?" The queen sighed, and reluctantly nodded. "So wouldn't it be best to have him trained, just like the king would have? The king might not be embarrassed by a son who didn't have that training, but Telemachus would be."

"I—I know you're right. It's just—well, it's hard. You feel as though if he doesn't know any of that, then he can't be taken from you, the way they took Odysseus away." She sighed again. "I know, that isn't right. You'll think I'm a fool, to act this way."

"You aren't a fool," Gabrielle said warmly. "And mothers can't help feeling protective of their sons. At least you aren't being silly about it, the way some mothers have been.

Haven't you heard the tale about how your husband tricked Achilles' mother when she tried to keep him back from going to Troy?''

The queen stared at her. ''I—of course, I—'' She blinked, let go of her hair, and began to comb through the tangled mass with her fingers. The servant came across with a comb, but Penelope waved her away with a faint smile. ''When did he do that?''

Gabrielle settled her back against the wall. ''Well! It was just after King Menelaus' messenger tricked the king into going to Troy. Now, I hadn't heard about that until Xena told it to me, just as Odysseus told it to her. But I think I was in Athens when I heard about what happened after that. Anyway, Odysseus began assembling his army, and when it came time for him to get some of the heroes to join him, Achilles' mother, Thetis, was so afraid for her son that she made him dress up like a girl and hide in her apartments. Well, Odysseus knew he was in there, and he had a hunch what Thetis had done—she's a Neriad, you know, and they can be a little, well, flighty.'' *And Thetis knew, because the gods told her, that her son would die if he went to Troy,* she remembered with a sudden pang; well, the queen didn't need to hear *that* part of the story. ''So, your husband got himself up as a peddler in a plain tunic and a ragged old hat to shield his face, and he came in with boxes of silks and threads and ribbons, and one separate little chest of fine daggers. Poor Achilles; he was all muscle and hot temper, no brains. He didn't have enough sense to coo over the silks like the women were doing, and leave the knives alone.'' Silence, as Penelope considered this story, and finally shook her head in bewilderment.

Gabrielle spread her arms wide and resettled, cross-legged, on the cool floor. ''Well, *your* son isn't like Achilles; he's got brains and looks. But he's got that male thing, you know, he'd hate having his hero father finally coming home from the wars and discovering a son who's hiding behind his mother's robes." She paused. "But that isn't important right now. The important thing is that Telemachus feels coddled, and babied, and you know how hard young people that age take things. He'll try to be a good son to you, but eventually he'll get upset that nothing's going right, and he'll do something, *anything,* to make it better. But he won't know how to do that right." Silence.

Penelope sighed deeply. "And he'll die. Yes, all right, I can see that. I suppose. It's just so—it's so hard to let him walk into danger—"

"He's doing that anyway, he can't help it, with Draco and an army here on Ithaca," Gabrielle reminded her pointedly. She got to her feet and stretched. Penelope rose with her, set her shuttles and combs on the cushions, and covered the loom with a cloth.

"I'm forgetting my duties to a guest," she said, and clapped her hands once for the servant, who came hurrying over. "Ismene, is there any fruit left?"

"Fruit, and a little of the bread. It might be a bit dry, lady," she added to Gabrielle, who shook her head.

"After that boat trip over here, dry bread sounds just like the thing," she said.

With the door barred behind her, Xena moved quickly, through the queen's lavishly painted and well-lit corridor, then down a narrow, plainly whitewashed tunnel of a hall lit at odd intervals with small clay oil lamps. Servants' access. She paused briefly, sniffed the air. Lemon and spices teased her nostrils; the lamp oil had been scented. But underneath this, the pleasant odor of well-cooked meat, and bread. The kitchens—that way. She strode light-footed down the tunnel, paused at the junction of another, equally narrow corridor. This one went more or less the way she'd come but sloped down to the next level, and finally vanished around a corner. She could hear voices down there; men conversing in low tones—nothing of what they were saying yet. She set her shoulders against the near wall, glanced behind her and along the rest of the corridor. A door at the end; storage, perhaps. Barred from the outside. No other doors that way, no one in sight, either direction, or down the ramp. Another long look; she had an unexpectedly good line of sight from here, and the floors were plain tile, the kind of surface that would make plenty of noise when someone walked over it in boots; the sound would echo. More than enough early warning. She moved quickly down to the sharp bend, listened intently for a moment, then eased around the corner.

The floor sloped even more steeply for a short distance, five or six long strides' worth, then flattened out. Here was a torch jammed into a bracket, and an oil lamp guttered well back in a small niche. Cooking smoke eddied in the yellowish, wavering light before sliding across the ceiling and out through a high, narrow slit in the wall. The smell of freshly baked bread overcame almost everything else from here. *Can't remember when I last ate.* She smiled grimly. What better way to break a fast than this? She paused just outside the partly closed door to listen, then moved so she could see into the room.

The kitchen was a vast chamber; clay ovens and braziers took up the far wall, where large window openings allowed the sea breeze to take the smoke away. Tables and benches lay everywhere; there was room enough here for a dozen or more cooks, and for twice that many servants or apprentices to manage the lowlier tasks of peeling tubers or washing. The two black-clad men who worked over something in a steaming pot in the far corner looked very lost indeed. The smile widened briefly; she pulled the door open, stepped into the kitchen, and hauled it closed behind her.

The two whirled around as one, knives in hand. Xena waved empty hands at them and leaned back against the door, arms folded. "Lemnos, isn't it? Nothing nice to say to an old colleague?"

Lemnos, a very small and extremely dark man—nearer blue black than brown—with a shaven skull and neat little hands, gaped at her. She didn't recognize his companion—he looked Egyptian, that bronze coloring, the arrogant, pale eyes, the hawk's beak of a nose. Silence for a long moment; Lemnos finally uttered a nervous little laugh, jammed his knife in the wooden rack behind him, and spread his arms wide. "I'll be—Xena! How'd you get here?"

"Xena? I've heard of her, what's *she* doing here?" the other asked suspiciously, and shifted his grasp on the knife hilt.

Lemnos caught hold of his wrist and laughed again; Xena smiled and gritted her teeth. *I'd forgotten how irritating that nasty little giggle of his is.*

"Rammis! Hey, it's all right, I know her. She's—" He seemed to remember something; the light went out of his face, but he rallied almost at once. "Draco and her was pals a while back. He'll be glad to see her. I'm glad to see her. C'mon, pal," he added in an urgent undertone. "Drop the blade before she does you, will you? I don't wanna have any part of some fight you pick—not with *her*."

"Pals, huh?" Pale brown eyes held hers. "Seems I heard some other things about her. Seems to me Draco might wanna see her, but not necessarily like a friend."

"One of the perils of a competitive business," Xena murmured throatily. Rammis stared at her blankly. "Sometimes we want the same thing—and neither of us wants to share. That isn't always the case, though. Like maybe now."

"Now—" Lemnos seemed to be struggling with the idea. He brightened suddenly. "You mean, maybe you're gonna rejoin us? Hey, would that ever be great!"

"Yeah," Rammis added suspiciously. "Great."

Lemnos nudged him with an urgent elbow. The Egyptian took a wary step backward as Xena sauntered across the kitchen; she stopped behind an enormous cutting table, leaned forward on her hands, and settled her shoulders comfortably. The little dark man's eyes bulged.

"I'd really like to see him, Lemnos. I know he's here somewhere—I just don't know where."

"I—well, I—well, sure—" Lemnos stopped short, swearing under his breath as Rammis nudged his ribs.

"How'd you get in here, anyway?" he demanded suspiciously. "Out here to the island? There's no way through mainland Ithaca, and we sank all the boats. And there's men everywhere out on shore!"

She smiled at him; he swallowed and fell silent. "I walked." She waited, but the little Egyptian seemed to have no answer for that. She then turned the full force of an extremely seductive smile on Lemnos. "So, where is he?"

"Ah—yeah! Well!" The little man was sweating, all at once, despite a cool wind blowing through his end of the kitchen. "Ya know, Xena, maybe you're right, and he'd really like to see you, too. But right now—well, you know how it is," he added with an abashed little smile, "he just hates it when someone breaks in on his dinner."

"Fine. Then tell him dessert's here."

Even the suspicious Egyptian was taken aback for a moment; Lemnos tittered nervously then, and his companion brought up the knife in a menacing grip, taking a step forward. "Dessert—right. In *real* small pieces!" he shouted

138

as he hurled himself forward. Xena threw herself across the table in a tight tuck, dropped just in front of him, and went to one knee just as he brought the knife around in a slashing arc. He yelped; the knife went one way and he went sailing the other; a small bench collapsed as he slammed into it; several dusty baskets fell onto him.

He sneezed, sending baskets and years of dust and cobweb flying; more baskets slammed into walls and floor as he cursed furiously and fought his way free of the mess. He spun quickly, came onto one knee, hands out and ready, blinking filth from his eyes. Something swam before his blurred vision. Legs. Pale, well-muscled legs, neatly booted feet; he looked up slowly, warily. Xena gazed down at him, teeth bared in a chill smile, his knife in one of her hands. "Lose something?" she asked softly, reversed the knife deftly, and brought the heavy metal knob down hard on his head. He fell, bonelessly.

Silence in the kitchen, except for a faint, nervous titter somewhere near the ovens. "Lemnos," she said finally, her eyes still on the unconscious Egyptian.

"Ah—yes, Princess?"

"Just Xena."

"Ah—whatever. Sure, Xena."

"Stop that stupid giggle."

"Ah—hch. Whatever you say, Xena. You—ah—you want me to go tell Draco you're here?"

She turned; he'd taken a step or two toward her, and he retreated at once, right into the nearest oven. He yelped, skittered to one side.

"No. Finish whatever that is you're fixing for him. Then you'll take me to him." She spared the Egyptian one final look, sauntered across the room, and settled on one of the low benches near the ovens. "And find me a loaf, will you?

That one's fine.'' She pointed to a small, dark mound that smelled like honey and fruit. ''I'm hungry.'' She bared her teeth; he whimpered, but scooped up the bread and set it before her without further comment.

9

It was clear that Lemnos didn't like the position he'd been put in; he just as obviously couldn't find a way out of it he liked any better. After a moment or so he sighed heavily and cleared his throat. Xena yanked off another chunk of warm, tough-crusted bread and popped the bite in her mouth. She had one ear tuned to the still-motionless Rammis and her eyes were fixed on Lemnos, eyebrows high.

"Oh, all right." The words came out too high, nervous sounding. He cleared his throat. "You're asking to get your throat cut, you know. Draco hates you. He hasn't had a good word to say about you in a long time." He gestured toward his fallen companion. "I mean, where do you think *he* got the attitude, Xena?"

"Rammis? Maybe his mother dropped him on his head when he was a baby, how should I know? I can deal with Draco," she added shortly. Pausing, she tore off another chunk of bread. "This is good; I didn't know you could bake, Lemnos." She gave him a sly grin. "You never baked anything for *me,* Lemnos." It was an attempt to lighten the mood in the windswept kitchen; it didn't work.

"My father was a baker," he replied gloomily. "In Thebes. He sold bread and the like to the rich, and he died very poor. Guess I never told you because you never asked, all right?" He sighed. "I shoulda stayed there, kept the shop after he died, 'stead of going out for gold and glory. Maybe I'd still be alive tomorrow. Right now I don't like my chances so good."

"Now, Lemnos." She hadn't expected such a heartfelt reaction from him. But Lemnos had always been a *nice* little man, at bottom. Response in kind would only shift things onto the wrong plane and he'd probably see sentiment from her as a sign of softness. She chuckled, gaining a startled and wary look from him. "Lemnos, you'll probably live forever. You're useful to Draco, you're keeping him fed. And he's practical. You know he'll protect you better than he watches over himself, so long as you keep him happy."

"Oh. Sure. And what if someone who does a better job comes along?" He swallowed hard, primmed his lips. "I nearly met my replacement last month; a man who could make pastry sing. Unfortunately, he doesn't—*didn't*—do so well with the pretty bits when he was drunk, and he had a powerful friend in a jug of wine." A brief silence. "He downed too much Aeolian sweet red and burned the crust."

"Too bad for him," she said coldly. "Don't tell me how Draco rewarded him. You about done there, my friend?"

"Almost," he replied absently; his fingers were moving at dizzying speed, folding bits of leaf around small pieces of fish or meat, twisting little sprigs of grass or branch around the whole packet to hold it in place, drizzling a pungent liquid over these. He patted leaves into a patterned bed on another painted wooden platter, drew a clay bowl from one of the ovens, and began setting shining, dripping slivers of meat in a glyphlike pattern across the flattened greenery, then drizzled ruddy oil over everything, to create yet a third pattern. "This isn't the meal, you realize," he said. His hands seemed to have a life of their own.

Xena watched, fascinated. Pattern upon pattern upon pattern . . . She scrubbed at her eyes, shook her head hard. "Gods, Lemnos, I hope not; there isn't enough there to keep a dryad alive!" Lemnos cast her a crooked grin. "Let me get something straight. He *eats* this—this stuff? He actually *likes* it?"

"Yeah." He considered this, and laughed despite his situation. "Okay, he claims to like it, but sometimes I wonder. Because—well, listen, you probably won't believe me, but . . . 'Bout a year ago we raided some rich guy's northern summer palace—two palaces he owned, this guy, one down on the southern Mylitos coast, another in northern Macedonia—"

"Macedonia? You guys are getting around, these days—"

"Sure. Anyway, this rich feller—wish I could remember his name, but anyway, two palaces. You have any notion, Xena, how much it takes to transport all your people, your special bits of finery, your special food, all that? To another location days or weeks distant? So you can do the exact same thing except somewhere else, and then do it again when the seasons change?"

"Lemnos—I think you're a Minoan at heart," Xena replied cheerfully. "Everyone equal, all money equal, land equal, men and women equal, possessions equal—what's the fun in that?" *Well,* she amended privately, *all but the one involving physical being* . . . Some simply couldn't manage if everyone started on a level field.

"Fun," Lemnos replied darkly. "You and Draco both wait until *we* find a way to redistribute the wealth!" He caught his breath sharply, suddenly remembering who he was—and who he was with. But Xena merely smiled and

143

waved him on. After a moment he cleared his throat and nodded. "All right—anyway. This noble had two complete palaces, and he was whining about losing one of 'em!"

"He wasn't whining for long, I wager."

"I don't bet! Well, not with you, Xena, you know that." He eyed her sidelong. "No offense, okay? So we bust in right in the middle of this *amazing* banquet, some kinda combination betrothal for his kid and a welcoming-back ceremony for—who's that, spends winter in Hades? The plant goddess's kid with the pomegranate?" Xena shrugged, not much interested. Lemnos wasn't very interested either. He waved oily fingers in dismissal. "Anyway, for this supposed virgin goddess and also because of the betrothal thing—it's the virgin crossover, goddess and betrothed kid, got it? Well, the old guy's filthy rich, and so, of course, lots of fancy food everywhere.

"Me, I'd've sent 'em all to Hades to chase gold coins across a *very* convoluted plain! A *hot* one—supposing there's a Hades and gods to run it; you can't prove that by *me*! Anyway, one of the guests—he could talk faster than a hungry bard—was trying to talk his way out of being spitted. The surprise was, so far it had worked. Bigger surprise, it's Draco standing over him and he hasn't cut the rich little slime's gullet—he's listening to this nonsense!" *Gabrielle's got a male counterpart out there somewhere,* Xena thought. *Now, that's scary.* The little baker snorted. "Me, I got no clue what he was saying, I just know the result. The lippy barstid goes free, and all of a sudden Draco's going for all this kinda pre-meal nonsense himself— just *for* himself, of course; he's still Draco and he ain't about to waste this kinda time and supplies on your average stupid village flattener. He eats the stuff, gabbles about the this and that of it—I don't know what half that stuff means, I just figure, he eats it, doesn't offer to kill me, and it's

144

okay, you know? Pour whatever wine he wants with it, then come back down here and break out the big platter with the baked joints. Last night''—he enumerated on dripping, sticky fingers—''it was four partridges, a quarter of boar—well, you get the idea.''

''Same old Draco,'' she murmured.

''Well—not really,'' Lemnos temporized; he licked his fingers absently, made a face at them, and dipped them in a bowl of water, then dried them on his britches; shiny tracks ran along both thighs from knees to the hem of his shirt. ''Oh, he's just as cold-blooded and evil-minded as ever; you wouldn't *believe* what he did to everyone else in that summer palace, let alone some of the tricks he pulled getting us all across mainland Ithaca, just so's we could reach the shore back there!''

''I'd believe it,'' she replied flatly.

''Ah—sure.'' He seemed to remember who he was talking to, all at once. ''Okay. He's—I dunno. Used to be, he talked about nothing but taking over the world, or how to mangle a village or a palace properly, so everyone would know he'd done it, you know: leave his particular mark and he didn't have to bother leaving witnesses alive to spread the terror. It made him a proper social leveler. Now, I liked *that*. Coin redistributed, those with too much made to share—I saw the whole thing that way, and I thought he did, too. Lately, it's been— well, I don't like to say.''

''Tell me.''

''You wouldn't believe me. More—oh, how's history gonna see him; how're the bards gonna play this one? Not—understand me,'' Lemnos added hastily, ''he's not getting old, or looking over his shoulder for Ares to cart him off, like he useta joke about, nothing like that. He ain't one bit soft.''

''I wouldn't be fool enough to think that, Lemnos.''

"Well, sure, I know that. Just—ya know—" He looked quickly around, then went on in a very low voice, "He's been a little—different—since the last couple towns we hit, before Ithaca, I mean. I think something got him thinking about his—what'd he call it?—his legacy, that kinda stuff."

"Mmmm." She considered this for a long, silent moment, finally picked up the last of the bread, and tore it in half. "Good stuff." She tore the half into two more pieces, popped one in her mouth, then spoke around it. "I don't know, Lemnos. Doesn't sound like the Draco I know . . . You're not trying to fool me, are you?"

"My heart to the gods if I lie," the little man replied solemnly. He cast her a quick, suspicious glance. "And I'm not Draco; I got one. Heart, that is."

"Thought you didn't believe in gods."

"I don't." A smile tweaked the corners of his mouth. "Why I'd make a vow like that, right?" He turned back to his preparations, a frown etching his brow. "Draco, though; it's not—I mean, it's like the food thing—it's not a big thing, it ain't always, and he hasn't changed that much, it's just, if you know him, you'd know he's kinda gone odd." He balanced the small platter on the corner of the larger one and began the cautious process of picking them up.

Xena leaped to her feet, took the smaller from him, and inclined her head. Her smile was ironic. "So—lead the way."

Lemnos cast his eyes up, fastidiously readjusted two bits of slivered meat so they did something to the pattern, then straightened the platter and crossed the chamber to lead the way out the door she'd entered. Rammis was beginning to stir, groaning; his eyes fluttered open and he tried to lever himself up on one trembling arm; his other hand was feeling around for his knife. Lemnos sighed in exasperation and gave him a wide berth; Xena leveled a kick at his chin that snapped his head back into the wall with a sickening crack. He slid bonelessly to the floor, moaned once. Lemnos gazed down at him, his face expressionless—he was good at that, Xena remembered, the little wealth-redistributing Minoan rebel—then eyed her thoughtfully. "Still breathing," he murmured.

"Planned it that way," she replied. "He's not worth killing. Lead the way." He sighed, very quietly; she raised an eyebrow at him, gestured toward the door with her chin.

The chamber Draco used for his meals was at the far end of the hall from the queen's apartments. Torches and lamps were everywhere, lighting pale blue walls that had been painted with scenes of the sea, where ships rambled across a stormy surface, while beneath the waves swam monsters and fish. A pale-faced, gray-bearded palace servant attended the long, low table and its only occupant. Draco reclined on a soft couch, his bronze, sculpted chest and arms bare; a pair of soft suede britches hung loose around his hips. He waited while a deeply purple wine was poured for him; he lifted the small cup and before drinking, sniffed the contents, then set the cup down and shook his head. "I like the other; leave the bottle." The brown-clad old man backed away and moved as quickly as trembling legs would take him, through the door Lemnos had just opened.

The warlord looked up as his cook cleared his throat, rather tentatively, and held out the tray. "Ah! What have you for me tonight—by Ares, Lemnos, are my eyes going?"

Xena eased around the little cook, tray balanced on one hand. "Draco, didn't your mother ever tell you to wear a shirt in the dining hall?"

He stared at her for a long moment, eyes wide; torchlight made a ruddy highlight of recent pouches under his eyes and long marks from nostrils to the corners of his mouth; the scar that ran the length of his sun-darkened face, forehead to chin, was pale by comparison. The mark she'd put on him. All was silent for a moment. Then he let his head fall back and laughed uproariously. She waited him out; Lemnos set the tray at the warlord's elbow, and, with one unhappy look at Xena, backed away, one wary step at a time. He finally turned, just short of the door, and walked quickly and quietly out, easing the heavy carved panel closed behind him.

Draco came up onto one elbow, then swung his legs down to the floor and used both hands to wipe his eyes. "You know," he said finally, "I always expect to see you just—happen into a room or my tent, just like this, *poof,* a magician's trick. And there you are. You still caught me by surprise!" He wiped damp hands on his chest and grinned hugely. "To answer your question, my mother died while I was still puking breast milk; I'd have a hard time remembering anything *she* told me. Besides, this isn't the king's so-pristine family dining hall; this is the old Trickster's private hideaway. You know, one for dull family life then and this—where he'd entertain the boys. Lots of wine, dancing girls, the whole bit. Compared to what garb some of those guys still had on by the end of a long night, I'm positively decent."

Momentary silence. Draco broke it. "Hey, that reminds me." He slapped one knee, swung his legs back onto the couch, and dropped onto one elbow. "Someone told me they'd heard the damnedest thing about you recently, that you'd climbed into a dancer's sheers, veils and all, and entertained some king's old pig of a throat-slitting adviser—and all that so you could rescue a *baby*?"

148

She set the tray on the table before him, then settled one hip next to it, her free leg swinging. Draco watched it, fascinated, then blinked furiously and brought his eyes back to her face. "You know I can dance, Draco."

"I've *heard*," he corrected her.

She flicked him a smile, eased farther back onto the table; his eyes had gone back to the swinging leg once more. "Maybe it was my baby."

"Your—" He gaped, wide-eyed, then slapped his knee and laughed again. "That's a good one! Yeah, when I heard that story, I thought, there's another one of those myths growing up around Xena." One enormous hand slammed the table, rattling cup and painted clay bottle together; he caught the wine before it could spill. "I don't know how you do it, Xena. You've got a lot of stories out there. More things than you could ever've done. Me—" He patted his bare chest, grimaced. "Me, half the time, they don't even know who it was hit their village, or took out all their girls, or their hidden cache of gold, or—or whatever. Lot of stuff I've done, it's credited to some god or other, or maybe another warlord. Worse yet, some little creep like Hesiod gets his name on the job."

Xena smiled, raised her eyebrows. "Well, that's one you won't have to worry about stealing the light from your torch. Last I saw of Hesiod, he was a grease splotch on a back road."

"Oh. Really?" She laughed quietly; he laughed with her, much more loudly. "Say," he added in a suddenly serious voice. "How'd you get here? I've got all but three of the boats in Ithaca sunk to the bottom of the bay out there, and men watching for anything coming from the mainland or out to sea."

"I told Lemnos I walked." She let her gaze scare him for a moment before her mouth quirked, and he laughed

149

again. "You want the truth?" she said, when he had gained control of himself. "The queen sent a message out a while back, to King Menelaus of Sparta—"

"I know what he's king of," Draco interrupted flatly.

"All right." Xena crossed her arms and leaned back, her shoulders squared. Draco blinked, went very quiet indeed. "She wanted to find out where Odysseus might be, because he surely wasn't home. Menelaus—" She considered the humor of it for the first time. *Helen's brutish, arrogant husband, fresh returned from Troy, and after all that fighting, still no wife—and no idea that I'm part of the reason he doesn't have his wife.* Amusing. Distracting. "He sent word for someone to go to Ithaca, find out from the queen what was going on here." She gave him a cold little smile. "I found his messenger before anyone else did. Lucky me."

Draco frowned slightly. "Lucky—how?"

Her smile broadened. "Very lucky. Ithaca wide open— once someone dealt with a few freelance brutes who only needed to be killed, kicked out, or brought under control. My control, of course." She raised one eyebrow, gestured toward the two cooling platters. "If you want any of that, you'd better eat it before it congeals."

"Oh. Mmmm, right." He selected one of the wrapped and oiled bundles, popped it in his mouth, and briefly closed his eyes to properly savor the tastes; less than a heartbeat later one eye opened and fixed warily on his companion. Xena laughed quietly and edged back farther from him. "I'm not here to run you through, Draco. Not today, at least. Here—eat. Lemnos went to a lot of trouble, playing with all that, don't let me get in the way of your culinary pleasures."

"Mmm. Maybe if you were on the other side of the bay, or better yet, the great gray sea of Atlantis, maybe then I'd trust you.'' He chewed, swallowed, made a little displeased face, but squared his shoulders and finished the stuff, washed the last of it down with wine. ''Delicate—yet pleasing to the palate—''

Her laughter drowned him out. ''Come off it, Draco! Eat the nasty little bits if they please you, but don't try to impress me with your vocabulary or your taste buds. I know both.''

''Ah—hmmm. Yeah. All right, it's raw fish and whatever he's dipped it in, it still tastes like raw fish. Oily fish.'' He smiled crookedly, though his eyes were dark. ''This is a lot more fun without *you* sitting there and laughing at me.''

''I'm sure it is. I hope for your sake the fish was fresh. So, what do you have in mind for the rest of Odysseus' palace? From the looks of you, you're planning to take it all over, slide a crown onto your handsome forehead, and be damned to Menelaus, Nestor, Agamemnon, and all the rest of them.''

''That's about it,'' Draco replied cheerfully. His eyes narrowed. ''All right—I see you taking over the mainland, either terrorizing the grubby peasants or protecting them from all comers. Whichever mood is currently taking you. Why here, though?'' She picked up a sliver of meat from the second tray, smiled, and held it to his lips. He laughed softly and ate it.

''Maybe I didn't know you were here until I stepped off my raft.''

''Sure.'' He snorted. ''You don't do things that way. You knew an army was out here, and I'm ready to bet you knew whose. You don't fool me, Xena.''

''Who said I was trying?''

He scooped up more of the meat slivers, popped the lot into his mouth. ''Not bad, those,'' he mumbled around them. "Help yourself." She picked up one, sniffed it, shrugged and tossed it back onto the platter. Draco grinned and chewed, swallowed it with some wine, and leaned back. "So, why *are* you here? You can't hope to take Ithaca away from me; you can't rob the old king's vaults because even I haven't found them yet, let alone a way into them. And forget taking the queen and her whining brat away from me, if that was your plan."

"Got it all figured out, have you?"

"Enough of it. Not that I'm too worried, Xena; I'm the one with an army out there. It's not as big as some I've had, but it's the best bunch of fighting men I've ever assembled."

She picked up the sliver of meat she'd dropped, smiled, and held it tantalizingly near his nostrils, wafted it back and forth just above his head, then lowered it into his open mouth. "Maybe this is just where I wanted to be."

He choked, nearly splattering her with bits of marinated goat. "I offered you that chance well over a year ago, and you turned me down in damned convincing fashion! You're lying. Why?"

"I'm not," she replied evenly. "So I don't need to prove anything, do I? But last time you offered me half of your bed, the exchange rate was a camp full of grubby lowlifes like Hesiod and nasty, mouthy little Rammis."

"Rammis—you met him, did you?" She nodded; he sighed faintly. "Just great. Where'd you leave the body?"

"He's still alive. Next time he may not be. I don't like little men with big attitudes and bigger knives. Forget Rammis. You've got more to offer me this time."

"Oh?"

"Sure." She shoved the large tray aside and eased down onto one elbow, set a finger under his chin, and smiled into his eyes. "You couldn't offer me a crown before. Now you can.'' She smiled, exposing neat, white teeth. ''Queen Xena. I like the sound of that. Don't you?''

He considered this in silence for a very long time, narrowed eyes fixed on her face as he felt for the wine jug. He poured some and drank it down. ''Maybe. I'm still wondering why you think I'd trust you that much, though.''

''I don't think that.'' She let go his chin and sat back, one foot braced on the edge of the table, the other swinging loose. ''Any more than I'd trust you, Draco. We start from here, take it a day at a time, all right? I'm not offering to warm your bed tonight.''

''As if I'd accept.'' He laughed shortly, though his eyes were suddenly all pupil and his voice sounded odd. *Not thinking with his brains anymore,* Xena thought in satisfaction. *Nice to know you can still twist him that way.* Even if she didn't mean to take advantage of the situation. ''Ah—well. Actually, you know . . .'' He poured more wine, leaned back again on the soft cushions. His eyes had never left her face. ''Actually, I'm planning to marry Queen Penelope.''

''She's said she'd agree?''

He sat up. ''Are you jesting? She's said several things to and of me, words that I didn't think a queen would know! But she's got two problems: a long-missing husband who may or may not ever show up, and if he does he won't be in any condition to battle an army that's dug in here. And the other is that pampered, spoiled kid of hers.''

''I met him,'' she said evenly.

''Then you know what I mean. So I figure, I marry her, she has to claim me as a lawful husband, or the kid's fish bait. Then even somebody like old Nestor—he's supposed to be so damned upright and honorable—well, even Nestor wouldn't challenge her word, would he?''

''He'd probably know full well you'd coerced her, but

none of them would start a war for Ithaca. Especially not now; they lost too much in Troy. Telemachus is too young to count; Odysseus can't call in any favors if he's dead. And Penelope's male kindred are from somewhere beyond the horizon—no brothers and uncles to stick up for her. But—why bother with Penelope? You said she doesn't like you. . . . And you don't like the boy.''

"I'd probably live a lot longer with *her* on the throne next to me.'' Draco stretched, eased back down onto his couch, and clasped his hands behind his head.

Xena let her eyes drift over the bronzed male scenery sprawled over the couch, and smiled. *Not as wonderful as he thinks—but it's not that bad. Reasonably exciting.* Too bad the rest of him went with it. She squared her shoulders, met his eyes directly, and let the smile warm. ''So. Penelope doesn't take knives to bed with her—but I don't either. Not unless it's called for. What's she got that I don't have?''

He rubbed his shoulders against soft cloth and chuckled. ''You don't give up, do you?''

''You haven't given me reason to think I should.'' She looked up as the door opened. Draco came partway to one elbow, one stealthy hand under a dark cushion, but it was only Lemnos with a heavy tray, two bowls balanced precariously on top of it. He eased the door closed with his shoulder, staggered across the room.

Xena smiled, let Draco see she'd watched his stealthy hand movement, that she knew at least one throwing knife was under the cushion, then she rolled across the table and dropped neatly onto the low couch opposite his. Lemnos set the tray down with care, shook out his weight-numbed hands, and set the bowls next to it. The warlord sat up and slid the tray across the table. ''Here. Ladies first.'' Lemnos rolled his eyes; Xena laughed raucously.

"Draco, you always were a comedian!" She bared her teeth at him and chuckled briefly, then glanced at Lemnos. "Find a cup and get me some of that wine he's been swilling down."

Dracos laughed sourly. "Since you've watched me drink, the wine's all right, that it?"

"*Possibly* all right," Xena countered softly. "No guarantees between you and me, remember? And I don't know about what's in the jug over by the door, do I? But since you weren't expecting visitors tonight—" Lemnos sighed, fetched the jug, poured some into Draco's outheld cup, and settled the container in a hole that had been cut for it farther down the table. Xena watched him, shifted her gaze to Draco, who ostentatiously took a drink and set the cup aside. "Fine. You take something off the platter first—then I'll think about it."

He sighed; his eyes were ironic. "I just don't want you to wonder if I've forced a choice on you. Too much meat, too little time." She kept her eyes on his, glanced at Lemnos, who was all but wringing his hands, took hold of one long joint, then a thick cut of goat that would be very red and bleeding in the middle. No reaction from either; Draco might be able to hide his emotions, but Lemnos—she doubted it. She shrugged finally, took the long joint, then waited until Draco caught up another long joint with blackened, crisp skin. He gave her an amused look, bit into the joint like a northern barbarian would, chewed and swallowed, washing the bite down with a gulp of wine. Xena smiled, shrugged faintly, and tore a bite loose. As she chewed, she could sense Lemnos eying both of them with resignation.

"Tasty," she said finally. "Young goat?"

The little black cook spread his arms. "Very young. Kid." He turned to Draco, who waved him off.

"Good work, as always." He paused, grinning. "How's Rammis?"

Lemnos swallowed. "Well, I—ah—I thought you wouldn't mind if I left things for a little while so I could pack him over to the physician's tent, get him pinned back together. . . ."

"If he's stupid enough to tangle with *her* more than once in a night, I'd rather you dumped him off a wall and into the water."

Xena set her joint down, pulled out a dagger, deftly wielded the blade to swiftly cut a pile of very neat slices. Cook and cook's master watched. "He's stupid, Rammis— but I pushed him. And you've pushed me more than once in a day yourself, Draco. Let your cook keep his company." She jammed the dagger upright into the table boards and popped meat into her mouth; she leaned forward on her elbows, eyes fixed on his.

Xena's eyes: they were the most amazing things, Draco thought. That rare, pale blue ringed in deep azure—his mouth was suddenly much too dry. He drank deeply, waved a hand at his cook. "Ah, go on, get him out of here—just keep him out of my sight! Wretched, filthy, conniving Egyptian!"

Lemnos was trying to stutter out some kind of thanks and back away at the same time. Xena's cool voice stopped him. "While you're at it, Lemnos, you'd better send someone down to the ship that came in today. There's good wine and new wheat on board—and I'll wager both Metrikas and Krinos are getting stiff, tied up in the hold all this time. Cross, too."

Lemnos' lips moved; no sound emerged. Thought of a cross Metrikas didn't do anything for his coloring. He turned and fled, the slammed door echoing behind him.

The room was quiet for some time after that—a fairly

companionable silence as they finished the meat. Xena shoved her knife back into its hidden sheath, took grapes from the nearest bowl, and popped one in her mouth.

Draco laughed quietly. "Stepped off your raft, huh? And what—you didn't wait for me to taste one of those first?"

"Comes a time you have to take *some* chances," she murmured, and ate another.

"Chances." He drank the last of his wine, refilled the cup, and settled one arm on the table. "So—how many chances are you willing to—?" He hesitated.

Doesn't know what he wants—or how badly he wants it, she decided. Good. An off-balance Draco was exactly what she wanted. "Not that many," she cut him off flatly. She smiled, then. "You don't want *me* tonight—me, in the"— she drew a deep breath, exhaled grapes and wine in his flushed, upturned face—"*flesh.* Remember, you have to sleep sometime. With your eyes closed."

He laughed, baring fine white teeth. "So do you."

"Exactly. That's why I prefer to wait. Right now," she added sweetly, "I trust you as far as I could spit you, Draco. And I'd say that goes for you, too."

"Forget all that," he said cheerfully. "Have more wine."

She set her hand over the cup. "I've had enough. So— you sleep in the palace, or just eat here?"

"My men sleep out there—Odysseus didn't keep his army in the house, either. Once things are settled, I'll let 'em build barracks. As to me—well, wouldn't you like to know?"

"Not really. Not yet." She rolled off the low couch and flowed to her feet. "That was good, Draco—a nice, quiet, long meal where neither of us tried to murder the other. We'll have to do it again sometime. But for now, I'm going to bed."

"Bed . . ." His mouth was dry again. He blinked, swallowed, and swung his feet to the floor. "Where are you sleeping?"

She walked around the table, stopped short of his couch. "Maybe I won't be. Sleeping. Maybe I'll be keeping an eye on you." She shook her head before he could say anything else. "Maybe I'll be in the queen's apartments. They seem to be the safest place in the entire palace, and the decor's nicer."

"I—see." He didn't believe her; she smiled coldly.

"Do you, Draco?"

He shrugged, poured a thimbleful of wine, swirled it in the cup. "If you plan on getting it out of her, where Odysseus' treasury's hidden, it won't work. I tried that." She laughed, shook her head, started for the door. "I'll be watching every move you make!" he shouted after her.

She turned with the open door in her hand and smiled. "Do that," she said quietly, and was gone, the door pulled mostly closed behind her. The smile widened as she gazed down the empty corridor. It was deathly silent back in the Trickster's party hall. Draco hadn't moved; she was sure of it. Just as sure he was staring after her, still. "Nice to know you've still got it—even when you don't want to use it," she murmured, and with a quick glance back down the corridor and at the door behind her, she set off quickly toward the queen's corner of the palace.

10

Twenty long strides down the main corridor brought Xena to another of the narrow servants' tunnels, this branching off at an angle that would take her out toward the front of the palace. She hesitated, listened for a moment, finally shrugged, and with another cautious, swift glance up and down the main hallway, slid into the tunnel and ran part of the way, then covered the rest in long sidesteps, her back to the unbroken wall, eyes moving from one end of the tunnel to the other, quickly searching the small openings dotting the hallway on the opposite side: storage, for the most part, she thought. Air slid past her, cool and salt-scented.

Most of the little chambers were empty and dark, and one appeared to be filled with racks of clay jars. Sound behind her; she leaped across the tunnel and melted into shadow. The little room reeked of lemon. *Lamp oil.*

A scraping sound back in the main corridor, followed by a muffled curse. "Stow it," someone muttered angrily. "He said keep an eye on her, make sure she went where she said. He said be quiet about it."

"So shaddup!" the other snarled. A moment later two men strode down the main hallway; one of them glanced briefly down the servants' tunnel but kept going. The other didn't even seem to notice it was there. Xena grinned, a flash of teeth that didn't reach her eyes, slipped out of the oil storage chamber, and kept going.

The tunnel ended a short distance on; to her right, a ramp descended and on her left a mere indentation in the tunnel wall. Most of the space was taken up by a low, rough bench piled high with empty baskets. Somewhere behind the stack, air moved; the topmost basket, a small, rope-handled, lidless affair, trembled and toppled to the floor. Where it had been—an opening in the outside wall.

She stood very still a moment, listening intently: no sound from below or behind her; the faint sound of men laughing came through the window. She shoved baskets toward the inner end of the bench, edged past them for a look. The window wasn't much more than an air vent, long and thin, deep-silled, just wide enough for her to lean both elbows on the rough surface and gaze into the night. Twenty or more fires dotted the hillside, farther away than she would have thought—effect of the rocky ledge behind them, likely. She leaned out as far as possible, slewed around to look up. A balcony just above her and one off to the side from that. And just above that, the flat roof. She considered this, smiled, shifted her weight, and climbed onto the sill. No outer ledge here, and nothing below her for ten paces; the ground sloped but there was a hedge of tall, slender trees not far out. She eyed the balcony once more, shrugged, and dropped to the ground. Once there she ran quickly along the inside of the hedge to the nearest low porch, pulled herself onto that, and leaped to the upper balcony. Moments later, she eased over the lip of the roof.

No one up here, either. Draco'd said he was keeping his

men out of the palace for the most part. Maybe he hadn't lied about *that*. She took a moment to orient herself, glanced back at Draco's camp. Movement down by the water; Socran's ship lay higher aground now, and nearer, several men were helping two others stagger up the sand. One of them dwarfed his companions. *Have a nice night, Metrikas,* she thought sardonically, and turned away.

The queen's apartments were still well lit; curtains were billowing onto all four balconies. For the moment, it was quiet down there. Another quick look around the roof—no one here but her. She swung over the edge, dropped quietly, stood very still long enough to make certain the main room held no surprises. Gabrielle was curled up, asleep in a pile of cushions, a silvery-blue robe draped over her. Very faintly, women's voices came from the next room—a dressing or bathing chamber, perhaps.

She took one step forward, hesitated; someone was standing just out of sight on the other side of the wall; she could hear breathing. *Probably that boy.* She shook her head faintly, backed up to the railing, and dove through the curtains in a tight tuck, rolled, and came up and around, hands out, ready to attack. Telemachus hadn't moved; he was staring at her, eyes very wide and his jaw hanging. A painted jar dangled from his fingers. She grinned mirthlessly. "Nice idea," she said. "Been there long?"

He flushed and bit his lip. "Just—since I heard a sound, something out there. I thought, maybe it was one of *his* men, and maybe if I could get behind him when he came in . . ."

The swift slap of small sandals interrupted him. "Oh, son!" Penelope's reproachful voice. The warrior glanced at her, turned back to the prince.

His face was an even deeper red, if that were possible. "Mother, I thought one of those men—" Xena kept her eyes on him, and when he glanced at her, she held a finger to her lips, sent her eyes sideways to indicate the queen behind her. His eyes shifted, fixed on the floor before his sandals.

"Telemachus, you are not to even speak to any of those men, I told you that! Let alone to offer them violence! For you to even think of going against a—a butcher! And—and with a pot in your hand?" Xena held up a hand and she subsided.

"It's all right, nobody got hurt. I'll talk to him."

"I—please do, warrior. He might listen if *you* tell him!" Telemachus stirred; Xena shook her head minutely and touched her lips again. The queen's steps receded, were gone; they could hear her unhappy voice, the servant's low replies.

"*You* can't tell me just to—to—"

"To hide behind your mother's robes? What makes you think I'd tell you that?" Silence. "I didn't make any specific promises to your mother." She glanced at Gabrielle, who was fighting her way upright, blinking sleepily. "It's all right, Gabrielle; go back to sleep."

"Mmmm. Thanks." She settled back into the cushions; Telemachus moved light-footed across the chamber and pulled the robe over her shoulders again, then moved quietly back to the warrior's side.

"She's a very nice person. Mother liked her tales; I haven't seen her laugh like that in a long time. And Gabrielle knows so many of Father's adventures." Xena beckoned and led him to the opposite side of the vast chamber. She fished the cushions from a chair and threw them against the wall, then dropped onto them, indicating the floor next to her. Telemachus snared the pillow from his mother's weaving chair and sat. "I mean, did you know he'd wrestled a half-immortal lion in Nemea? Or that he went into the underworld and stole three-headed Cerberus right away from the banks of the Styx? Or that he—''

''I've heard most of it,'' Xena replied. She had; of course, those particular victories had all belonged to Hercules. *I hope the boy doesn't ever hear differently—not while he's young enough for it to matter. But it's nice to know Gabrielle and Iolaus spent some of their time alone talking while Hercules and I were rescuing Prometheus.* Gabrielle'd done the right thing, though, with her stories. As always; the boy's eyes were absolutely shining. Maybe if Odysseus ever got home, the boy would hear new and better stories from his father, and forget these. *If the boy lives through this.* ''You had the right idea over there— partly. The way you did it would have gotten you killed, if it had been anyone but me coming off that balcony. You're no use to your mother dead.'' The light went out of his face.

''I'm sorry.''

''No, don't be. You weren't killed. And I told you, you had the right idea. You and I will work on it; I'll show you how to jump someone so you don't get a knife in the ribs. I'll teach you as much as I can.'' She held up a hand as he strove to speak. ''It may not be much, there's a lot going on and I have a lot to do here. Still, you're young, you think on your feet, and you can move well. That's a start.''

''I—my mother won't be pleased.''

''I talked to her earlier. I thought I got through; I understand why she's still worried, though, because you're all she's got until your father comes home. If he never came home, you're all she has to remember him by. But knowing that doesn't make things any easier for you to bear, does it?'' He considered this gravely, finally shook his head. ''I'll talk to her again, tomorrow. Meantime, I want to warn you; you're going to see me out there tomorrow, the day

163

after—every day until this is settled and Draco's gone, however long it takes. It might look to you as if I'm on their side. I'm not. I know a lot of them and I'll be doing what I have to, to convince them to trust me. You may not like the way it appears.''

''I—all right.''

''If we cross paths out there and you feel like showing you don't like it, feel free. It won't convince Draco of anything, but he's smart. Most of his men aren't that clever.''

''There's a lot of them, maybe two hundred,'' he said finally.

''I know that.''

''If you get killed, that won't help my mother at all!''

''I won't. I don't intend to start a war here. Not a straightforward one, anyway. I don't intend to lose, either.''

''Well—but, what are you going to do?''

She shrugged. ''Don't know yet. Maybe I'll figure it out, if I sit here and think about it. Go get some sleep.''

For a moment she thought he was going to argue some more; he finally nodded, got to his feet, the pillow trailing from his fingers. He dumped it on Penelope's chair, glanced unhappily toward the little room where his mother's still-displeased voice could still be heard, then walked out onto the balcony. Xena heard the dull thunk a moment later as his sandals hit the next balcony—and then another. Nothing after that.

The queen's servant came into the room, a length of bright yellow silk trailing across her arms; she settled this over the bed, then retraced her steps. Moments later the queen came out, robed for bed in the same yellow. Xena came to her feet. ''Warrior,'' Penelope said softly. A glance in Gabrielle's direction assured her that the girl was asleep.

She crossed the room and settled on her weaving chair. "Where's—my son?"

"He's gone—into the room two balconies down."

She sighed faintly, closed her eyes, and shook her head. "That's all right, then, it's his room. I wish he wouldn't go that way, but he first learned that trick when he was eight, and I've never been able to keep him from doing it." She looked at her motionless, quiet companion. "You don't have to say it; I know what you must think of me. I told myself tonight I wouldn't treat him like a baby, that I'd let you do what you could to instruct him, if that was what you really wanted. Gabrielle—she's told me a lot about you."

"I'm not surprised," Xena murmured.

The queen smiled briefly. "She was very kind; I haven't had such a pleasant visitor in some time. Hardly anyone's come to Ithaca since my husband went to war—until that—" She seemed to be searching for a word, finally dismissed the effort with a turn of her hand. "I wasn't going to chide poor Telemachus anymore. But just now, when I saw him, the look on his face, that jug in his hand—the words just came out."

"The thought's a place to start; I don't expect you to change that quickly. And he knows why you want to protect him."

"Oh." Penelope considered this, then stifled a yawn neatly with the back of her hand. "You wouldn't think a woman could grow tired, barred inside this chamber all day. I'm used to walking for hours, all over the island, and hardly noticing. But the past days, since *they* came, I'm exhausted by this hour."

"Fear's tiring," Xena said. "And you probably haven't slept well for worry. Go, sleep. I'll know if anyone's around."

"Thank you," Penelope replied simply. She crossed the room with a young stride, settled under the thin cloth, and closed her eyes. Xena went back to her place against the wall, rubbed her shoulders across the slightly sandy-feeling surface, and gazed up at the dark-beamed ceiling. "So," she murmured. "What next?"

She sat and thought for a long time; Gabrielle tossed and turned and occasionally moaned in her sleep. Xena got to her feet, crossed over to the cushions where the girl lay. The warrior's presence seemed to comfort her. The queen hadn't moved much; possibly she hadn't slept, either. Xena passed her, stepped onto one of the northern balconies, and stood in shadow, listening. She could still hear the camp, but the noise was muted. Half of them passed out, probably. *I wonder who's out there.* She'd find out, come morning.

Movement in the blackness surrounding the tree hedge: a man carrying a short spear came into the open, gazed all around, out toward the camp, up at the balconies, then along the roofline. Apparently satisfied, he turned and stalked back into shadow, finally vanishing around the corner of the palace. A single lamp burned in the chamber two balconies down, but she couldn't hear anything. Nothing on the roof. She finally went back in, shoved pillows with her foot until they made a stack in one corner near the door. She checked the bar, then eased down, settled her shoulders, crossed her legs at the ankle, her arms across her chest, and closed her eyes.

Early sun touched the pale curtains and a light, warm sea breeze ruffled them. Xena stood on the balcony, her head tipped back to catch the first rays, and stretched mightily. Behind her, she could hear the queen's woman bustling around, talking to the old man who'd poured Draco's wine the night before and who had just brought Penelope's breakfast.

She herself had already eaten. A tap on the door in the gray hour before sunrise had brought her alert and on her feet. When she'd listened cautiously, then eased the door open, it had proven to be Lemnos, in his hands a small tray bearing one of his round fruit loaves, still warm from the baking, a large flagon that was a little wine and mostly water, and a bowl of pale purple grapes. He'd waved aside thanks as she took the tray. "I don't think anybody but me likes Rammis. This is part of my thanks to you—I'll keep him out of your sight." He was gone before she could say anything.

Surprising. She'd eyed the loaf dubiously for a moment, but no longer than that. Lemnos was an artist; he'd no more poison that loaf than—well, he wouldn't. "And you have to eat something on this island, sometime." She'd inhaled bread fragrance deeply, settled back down cross-legged on the cushions where she'd slept, and tore into it.

Gabrielle came out to stand beside her, one hand shielding her eyes against the dawning, level sun. "Hope you slept as well as I did."

"I did all right."

"I don't know what a queen can afford to stuff in a pillow that the rest of us can't, but it's great; it was like sleeping on clouds." Gabrielle leaned on her arms and gazed across the grounds. "So—I missed you last night, guess I was already trading stories with Morpheus by the time you got back." Not quite a question in her voice; Xena smiled and ignored it. "Well! Anyway. We had a very nice time while you were gone."

"So I heard."

"Oh. Did—ah, did you come up with any—well, with a plan?"

"Not really." Xena yawned hugely. "I ate dinner with Draco."

"Oh?" Silence for a moment; Gabrielle glanced back into the queen's apartment, lowered her voice. "So what does he have in mind, here? She wanted to know—I had to really talk fast to kind of distract her, and I'm not sure it worked that well."

"Probably not. It's her island, after all. Her son. Her people. Draco's pretty happy here, seems he's decided living in a palace is the only way to do things."

"Mmmm. That's not good."

"Could be worse—could be he was letting his men live in here, too."

"Ah—I get your point. Good one, too." Gabrielle hesitated, glanced over her shoulder once more, then added, "Queen Penelope thinks he wants to marry her. Imagine!"

"Not hard to imagine, since that's exactly what he has in mind. Marry Penelope, keep Telemachus close to be sure she'll act like that's what she wants, too—King Draco of Ithaca."

Gabrielle wrinkled her nose fastidiously. "King Draco? Who's going to go along with that?"

"Who's going to care, once he's settled in?"

Gabrielle stirred indignantly and opened her mouth, but no sound came. After a moment her shoulders slumped. "I guess you're right. Nothing here but women, children, and peasants; who cares what they think? And—okay, so how do 'we' fix it?" The sarcasm was evident in her voice.

"Yes. We." Xena cast her a sidelong smile. "You and me. It's a job for both of us, Gabrielle. You have the hard part; you stay here and keep Penelope's spirits up, keep her mind off Draco and all those tents out there. Give me a

168

chance to get out there, among Draco's men, see who I know, how well and why; look things over, come up with a plan."

"Sure. Simple stuff. I always get the hard part," Gabrielle grumbled good-naturedly.

Xena laid a hand on her shoulder and waited until the girl smiled up at her. "I know it's hard, sitting and waiting. But what you're doing is important, and it's something I couldn't possible do. Last night, you took her mind off her problems and you made her very happy, telling her all those tales about her husband."

"I did?"

"Made her believe that Odysseus might actually be on his way home. Made Telemachus proud of his father. You heard him yesterday; what you did with words to change that boy's mind wasn't much short of magic. Keep talking, and enjoy living in the queen's apartments in a very nice palace while you can. You won't get a chance like this very often."

"It's a point," Gabrielle conceded promptly. "Did I mention the pillows smell like violets and roses?"

"Sounds great. Tonight maybe I'll sleep lying down instead of propped against the wall." She turned to go, thought of something, and turned back. "Any of the servants come in here—get them aside, out of the queen's hearing if possible, and try to find out anything they might know."

"They may not want to confide in me."

"That's your job: convincing them you need to hear things the queen doesn't—so you can pass them on to me. Anything at all; I don't know what's going to shift things our way at this point."

"Servants," Gabrielle echoed, then nodded energetically. "Got it. Where you going to be?"

"Finding out what Draco's men know, of course."

A short while later she stepped out onto the south-facing portico and stretched hugely. Sun; wonderful at this hour. In another, without a fresh ocean breeze, it would probably be unbearably hot. She let her head fall back, let the sun turn her closed eyelids red, felt the heat against her armor, her hair.

A faint jingle of harness coming down the broad, shallow steps of the portico. She blinked, stretched again, and said, "Hello, Draco. Sleep well?"

He hesitated briefly, then came down the last steps to join her. "How do you *do* that?"

"How I knew it was you? Easy. The way your sword clinks against the metal rings you had fixed to your britches. No one else sounds like that when he walks."

He cast her a startled glance, then smiled. "So—you must have slept well, to be out here so early."

"Maybe." She eyed him from under dark lashes. "Maybe I just want to get out here and see what you've got for an army while it's still sleeping off last night's wine."

He laughed sourly, gestured toward the motley camp of tents. "I haven't cut it down to something reasonable for here, such a small island—I will, soon. For an invasion force, they don't have to all be pretty or top class, just numerous. Cow the invadee, and you've won already."

"Skip the lecture," she replied, her voice edged with amusement. "I know how it's done, remember?"

"You used to. I'm not so sure you do, anymore."

She sighed. "Draco, I don't care about your doubts, and I'm not gonna let you push me."

"Who says I was trying to push? Maybe you're interested in helping me winnow out the chaff?" He gestured toward the tents.

She considered this, let her eyes move slowly across the sprawl of army. "Maybe. Let's see what you've got."

The camp already smelled bad—she'd forgotten how little time it took for a place like this to develop a powerful and unpleasant aroma. Draco stepped around a pair of leather-clad men sprawled next to the fire pit that served four surrounding tents; one still clutched his wineskin and both reeked of sweat, wine—and things she'd rather not think about. "Any of these guys ever bathe?" she demanded as they moved on.

"Why should they? No one's paying 'em extra for that."

"Point," she conceded. She moved on to the next clutch of tents, hands relaxed but ready, eyes moving constantly—for any sign of problem, anyone here who might bear her a grudge. Draco stayed just behind her and to her right—where she could easily take him, if that was what she wanted. *Subtle,* she thought dryly. *You were always good at the subtle things, Draco, but you're getting better with age.*

He was upwind of her; he smelled very faintly of lemon and warm skin.

They moved through the camp. Too early for most of them, she decided finally. Near the southwestern edge of the camp—a boundary delineated by piles of stone, set at exact intervals—she slowed as angry voices rent the early-morning quiet.

This particular tent was larger than the rest, marked with a caduceus: twin snakes twined about a spear. Hospital tent. Several voices spoke at once; a thunderous roar topped them all.

"By Zeus himself, if my brother thinks you can keep me in here—!"

Draco eased around her, shoved the flap aside, and went

171

in. Xena glanced back toward the palace—there was no sign of life anywhere along the sprawling whitewashed edifice—then shrugged and followed. Draco was arguing with a man who seemed at first glance even more massive than he. Partly the beard, the cut of his armor, and that overwhelming voice, she decided. Draco's sword was out and up; physicians and boys scattered. She caught hold of the commander's arm, smiled up at his furious adversary. "Hello, Metrikas. How's your head this morning?"

His eyes bulged. "You!" he breathed finally. "I will—"

"You will be silent," Draco topped him harshly. "Or you and your brother both will find yourselves swimming back to the mainland."

"My—" Metrikas snapped his fingers. "*That*—for my brother."

Draco smiled at him, bared teeth beneath chill eyes. "And for me?" he added softly. Metrikas was suddenly quiet. He swallowed. Draco watched him for a very long moment; the big man's eyes flickered away from him, found another resting place.

"This—this female!" he snarled.

Xena folded her arms and smiled lazily. A wildly furious, oversized brute wasn't that much problem; anything that big could be overbalanced, one way or another. *So get him off balance again,* she thought dryly, and let the smile broaden. "Next time, stick with fighting sailors, you'll do better."

Almost enough—not quite. Metrikas was teetering on the balls of his feet, but with a sidelong, furious glance at Draco, he subsided. Narrowed eyes nearly vanished beneath brushy eyebrows. "Names, woman," he hissed. "I want names. Who were those filthy sailors and how did they come up with a plan to trap *me*?"

"Because *I* told them what to say, of course," she replied flatly. He continued to stare at her for a very long moment, finally backed up a pace, then a second, and with a mumbled curse and a wave of his hand, stalked off, shouldering his way out of the tent. The two physicians—small, elderly Egyptians by the look of them—exchanged resigned looks and retired to the bench at the rear of the tent, where a boy barely old enough to grow a sparse beard lay moaning. Xena glanced at the boy, turned, and left. She could hear Draco behind her, talking to the physicians.

"I'll deal with Meronias; he should know you can't control his brother." A moment later he was with her again.

"That was amusing," she said. "What next?"

He shrugged, spread his arms to include the entire camp. "Your decision—I'm following, remember?" She cast him a sidelong, sardonic glance, turned her face toward the palace, and began working slowly up the low hill. "In a way," he said after a while, "I'm glad for that little exchange of pleasantries. Next time the ship goes out, I'll send an escort with it."

"I'm surprised you didn't think of that before this," she replied dryly.

"I would have—I was letting Meronias handle the details; he must have passed that one on to Metrikas. Metrikas," he mused quietly, "is about to make himself a liability."

"About to?" She laughed shortly, edged between two tents and onto the open hill above the camp. "You're getting soft, Draco."

"I find Meronias useful; he's too fond of Metrikas. And he knows I know that. It keeps him—in line."

"Subtle stuff," she scoffed. "What happened to the old Draco?" She turned to face him; the breeze ruffled his hair.

He smiled, but his eyes were calculating. "He's still there, don't doubt it. It's—it's a different thing, conquering

173

everything in sight and killing everyone, from what I'm doing now. I want a base army I know, down to the least mess boy; I need captains I can depend on, and if the trust isn't straight, man to man, then the trust I put in Meronias is almost as good." He shrugged. "Eventually, I'll replace him—when I find someone better. Someone I don't have to bind the way I bind Meronias."

"Is that an invitation?" she demanded.

"It could be." Silence. He turned away from her, strode across grass and flowers to stare toward the western shore of the mainland. "You don't want to be Queen of Ithaca, admit it."

"Why not? There's no reason *I* have to sit in pretty apartments and weave all day, is there? Why not queen and commander both?"

He sighed heavily. "Reverse the position. You'd never give me that much power."

"No—probably not." She smiled. "Think about it anyway. Maybe it answers a lot of your problems."

He laughed; there wasn't much amusement in the sound. "Maybe it creates more problems than it solves." He met her eyes levelly; his were opaque, his face expressionless. For a moment she thought he might say something else, but he turned abruptly and strode back down the hill.

11

ena stood motionless, watching until he was out of sight,
ack among the tents of his army, then turned slowly, to
rient herself and to check the terrain for Draco's guards
nd for places she herself might use as watchposts. The
ope where she presently stood continued in a gradual,
rassy way for some distance, then reared up abruptly in a
umble of massive, raw stone; the peak was a low one, but
as the highest spot on the island and well above the sea.
ot much short of the rocky point, near the eastern edge
f the slope, stood a grove of several ancient, spreading
aks; well down from that, perhaps a hundred long strides
om her present position, two more vast oaks and a number
f saplings grew near a drop-off that formed a narrow, steep
avine ending near a rocky shoreline facing west. She could
e a single hut down there; a few pigs grazed around it.
othing besides pigs moving, except the surf, which slid
zily across the pebbly shore.

To the other side, across the water, a dark line that was
ost likely the mainland; on this side of the island the slope
as more gradual and much longer. Men—Draco's

men—grouped around a pair of open fishing boats; the ship she and Gabrielle had ridden the day before was being nosed onto the beach next to the smaller of the open boats. Two sailors on the deck and one of Draco's men—she couldn't make out any more from this distance.

Behind her, the camp was fairly quiet.

She moved quietly and swiftly, gained the nearest grove, stood very still in the deep shade, listening. No one here. She leaped up and caught hold of a branch running parallel to the ground, swung onto it, climbed high enough on the main trunk to make out the palace and the camp when the leaves moved in the light morning breeze, then settled her back against a join between a good-sized branch and the trunk.

From this vantage, she could also just make out the village where the palace servants lived—a collection of ten or so huts across a low, grassy ridge from the tents. They appeared well constructed to withstand the winters, sheltered from the western and northern winds. Low fences of sticks and brush separated the track leading to the fishing boats from houses and from the garden plots set high on the south-facing slope; beyond the gardens, another thickly entangled fence contained two pigs. No movement down there; not surprising, she thought, no doubt anyone who wasn't on duty with that ship, or at the palace, was hiding behind a barred door. She rubbed an itchy shoulder against rough bark, found a more comfortable position, then let her eyes move back over the ridge to scan Draco's camp again.

The sun had nearly reached its zenith before there was much sign of life in the camp: four men staggering down to the shore to fall into the waves; another two carrying buckets and crossing the ridge behind the hospital tent. They slipped into shadow, down the steep-sided ravine, but appeared a moment later, working their way down. A well there, she decided. It must be hidden in one of the tight turns the cut took, around slabbed stone; they were out of sight down there for some time, but finally came back up, buckets sloshing.

All very quiet; almost peaceful. Moments later someone bellowed out a curse, and a boy came running out of one of the tents, arms flailing, and went flat in the dust. Someone laughed, someone else shouted him down. The boy picked himself up, eyed the tent briefly, then hurried downhill. She studied the camp, waited a few moments; the boy didn't show anywhere else.

Time to look over the rest of the island, she decided, but before she could ease down from her perch, more movement just past the hospital tent. Metrikas stalked up the hill. A slightly smaller man in well-constructed armor, his hair the same flame-red as the big man's, came after him, but he was a fair distance back and losing ground with every long stride the enormous Metrikas took. The second man waved his arms and shouted furiously; Metrikas ignored him, but once he reached the shade under the first oak, he slowed, then turned and leaned against the trunk, arms folded across his chest, legs crossed. The smaller man was almost running by now, and she could finally make out what he was saying as he skidded to a halt and dropped cross-legged to the ground a distance from Metrikas. "—trying to get me *killed*! Draco doesn't need even me that much, brother!"

"Tell him to—"

"Tell him yourself, go on, get your throat cut," the seated man broke in. "He's angry, I tell you. I spent the past two years getting in good with Draco. I won't have you ruining things for me."

Metrikas uttered a bark of laughter. "Don't try to fool

177

me, Meronias. He needs you to keep that pack of rats down there in line.''

''He could do that himself, if he wanted to. In which case—'' Meronias drew a meaningful hand across his throat. Silence; the brothers looked at each other. Xena couldn't make out anything of Metrikas but the wild snarl of red hair and his bulky shoulders. Meronias' face was upturned, still red from exertion and anger and his eyes were black. Other than the red hair and the eyes, he didn't resemble his much larger brother at all; without the hair, he'd be just another unremarkable mercenary. ''Look, Metrikas,'' he said finally, in an abrupt change of mood. ''I don't ask much of you, do I? Keep your own following in line, don't bother the servants, help me keep those slobs down there inside the line of tents and away from the women when they're drunk, keep them clear of the herds at all times. You've set up a full-time watch on the fishing boats and I'm grateful for that. But going against Krinos' orders—''

''Maybe Krinos woulda needed a full day to get over a sore head,'' Metrikas growled. ''I don't.''

''Well, next time—if there *is* a next time—don't start tearing things up just as Draco comes around.'' The larger man snorted; Meronias sighed in exasperation. ''All right, I know! You *told* me, you didn't know he was there.''

''And that woman. She's the one who—''

''I know who Xena is, and I know she pounded you flat and tied you up in the stinking hold. The way you've yelled it around the camp, everyone knows it.''

Metrikas swore furiously. ''*She* knows who was on that boat—''

''Be your age, brother, of course she does. She'd tell you as soon as Draco would, you're wasting time and energy being angry with *her*.''

"Krinos should've gone down to that village, found the—"

Meronias jumped to his feet and closed the distance between them. Metrikas loomed over him; Meronias appeared not to notice. "Look, it's done, over with. Krinos should have taken the names of every mother's son aboard before that ship ever left for the mainland. He knows that now because I chewed on him real good this morning. What happened yesterday and last night is past fixing, and if Draco's unhappy about Xena coming in with the wine, he hasn't said so, has he?" Silence. "Well, he hasn't. He hasn't busted any heads over it, he hasn't run anyone through. So maybe he never planned on this Xena showing up, but it *doesn't* matter. Not to me—and not to you." Another silence. This one stretched. "I want you to swear to me you'll drop it, brother."

"Like Hades, I'll—"

"No!" Meronias overrode him angrily; somewhat to Xena's surprise, the larger man fell silent. "Swear it, or I swear I'll see you and your rough little band over on the mainland once more, stealing scrawny sheep to stay alive. You're good at keeping men under your control, Metrikas. Now try and do the same for yourself."

"I—" The big man slumped back against the tree. "That's not my fault; you know how many bands of men there are out there? Just like mine? Man's gotta figure out where to go that hasn't just been picked over, gotta keep his followers happy—"

"*You* don't have to do that anymore. I told you, long as I have a say, you stay with me, you eat good, you get a share of decent spoils, you remain captain of the men you brought with you. Only thing I ever asked, stay out of Draco's way, don't draw his eye." Another silence. The big man finally nodded once. "Swear, I said."

179

"All right," Metrikas mumbled. "I swear."

"Good. You won't be sorry."

"I already am." Metrikas sounded peeved. "You got any idea how bad my head hurts?"

Meronias clapped his arm. "You eat anything since last night?" Metrikas shook his head cautiously. "I've got bread and I think there's some fish broth left." He turned and started down the hill.

Metrikas let him get a distance away, then gazed out toward the eastern shore, where men were hauling the sturdy little ship higher onto shore. "Swear," he growled. "I swear she'll pay for last night. In blood." Meronias shouted out his name; he clutched his head and yelled back, "All right, I'm coming!"

Xena remained where she was for some time, considering what she'd just seen and heard; a faint smile tugged at her lips. "Dissension within the ranks—always useful." How to best use it, though. If at all. She finally shrugged, took one last good look around from her perch, then dropped rapidly from branch to branch, back to the ground. She hesitated momentarily. Up the mountain, or back down? It didn't really seem to matter; the day was clear and bright enough, cover sparse, anyone could see her. *Let them; get them used to the sight, most of them will take my presence for granted by midafternoon.*

There wasn't much new to see from the peak—not much new and useful, anyway. The north face of the mountain dropped nearly straight to the sea far below; the western slope was a dangerous scree of loose stone barely held in check by a few windblown pines and sparse bushes. East: a clearer view of the distant mainland, a narrow beach well below her feet that was rapidly vanishing under the incoming tide; possibly a narrow path leading up from wet sand, along a low, grass-tufted ledge, but her angle was bad, and if it was a path, it vanished almost at once behind rock and under low trees, bearing south.

"Ideas," she grumbled. So far, she didn't have one. Nearly two hundred men down in that camp to her one.

The camp wasn't visible from the high rocks, except for the very tops of two tall tents and a single wisp of smoke. The palace seemed deserted from here, and she couldn't see either the village or the boats from this vantage point. She sighed, started back down the hill with a ground-eating stride; a slight detour took her through the higher grove. There was sign someone had recently grazed pigs or goats here, nothing else. "You didn't expect to find help out here, though. Go back to the palace, think," she ordered herself. But as she emerged from the trees, she could see Draco coming toward her; she leaned back against the nearest tree and waited for him.

He was smiling broadly as he stepped into shade. "Checking things out, are you?"

She shrugged. "I always do. Looking for me, or just looking?"

"One of the boys down by the boats saw you up top. I thought you might like bread and wine with me and my captains." She considered this, shrugged again, then gestured for him to precede her. He moved ahead, but couldn't seem to keep his eyes on the trail, and after a few paces, to her amusement, he dropped back to keep step with her. They were most of the way back down the slope when he spoke again. "Find out anything interesting this morning?"

"You've got a lot of men down there. It's a long way back to the mainland."

He laughed shortly. "Don't try to convince me that's got you scared."

"I wasn't. I was stating facts."

"Stating the obvious." He stopped short and turned to

181

look her squarely in the eye. "You know, I've been talking to my men this morning. You caught me by surprise, back in that village a while ago. Last time we met."

"Oh?"

"I could see you maybe thinking you'd done enough killing for a while. Some people do, but it doesn't last. Or wanting to go home to mother. But all the stories out there, this hero business."

"I hear strange tales about you, too, Draco."

"Sure. But not as strange as some of the ones about Xena. I never believed you'd stick with the hero act for long. You tell me you haven't, but it's hard to figure from the stories circulating out there whether you're for real or not."

"You know how stories are," she said, and waved a dismissive hand. "You don't always get credit for what you did, and sometimes your name gets attached to something you didn't. What you did gets blown out of proportion."

"Sure. Like I said. But I've got men in that camp who've seen you out there recently, or fought you; I've spent the morning talking to them. And now, after everything I've heard today, I'm seriously wondering why *you* say you've turned back."

She sighed heavily. "You get what you deserve, listening to rumors. You've got men out there like anywhere else, they lie just because they know how, and because maybe it starts trouble. I told you last night what I want."

"Oh, sure. I can see you as Queen of Ithaca—just not as *my* queen. Not as anybody else's either. You yourself running the island—sure, that fits."

She held up a hand, silencing him; her eyes were black, her whole face sullen as she turned away to study the palace, its entire western face now brilliantly sunlit. "I don't care what you believe, Draco. I'm not playing games with you, though. You start pitting what I say against what one of your grubby little men says, forget the whole thing. The same boat that brought me over can take me back to the mainland.''

''Maybe—maybe not. It's my boat, remember? And it's a long swim.''

''Is that a threat?''

''Me—threaten you? Why?''

''Because it's what you do best, maybe.''

''I'm still thinking about it,'' he replied genially, and started down the hill again. She eyed his back narrowly, then shrugged and followed.

Draco's tent had been placed on the easternmost edge of the camp, where it would get afternoon shade; the sides had been raised to allow what breeze there was to cool the interior. His bedding was rolled into a corner; a long bench filled most of the open space. Two plain pottery jugs and a large basket of cups took up one corner, another basket piled with rounds of baked flat bread next to them. Draco snared two cups, poured wine, extended his hand. ''Your choice,'' he said dryly.

She smiled faintly, took one, waited until he'd drunk before tasting her own. He eyed the basket of bread, shrugged; waiting to see if she'd wait for him or not, she thought. *Everything's a game, with him. Everything like that platter of nasty little strips of oily meat: patterns within patterns over patterns. You think you have him figured, he's already heading back the other way.* It made for a warlord who won his battles—but at the moment it was damned tiring.

Maybe it was still a love-hate thing for him, the way it had been last time they met. *I'd just like to get this done with, and be done with him. For good.*

His eyes had narrowed as they shifted to a point behind

her and to one side; she turned as Meronias stalked into the tent and inclined his head slightly. Draco gestured toward the baskets and jugs. Meronias poured a swallow of wine, tossed it off, and set the cup aside. He cast Xena a smoldering glance, then ignored her. *Fine by me,* she decided. He wasn't the type to force a confrontation; she didn't have time or inclination to take on the whole camp a man and a grudge at a time.

Draco refilled his own cup, drew a leather stool over, and dropped onto it. "You got my message earlier?"

"I got it, sir," Meronias replied stiffly. "I talked to him."

"It's his only chance," Draco said; his voice was very soft, all the more deadly for it. "Anyone else, he'd be a league that way and all the way down." He gestured toward open water.

"He knows that, sir."

Xena laughed sourly. "You fighting my battles for me now, Draco?" Meronias' shoulders went stiff and still momentarily; he poured more wine, crossed the tent, and settled on the edge of the bench, opposite the warlord.

"I'm keeping order in my own camp," Draco replied shortly. He glanced across the bench. "Remind your brother he's still alive to hold that grudge. A lot of men aren't."

"He knows that. Sir."

"Good." Draco snared the basket of bread, tore the top loaf in half, and took part to dip in his cup. He glanced up as two more men came in.

Xena studied them in turn. One she knew by sight; he'd been in Draco's camp outside her mother's village and he'd been in the hall when the two had fought. The other—Polyces hadn't changed much since she'd seen him last. Maybe a strand or two of silver in his dark hair, more lines in the sun-darkened skin around very brown eyes. His armor, which was made up of bits of leather, brass plates—anything a man could scavenge up and cobble together to protect himself. Right on his heels came Lemnos, carrying a pottery bowl of grapes. He set the bowl in front of Draco, then turned to face Xena. His face was set, his eyes all pupil.

"I was talking to a couple of the men this morning," the little cook said abruptly. "They—told me about Marcus."

"Oh?" Silence. "I didn't realize you knew him, Lemnos."

"I might've known you'd be that—that casual about it, Xena," Lemnos replied bitterly. He set the grapes down with a clatter, shoved fists against his waist. "Marcus taught me how to fight, years ago, when I first left Thebes. He—was a good friend." His eyes narrowed and there was suddenly a long-bladed knife in his hand. "And you murdered him!"

Polyces jumped up and backed warily away. Draco started, one hand reaching for his sword. Xena flicked him a hard-eyed look that said, Back off, then closed the distance between herself and Lemnos, one hand twisting his knife hand down and away, then up behind his back, the other snatching a fistful of shirt as she hauled him onto his toes. Polyces started to say something and she snarled, "Back out of this! It's my business, not yours!" Her eyes met Lemnos' squarely then. "You heard all that, did you?" she spat. "Who told you?"

He was sweating freely but fury still held his voice steady. "Metrikas; he knew I was a friend of Marcus'. But he only just got that from—you're choking me!"

"You're that far from dead. Just got it from who?"

"From—from a guy named Kalamos, he—just landed, buncha men with him, said—he'd been there when—"

"Marcus was *my* friend," she whispered, so softly no one else could possibly have made out the words. "I killed the arms merchant who murdered him." Silence. "Ask yourself, Lemnos—Metrikas doesn't owe me anything good, neither does Kalamos. Why bother to tell you this?"

"What—what really—"

"Later," she said in a low, sharp voice. "I don't owe Draco that part of my life." She let him go with a shove that sent him staggering back into the bench, then turned away from him. "Draco, Lemnos tells me Kalamos just got here. I didn't know you were recruiting that class of scum."

His eyes narrowed; he rose, dropped the half-eaten bread, and adjusted his sword belt. "I'm not. Lemnos, where'd you leave him?" The little man gestured, his fingers trembling. Draco smiled faintly. "You want any part of this, Xena?"

She smiled back, though her eyes were still furious. Kalamos was a problem she didn't need just now. "I just honed my sword; I'm not wasting all that work on Kalamos."

Draco gestured sharply and left the tent. Meronias, his own face grim and pale, went with him. Xena let her eyes rest briefly on Polyces, who was trying to look as though nothing odd had just occurred; he was pouring himself wine, concentrating on the liquid.

"Polyces, my good old friend," Xena said. He glanced up at her, forced a tentative smile before turning his attention to the wine again. "Tell Draco I've had enough cute little games for one day. I'll find him later—maybe."

Her eyes slid over Lemnos, who looked briefly as though he might say something; he let his eyes slide toward Polyces, then began backing warily away. Once he was past the canvas roof, he turned and fled. Xena strode rapidly in the opposite direction, through the maze of tents; but once she reached the road, she headed for the palace.

Behind her, on the shore, she could hear Kalamos' high, cutting voice, then Draco's bellow. Metal clashing against metal, but the sounds of battle faded very quickly. She smiled grimly; she hadn't suspected even Kalamos of such stupidity as to come here. *Enjoy your trip to Hades, Kalamos.*

The afternoon had turned unpleasantly warm and windless, the sky an unusually deep blue. Xena blotted her forehead with the back of one hand, gained access to the queen's apartments via the roof and the eastern balconies once again.

No Telemachus; not behind the curtain, inside the main chamber—nowhere in sight. She sighed quietly, cast her eyes toward the ceiling. *Now, where is he?* No answer at the moment. Queen Penelope's fingers moved rapidly, shifting shuttles from one hand to the other, moving them across a complex fabric as Gabrielle spread her hands and spoke as quickly as the other's hands moved.

"... and so, the princess told her father, 'I had a vision last night, from the goddess Athena, and Athena told me, "If you want this marriage to last, and the union of your kingdoms to hold, then you must do me a special honor. Weave your own wedding veil." ' "

Penelope laughed cheerfully and clapped her hands together; she had to move quickly to retrieve the shuttles about to slide from the frame and from her lap. "And then?"

"Just what you'd expect," Gabrielle replied, no less cheerfully. "She worked on the veil every day—everyone said how diligent she was at it, too, how complex the pattern, how pleased Athena must be. . . . But every night, she unpicked most of the rows, and no one was ever aware of

187

what she'd done. Eventually, her true lover came to rescue her, the false prince went away in shame, and—'' She shrugged and laughed. ''And of course, she completed the veil in record time, so she could marry Prince Thereus.''

''Oh. Oh!'' Penelope laughed once again, and her bell-like giggle lightened and cooled the atmosphere in the apartments. ''Such fun! But that wouldn't *ever* work in the real world, would it?''

''What—weaving all day and unraveling at night?'' Gabrielle considered this. ''You'd have to be careful not to unravel too much, so no one would suspect what you were doing—but I'd wager *you* could do it, if you had to.'' She turned to Xena and smiled. ''I was hoping you would come back and talk to us. It's so *quiet* in here!''

''Better than an adventure at the moment, isn't it?''

Gabrielle nodded. ''Ah—you have a point. Thanks. All the same—it's hot, there's no wind, there's not much to do—''

''She's been telling me stories,'' Penelope put in; she shifted one shuttle into her free hand, dropped the other onto her weaving, and clasped the girl's hand. ''I can't tell you how exciting her stories are—I don't recall a morning and part of an afternoon that have gone so quickly, not since my Odysseus went to Troy.''

Xena raised an eyebrow; Gabrielle gave her an abashed grin and shrugged slightly.

Faint noise behind them; the two women started and Xena whirled around, hands flexed, but it was only Telemachus, who'd obviously just swung down from the roof. He pushed aside pink curtains and entered the chamber. ''I saw you do that,'' he said mildly; his color was high. ''It seemed—a sensible alternative to jumping from ledge to ledge. Sometimes, at least.''

In spite of herself, Xena smiled. ''You're a quick study,''

188

she said. His smile faded and his cheekbones were suddenly a more pronounced red. *He thinks I'm making fun of him,* she realized, and stifled a sigh. Boys could be touchy and exasperating creatures.

"Only because I have to be—"

He would have gone on, but Xena held up a finger and he fell silent. She cast a meaningful glance at Gabrielle, who turned her eyes to her fingers and flexed them in an experimental fashion. "I think you were going to show me how you manage that pattern with one color on top and the other beneath?" she said.

Penelope blinked, then managed a smile for Telemachus as she picked up both shuttles again. "Hello, son," she said, then turned her whole attention to the loom and the young woman at her elbow. "Well, Gabrielle, it's really simple when you understand how these things work."

"I wish I did. I've tried to weave complex things before," Gabrielle murmured apologetically as the older woman paused, "but anything past your basic basket-weave—I just can't *see* it, if you know what I mean."

Xena smiled, cast her companion a wink once she was certain Penelope was too involved in the pattern on her loom to notice, then beckoned and walked back to the door. Telemachus, his color still high, went with her. Xena leaned against the bar, arms crossed over her chest. "I'm sorry," he mumbled. "I wasn't trying to—"

"I meant just what I said," Xena replied. "Don't bother sorting my words for extra meanings, I don't do that. Quick study, I said—it's a gift, the ability to see something once and act on what you've seen. You'll be good with weapons, probably good at unarmed fighting. I said I'd teach you what I can. I will. At the moment I don't know when that will be, because I don't know yet how I'm going to deal with Draco."

"How *we*—" Telemachus began sharply, but she gestured for silence once more, shook her head.

"You're intelligent, I won't insult that intelligence. You'll be able to help me, but not by fighting. You can't learn weapons overnight, or use novice training to kill trained men like Draco's. People who try that wind up dead." Silence. She watched him; his eyes slid from hers almost at once, fixed on his hands. Finally, he sighed.

"All right. I can see that."

"There are other things you can do; skills you already have. You know this island, the palace. You know the people who live here. One thing I will want you to do as soon as it's dark is go find Socran and the other three sailors who came back with the ship, and their families. They've been hiding—a cave that can't be reached except at low tide?"

"I know it," he said as she paused.

"Good. Draco doesn't know who was on the ship; his men don't. With one exception, they don't care."

"Exception—the big man?"

"Metrikas. Don't worry about him."

"Ah—no." Telemachus didn't look very convinced.

She smiled. "He won't see you or be able to follow you out there—he's big and awkward, you'd hear him. And you can outrun him."

"Oh. Good."

"Find Socran and bring him. Where's a good place for us to talk?"

"My rooms, the roof . . ."

"Find a place you can trust, then come for me." She was taking something of a chance, giving the boy that much free rein. "Remember your mother, and don't get cocky, or careless," she added. He grinned.

"I'll remember. After dark." He blotted his forehead and
is neck. "It's fog-making weather."

She was about to leave; his words brought her back
round. "What's that?"

He waved a hand toward the windows and the still cur-
ains. "No wind and thick air. It always means fog. The
eally heavy kind, warm and wet and you can't see anything
n arm's length away once it's dark outside; you couldn't
ell Gabrielle from mother's tiring woman." She eyed him
houghtfully. "Last time we had a fog maker like this, it
tayed thick for two days. But it doesn't go until the winds
ome back."

Fog. She smiled. "You've given me an idea, Telema-
hus. I'm going to go do some thinking. Meet me back
ere after sundown, before you go out."

He nodded gravely. Gabrielle and the Queen glanced up
s Xena slid the bar from the door, but were deep in weav-
ng and patterns again before she entered the hall.

12

By the time the sun was low in the sky, the air had become noticeably sullen and thick; from a shaded corner of the roof, Xena could see mist beginning to form in one of the sheltered little bays. Even the sea looked sluggish; foam slid quietly over sand and stones, slipped back out soundlessly. Xena leaned back against a low parapet and gazed out toward the mainland.

"It's a little risky," she murmured. Not as risky as a direct confrontation, of course. And Draco wouldn't fall for the same trick as last time—one-on-one combat, winner take all. "I could make him fight—" Maybe. The odds weren't that bad; Draco had about two hundred men in his camp, but not all of them would be willing to jump her, and all two hundred couldn't jump her at once. This was still better. Less danger to the others involved.

Because this plan would call for some help: Socran and his fellow sailors; possibly Telemachus, if she could coach him to do exactly what she wanted, and get his solemn word he wouldn't deviate from that.

She narrowed her eyes, came partway to her feet. The

mainland had vanished; nothing of the horizon was visible save a pale gray. She smiled, eased back down, and thought some more.

The sun was a deep orange ball sliding into mist when she finally dropped down from the roof onto an east-facing balcony, slipped through an empty chamber and into the hall that led to Penelope's apartments. But motion to her left brought her around; one of the narrow servants' halls cut through the opposite wall, and several paces back in shadow, she saw Lemnos. He took another step back, glanced over his shoulder warily, then beckoned. Xena eyed the broad hall in both directions, checked the corridor behind him, then slipped into the gloomy opening.

"I need to talk to you," he said in a low voice.

She gazed at him thoughtfully for a long moment, finally nodded. *He's no threat—but he doesn't intend to be, either.* The fingers that had hovered near her dagger hilt relaxed. "Not here," she said finally.

"No—ah, where, then?"

"Kitchens?"

He was already shaking his head. "Rammis is down there, cutting up tubers."

"This way," she said with a jerk of her head back the way she'd come. Lemnos didn't like crossing the broad hall, and his forehead was shiny with sweat once they gained the deserted chamber and the door was closed behind him. "Keep your voice low," she said.

"Right," he replied grimly. But he was quiet for a very long moment, unblinking eyes fastened on her shoulder or her arm; she didn't think he was actually seeing her, though, and his first words proved it. "Marcus found me on the road outside Thebes, must be—ah, it was years ago. Too many of 'em," he said finally. "My father'd died a season earlier, the bakery was more work than I'd realized, and I wasn't making much money at it—not interested in working as hard as my father had, I know that now. I sold it to his oldest competitor, took the money, figured I'd head for Athens or Sparta—somewhere I could take up a sword, earn my keep as a city guard. I used to think that sounded exciting. In Thebes, though, it was all political, who your father was, who your father knew or could buy.'' He shrugged.

''That ain't important. I got jumped not far from the city gates, four guys almost as big as Metrikas took my money and my knife and were stomping me flat into the cart tracks when Marcus came along. Me, I was too dizzy by then to see much of what he did, but two of them guys wasn't going anywhere except across the Styx and the other two wasn't much more healthy. I said something—I forget what, something dumb like, 'Thanks for saving my life,' and he just laughed. After he helped me up and shoved my coins back in my belt, he said maybe he oughta teach me how to use that knife, *that* would save my life proper.'' He swallowed.

''He—yeah. Well, he did that, kept me with him for about a year, then I decided to go on to Sparta. I never did join the guard, of course. I saw him off and on over the years, your camp and all, then—well, that was it.'' He shrugged again, turned away, and surreptitiously blotted his eyes. ''I shoulda known you didn't—I mean—''

''It's all right,'' she said quietly. ''Leave it at that.''

He nodded sharply, turned back to face her. ''I'm not working for Draco anymore, not after today.''

''No? Why, tell me?''

He spread his hands in an exasperated shrug. ''I don't know what you're really up to here, Xena; I know you got Draco wondering in fourteen different directions, and probably all of 'em wrong—he's thinking with his loins at this point, Xena. You do that to him.''

''I know.''

He grinned suddenly. ''Yeah. I bet you do.'' The grin faded, was gone. ''I think Kalamos was still alive when they shoved his boat back out to sea; all his men but one were dead. Draco thought the whole thing was pretty funny, me believing what that little scum told Metrikas, and trying to gut you like that. I—look, I swear I—''

''Forget it, Lemnos; *you* weren't thinking, you did something stupid. You're a lucky little man, though, you're still alive. Kalamos manipulated you—so he's paid for it.''

''Yeah—guess he knew just how I'd react—''

''That temper got you in bad trouble last time I saw you, Lemnos, you gotta put a hard rein on it. But this about you and Draco—why, tell me? You don't want to stick with Draco anymore, go steal one of the fishing boats, head for the mainland. That's probably your best chance—''

''No,'' he broke in flatly. ''You're my best chance, Xena.'' She took a step back, leaned against the door and studied him. His dark, round face was as solemn as she'd ever seen it. ''Most of Draco's men look at you, they remember what you was like, back when. Those who've heard this new stuff about you—well, most of 'em figure anyone can try dropping their old bad ways, but it ain't gonna take. Draco'd like things to be that way in your case, because it makes you—available. So no matter what he hears, part of him's still gonna figure you tried good and couldn't hold on to it.'' Silence.

''Maybe you misread things, Lemnos,'' she said quietly. ''Maybe that's how I did things, and you're as good as dead right now.''

''Maybe—fine, if that's how it is. Man can't live forever, especially in Draco's company. I already told you, he ever finds a cook he likes better'n me, I'm bait.'' Another silence; she could almost hear the pulleys shifting as he tried to pull his thoughts together and convince her. "All right, you were Marcus' friend, too. Maybe he never told you, maybe he never had the chance—was a time, way back when, he tried turning his back on all *that*." He waved an arm in the general direction of the camp. "For him, it didn't work, and it made him kinda bitter, you know? That was one of the last times I ever saw him; he was drinkin' a lot and soured on everything. I figure, maybe I owe it to him, try for myself. Maybe I don't have any better luck than he did. You aren't laughing at me, are you?" he added suspiciously.

Xena shook her head. "I wouldn't laugh at you, Lemnos," she said softly. "Not for that." He would have said something else, but she held up a hand for silence. "All right," she said finally. "What're you up to for the next little while—say, between now and full dark?"

He shrugged. "Go put Draco's meal together, make sure Rammis got the fire built right in the big oven and get the bread baking—"

"Rammis," she muttered. "What do you usually do with him, after Draco's fed?"

"Tonight, I wager he don't make it to that point, Xena. He's got this headache. . . ." He fell silent as she chuckled. "I mean, he's only down there 'cause he's more scared of Draco replacing *him* than I'm scared of that. *Was* scared of that," he amended.

"He drink?" she asked. Lemnos nodded. "Fine. Feed him some of that red Draco had last night; he'll be out until morning. Once you're free, bring a tray—bread, fruit, anything—up to the queen's apartments for me. Anyone asks, say I asked you to feed me there—after the party this afternoon and Kalamos showing up, I'm still a little angry.

196

Draco asks about me, tell him the same thing but that maybe I'm gonna sleep awhile, see him later on. You and I talk when you bring the food.'' She checked the hall quickly, then held a hand against his chest as he would have hurried out. ''I'm trusting you, Lemnos. Maybe I'm crazy. But if you're planning a fancy betrayal, if you're lying to me, I swear it's the last lie you'll ever tell.''

''My tongue to the gods—and both my hands,'' he replied solemnly.

''That's it exactly.'' Her voice was hard, her eyes chilly. ''But it won't be the gods who cut them off. Got it?'' He swallowed hard, nodded once, and slipped past her, moving quietly and swiftly across the hall to gain the servants' corridor. She gazed after him for a very long moment, finally shrugged gloomily.

He might be lying—she didn't think he was. *Maybe because of that story of his. Marcus did try changing—twice.* It was still hard for her to deal with all of that, without her heart aching and her throat getting much too tight. *Forget that, all of it. It doesn't help Marcus and it won't help Penelope. Lemnos is a good baker, a good cook; he's not an actor.* She shoved herself away from the wall, quietly eased the door closed behind her, and slipped to the queen's rooms.

The queen was nowhere in sight; a lamp glowed warmly from the inner chamber and low voices came from that direction. Gabrielle stood on the east-facing corner balcony, her chin resting on her crossed arms; she was staring moodily at the darkening sky and growing fog. As Xena came up, she straightened and stretched, then sighed.

''You know, I'm beginning to feel like I'll never want to talk again, once we get out of here.''

Xena smiled. ''Oh—I'm not too worried about that.''

"Yeah, right." But Gabrielle smiled back before she glanced over her shoulder. The smile slipped. "She's really worried, mostly for Telemachus, about what's gonna happen when Draco decides to push for an answer and she tells him no. I've tried to tell her that isn't gonna happen, but— she doesn't argue or anything," the girl added helplessly. "She just smiles and nods, but I can tell she's still thinking that—"

"I know. After tonight, maybe she won't have to worry about it."

"I *knew* you'd come up with a plan," Gabrielle said excitedly; she lowered her voice cautiously as the warrior held up a hand and cast a meaningful glance into the main chamber. "I mean, you always do, and even if it's just a few of us—"

Xena shook her head. "Not you, Gabrielle. Not out there, anyway. That's Draco's army, not a bunch of thugs like those louts Krykus put together to stir up war between the centaurs and the Amazons."

Gabrielle looked momentarily offended; then her shoulders sagged and she sighed. "Yeah—I know, I can see the difference. Still, there has to be something I can *do*!"

Xena nodded and laid a hand on her friend's arm. "There is. Who do you think's going to be in here, the last barrier between Draco's army and Queen Penelope?" Gabrielle's eyes went wide and her jaw dropped. "Understand me, it should never come to that. Nowhere close. But nothing's ever perfect, plans can go wrong. I'm going to need Telemachus out there. It's going to be foggy and he knows this island as well as anyone; I don't."

"That leaves me," Gabrielle said; her voice was low and steady, but her eyes were still huge. She made an effort to smile. "Well—hey! It's nice to know I won't just be telling stories while you're out there kicking—"

198

"Right," Xena said hastily. "I'll get you a fighting staff."

"Great! I—ah—mmm. There's the queen," she said suddenly. Xena turned to see Penelope standing in the center of her room, a deep blue cloth wrapped around her arms. "Asked me to just call her Penelope," she added in a low voice. "Nice lady." Raising her voice again, Gabrielle pressed past the limp, sheer curtain. "I'm out here, Penelope, but there's not much to see anymore."

"There may not be for another day or so," Penelope replied; her eyes were momentarily warm, then wary as they moved past Gabrielle. She sighed faintly. "Oh, warrior; I wasn't certain who else was out there. I'm—I'd never seen such fogs before I came to Ithaca, and they still make me nervous. More than ever, now that there really *is* something out there."

Xena smiled. "Maybe after tonight, there won't be." The queen nodded, but she didn't look very reassured.

"Part of me says you're right, that my Odysseus would do the same thing—attack them, take them by surprise. The rest of me wants to hide in my rooms and wait for King Nestor to send an army and drive this Draco so far away he'll never return." She wound blue cloth around her arms and caught at her hair with both hands. "But if we wait, he might—"

She hesitated; Xena nodded grimly. "That's why we don't wait. Because the longer we wait, the more danger for you, your people—your son. And there's no guarantee King Nestor will send an army."

"He—" She slumped, turned away. After a moment she nodded. "He might not have the men, or the ships. He might weigh matters and decide my husband is dead and Draco would make a better ally than Odysseus' widow and his orphaned son."

"You're a sensible woman," Xena said after a moment. "Your husband is a fortunate man. So is your son."

"My son." Penelope shuddered, closed her eyes. "What—will he do tonight, to aid you?"

"Nothing like what your fears suggest," Xena replied softly. "I need him to rally your servants and your villagers, and then to help me move from place to place without getting lost. I'd be hard-pressed to manage in mere darkness; fog makes it harder." Silence. "He'll be with me; I won't let him do anything stupid."

"You—I know," Penelope said. "It's just that—I know my son."

"He'll do what I say, and when I tell him to do it. He knows your life and your freedom ride on that; that knowledge will tether him better than anything else." Silence.

"Penelope," Gabrielle said, "He's got a better chance to reach an age to grow his first beard, this way. I've seen Xena fight, and I know her; she doesn't waste lives. Certainly not someone as young and untrained as Telemachus."

"Yes, all right," the queen murmured; an abashed smile tugged at her lips. "And he'd be shamed if I didn't step aside and let him do what he must, isn't that so? I won't thwart you, warrior, and I won't hold my son back. I know if you weren't here to aid us, Telemachus might already be—be dead."

Gabrielle make a faint, anxious sound. Xena spoke over it. "That's exactly right. Remember how I met him last night; he was trying to steal a ship from under Draco's nose. If Metrikas had been wandering the ship instead of unconscious in the hold, the boy—well, his heart's in the right place, it's a good start." She hesitated, then spoke again. "This is a battle I don't intend to lose, or I wouldn't start it. But sometimes things happen. The wind could come

200

at the wrong time and clear the fog away; someone could betray us. Battle isn't ever exact.''

"I know. My husband's told me about battle, often enough.''

"Good. Then you know that—whatever I intend, things might go wrong.''

"I know that,'' Penelope replied steadily. Her eyes flicked toward the barred outer door. "That—isn't worth much, is it? Not under real attack. And all these vast windows, all those balconies . . .''

"It won't come to that,'' Xena said, as evenly. "It shouldn't. If it does, though—''

Penelope's chin came up; dark brown eyes met pale blue ones steadily. "I suppose you have a spare dagger?''

Gabrielle made a faint, unhappy noise; Xena chopped a hand at her for silence, then freed one of her numerous small blades and held it out, hilt first. "You're a brave woman as well as an intelligent one. Take it. Don't even think of using it unless there's no other choice.''

"Unless Draco or one of his men is—yes. I won't be premature, warrior. My son needs me, and so do my people. And when my husband returns . . .''

"He'll be a fortunate man,'' Xena said as she hesitated. Her head came around; Penelope, dagger in her outstretched hand, froze as a faint tap came at the outer door once again. Gabrielle started for it, but Xena pressed past her. "Stay with her; keep her from listening.''

"Oh?'' Gabrielle demanded curiously. "You're expecting—?''

"Bread,'' Xena replied, and crossed the room. She pressed one ear against the door. "Who's there?''

"Lemnos. That you, Xena?''

"Who else?'' she asked dryly, and moved the bar aside. Lemnos, his dark face set, edged sideways into the room, waited until she closed the door and rebarred it, then held out the tray. Xena crossed to the pillows she'd slept on the night before, dropped down, and gestured for him to join her. "You first," she added as he held out a plain wooden platter that held two of the fruit loaves, a small jug of wine—heavily watered, by the color of it—two mugs, a very small bowl of grapes and one dusty purple plum, and several strips of very plain, very well-crisped meat—swine, from the savory odor rising from the platter, and still quite hot. She smiled again as he hesitated, and one hand swept meaningfully over the food and drink. Lemnos poured wine into both cups, waited for her to take one before he drank from the other, let her place a random strip of meat across his palm. He balked only when she held out the plum.

"That was—I saved that out from Draco, just for you!" he protested.

"We'll share," she murmured. "Nice little bite, my friend."

Lemnos grumbled, took the plum, and bared surprisingly neat, white teeth to take nearly a third of it off the pit. He chewed vigorously, sighed happily, and swallowed. "Gods of harvest and sweet virgin Demeter, but I adore those!"

"You did that on purpose," Xena remarked pointedly. "Bringing one single plum so you could be assured of some of it. What—doesn't Draco share the good stuff?"

"What do you think?" he growled.

Xena laughed and gnawed the rest of the fruit from around the stone. "Your information's off, too. Demeter's got a daughter, if I recall, so she's hardly a—"

"Details, boring details," Lemnos replied cheerfully and with an airy wave of one hand. "I don't believe in gods, remember?"

Xena set aside the pit, picked up grapes, and began separating them from the stems. "You're giddy, little man. I hope that doesn't mean anything I'd rather not hear?''

His eyes met hers; he looked extremely indignant. ''As in, that I just poisoned you? Or that Draco's just outside the door with forty handpicked brutes to personally turn you into swine feed? Xena—I *prepared* that food! And I already swore—''

''Yeah, all right.'' She laid a hand over his mouth, silencing him. ''I'm still finalizing plans. That means I'm itchy, anything's gonna set me off, all right?''

''I know that,'' he said earnestly. ''Look, Draco's down in his private dining room glowering at the walls and swilling down wine like—well, he's either suspicious or just plain old displeased about something. Probably you.''

''Good. I want him off balance.''

''He's already drunk. And getting mean. You want him so off balance he spits me if I look at him wrong, then comes after you?''

''He won't,'' Xena said quietly. ''Because you're gonna go back down there and push another jug of that red on him, aren't you?''

''I'm gonna push—you know what he'll—?'' Before she could say anything, he held up both hands, shook his head, and sighed. ''All right. I find a way to pour more wine down him. And?''

''And then you wait for my signal—''

''Wait where and what signal?''

''I was coming to that,'' Xena replied with exaggerated patience. Lemnos cast her a crooked grin and ducked his head as if ready to ward off a blow. *Damn the little man, I like him in spite of myself,* she thought suddenly, and with an equally sudden lift of heart. ''Once Draco's out cold, you find a way to be on the portico steps, north side, next to the pillars—where you could normally see the fishing boats—and watch for a torch waved back, forth, back, then down. It might be a while. You wait, you stay alert, you see what?''

''Back, forth, back, then down. Pretty hard to copy by accident,'' he said. ''Steps, pillars, north side, torch. It's foggy out there,'' he added suddenly.

''The torchbearer will get close enough to the palace to see the pillars, so you'll see the torch.''

''Ah—right. And?''

''And you meet me at the foot of the portico steps, and we go out into the fog and—well, you'll see.''

''Sure, Xena. And what's Draco's army gonna be doing all this time?''

''Let me take care of them,'' Xena said evenly, though a smile was tugging at her own mouth. ''Just pray the fog holds.''

Lemnos chuckled. ''I hear it's gonna be so foggy out there tonight, a man couldn't tell his own mother from the Hydra.''

''Draco's mother might've *been* the Hydra,'' Xena told him, but her eyes were wicked. ''You with me, Lemnos?''

He sobered all at once. ''I'm with you, Xena. With you, and in honor of Marcus' shade. I may not survive this night, but at least I can face him down there and know I tried to do something right. Right?''

''Good man,'' she replied gravely, and held out the tray. Lemnos jumped to his feet, took it, and eased the bar away from the door with one elbow. ''One last thing,'' she added suddenly. ''You got any notion where Polyces sleeps?''

''Polyces—oh, him?'' He shifted the tray, held up one hand, index finger turned down. ''Yeah, sure. Why you wanna know?''

She merely smiled and waved him out, then barred the door behind him, and went swiftly across the room to ease out onto the northeastern-corner balcony. It was getting noticeably darker out there; little visible close to hand but darker shadows in foggy shade that were the nearest trees. Faint, ruddy light to the west; the last glow of sunset. A nearer rash of red dots—any man who could be, would be inside his tent on a night like this, or huddled around his fire. She could hear voices from the camp, but they were muted. An unpleasant smile touched her lips, was gone. *Draco. Next time you'll know better than to play this game with me. Next time—* If luck and planning went her way, there would never be a next time. Not for Draco or his men, not this side of Hades. She smiled grimly, then composed her face and went over to talk to Gabrielle, who was watching and making pleased little comments as Penelope worked on her weaving.

By the time it was fully dark, fog was beginning to creep into the queen's apartment and the old male servant was crouched in the center of the fire pit, pouring oil on a stack of wood, while two of the women draped heavier cloth over the windows. Penelope and Gabrielle had retired for the moment to the queen's inner chamber. Xena stepped onto the northern balcony and tested the air; it didn't seem particularly cool out here to her, just damp. From the edge of the curtain, it was nearly impossible to make out the balcony railing. She slipped back into the main chamber, crossed to the smaller one, and looked inside. Penelope was on her knees before a large, open chest, showing Gabrielle some of her linens. Both looked up as the warrior cleared her throat. "I'm going. Make certain of the door."

For answer, Gabrielle held up the thick staff and gave her a rather grim smile. Penelope looked perilously near tears, but she, too, managed a smile, then squared her shoulders and turned back to the chest.

• • •

Telemachus was waiting for her in the lower hall; she held a hand against her lips, warningly, and he nodded, then swung around and pointed down yet another of the servants' tunnels. She nodded, followed. It went north for several paces, bent west, dove down.

After some distance, he slowed and murmured, "It used to be for the cooks to bring in supplies from the boats, before my mother had the new kitchens built. Comes out most of the way to the shore." A short while later he stepped aside, indicating a thick line of brush. Xena edged through this with care, stopping once or twice to listen intently, but there was no one near—no sound but the very faint lap of water against stone.

She tugged at his ear as he came into the open. "Who knows about this?"

"Everyone who belongs on the island. *They* don't." He bent to pull the brush back into line. "You can't see it unless you know it's here."

"Good." She took a few steps into the open, avoiding the softly surging water by sound and luck both. Out here, she could hear the camp better; a few surly voices shouting at a group of sloppily drunken singers. At least, she thought it was meant to be singing.

Telemachus found her by feel, brought his face close to hers. "The swineherd's hut is that way."

"Lead on." They slowed once; someone was stumbling around on the rocks, cursing in a low voice. Moments later they heard sloshing sounds, boots scrabbling on shifting stone; the sounds retreated, heading back toward camp. Another fifteen or so paces, the beach bent northward and the red pinpoints of firelight faded, then were gone.

Telemachus stopped and touched her arm. "Headland just there," he breathed, pointing toward the darkness behind them.

It was quiet here, with the slope between them and the camp. All at once Xena could hear the faint snuffling of pigs. The prince set out, moving very slowly and cautiously. Xena came behind him, still listening for any sounds behind them; the stones at the waterline here were larger and slick. The pigs were louder now, and she could hear a faint trickle of running water.

A little light, all at once, a tiny flicker showed all around the warped, ancient planks of the swineherd's door. Inside the little hut: Socran, his two comrades from the ship, and a dozen more sturdy, grim-faced Ithacans. As the two came into the light, the gray-haired little sailor got to his feet. "He said we can help you deliver our homes and our queen. What do we do?"

It took time, getting back across the island, around the palace to the sandy beach where two fishing caïques and the ship lay. There were torches here; two shoved into the sand flanking the little open boats, another on the ship's tilted deck. By that flickering light, Xena could just make out the cloaked guard who leaned against the rail, and the spear point that cast a faint shadow across fog. Socran edged up behind her, tapped her hand, and indicated the fishing boats. She leaned closer, nodded once, then settled down to wait. Men passed her—most of those who'd followed Socran, armed with garden tools or wicked-looking fishermen's spears. One brought up the rear, an awkward bundle making a misshapen monster of him: nets.

She waited, listening closely. A faint grunt, a thump—no other sound. She reached for Telemachus, then; he had stayed at her left elbow the entire time, quiet, well behaved, waiting. *Better than I thought,* she admitted to herself. Up on the ship's deck, the guard sat up and appeared to be listening intently, but after a moment she could hear him settling against the rail once more. She touched the prince's hand, indicated the deck and the guard with a quick gesture. He nodded, eased past her. Xena took one wary look around—wasted, she thought; the fog was thick enough that without the torches she could have passed the ship at two arm-lengths and never seen it at all. It was silent here; any of Draco's men coming this way wouldn't have any reason to be quiet. She drew her dagger and headed for the low side of the ship.

Telemachus had just pulled himself onto the opposite rail; the little vessel shifted slightly as the guard leaped to his feet. "Oh—hello," the boy said brightly. "I didn't know anyone was out here, I was getting bored back at the palace, and I—"

The guard interrupted him; his voice was gravelly and menacing. "Get off the ship now, or I'll throw you off."

"Well—sure, all right. It's not like I could steal it, though, is it?"

"Off!" the guard snarled; the ship lurched again and he started to turn—too late. Xena's dagger hilt slammed into his temple and he dropped to the deck. Telemachus stepped down to join her.

"Good work," she said softly. "Bind him and gag him. I'm going to go see how—" But at that moment Socran appeared just below them, his face barely visible in the flickering torchlight. He jumped up and caught hold of the rail, pulled himself on board, then held down an arm for one of his comrades. The scrawny little tillerman was next; he glanced at the fallen guard, then met Xena's eyes and drew his hand across his throat twice. She nodded. Telemachus got to his feet. "You come with me," she whispered. "You men, get the boats out. You're sure you can bring them in where we decided?"

"Within a finger's reach," the tillerman replied softly. He dragged the bound guard along the deck, ready to toss in the hold once the ship was afloat and the deck level, then moved into the stern to unblock the tiller. A moment later four men leaned into the bow and shoved the sturdy little vessel across soft sand and into the water.

Xena moved across rutted sand; the fishing boats were already gone. One torch had fallen over and was nearly out; the other flickered over two huddled, very dead men. She smiled grimly, turned back as Telemachus came up behind her. His face was expressionless, but she could guess how much that was costing him. After a moment he turned away and drew a deep, shuddering breath. The warrior walked him back away from the torches; fog covered the bodies after only a few steps.

A faint splashing and two low thumps just ahead of them and just to the east: men moving quickly through the low surge to jump onto the ship. More faint splashing and a creak as the oars moved stealthily into the water and the sailors began the job of backing blind into deeper water.

The prince touched her arm and leaned close, but she never heard what he was going to say; her hand clamped down on his fingers and she thrust him behind her as a faint clatter of stones came from somewhere up the path that led to the small village. "Farther out of the light," she whispered.

Telemachus backed away from her, turned and simply vanished. Heavy boots came down hard on stones, sand creaked as someone stalked toward the boats. Xena drew her sword and waited. A bare moment later, ruddy torchlight shone on a broad, long blade and wild red hair.

Metrikas stopped cold and stared down at the bodies, then wildly toward the fog-shrouded sea. He drew a breath to yell; Xena smiled and stalked into his line of vision. "Hello, Metrikas. How's your head?"

He roared wordlessly, raised his blade back over his

head, and leaped for her. She ducked under the blurring downslash with ease, closed the distance between them, reversed her sword, and slammed the hilt into his chin; his head went back with a snap, and he staggered, but kept his grip on his own sword. "I'll gut you, woman," he swore in a hoarse whisper.

"Like that? Don't make me laugh." She parried four wild swings, slapped his cheek hard with the flat of her blade.

"Traitor," he snarled, and changed his attack. Half a dozen hard, fast thrusts got him no further than the roundhouse swings had. He dropped back a pace, drew a long-bladed dagger, and began to circle, both blades describing intricate patterns in the air before her. She pivoted on one heel, watching, and drew her own dagger, her sword utterly still. Metrikas leaped; Xena sidestepped deftly, slammed one booted foot into his backside. He went flat, but bounded up again. She smiled, waited for him to scoop up his dagger, watched his eyes. He might think his movements surprises, but his whole body gave him away. *Slow and stupid,* she thought. He leaped again, but pulled to one side at the last moment and aimed a short, chopping blow at the side of her neck. She spun away, using his sword for momentum, and brought her sword hilt up as she came around. This time it cracked into his temple; he staggered, swore—but didn't fall.

He'd lost what little style he had with that last blow; now he was swinging wildly, hoping to overpower her with sheer size or maybe somehow to connect if he aimed enough slashes her way. He wasn't going to give up or go down, and any moment now he might realize all he had to do was yell for reinforcements. She sighed, blocked his sword high and away with her dagger, and lunged. It took him high in the belly and angled up; Metrikas swayed for a very long moment, staring blankly down at the sword hilt. His knees buckled and he fell, face first, onto the torch.

It went out, plunging the area into utter darkness. Xena swore under her breath, listened for a long moment. No sound except the water and somewhere behind her Telemachus' high, panting breath. Metrikas lay utterly limp; she swore again, rolled him over with her foot, retrieved her blade and the torch. Gutted—but there was still a glowing coal in there.

"Telemachus," she whispered.

"I—I'm here." Trembling, cold fingers found her shoulder. She clamped them to her arm briefly, then passed him the torch.

"You're doing fine. Can you get this burning again?"

"I can try." His voice sounded a little better this time. It took more time than she would have liked, but the beach was still quiet when he finally managed to blow a little life into the torch. "It got wet down the side," he began, then swallowed.

"I know it did." With Metrikas' blood. Great.

Telemachus swallowed again, then got a better grip on the smoldering thing and led the way back toward the palace.

13

Xena was effectively blind; she finally swore under her breath and caught hold of the prince's tunic as they sped away from the beach. He went straight for a distance, then slowed, and she could hear him whispering to himself— counting paces. He turned slightly, moving inland. The ground sloped uphill, just enough to make swift movement difficult; she brought her knees up a little higher and kept up with him.

The boy finally stopped and went to one knee. "Palace," he breathed against her ear. "Another forty paces, that way," he added, and took her hand, held it out a little to her left. He huddled over the torch, cupped his hands around his mouth, and began to blow on the ruddy embers. They responded, slowly at first. Black, sooty smoke was suddenly everywhere; Xena turned away to keep from coughing, drew a cautious breath of damp, foggy night. Flame licked at the tightly wrapped branch center, snapped once so loudly Telemachus jumped and nearly dropped it, then settled in to burn brightly. He stood cautiously, listened a long moment, then moved the torch, back and forth, back again, sharply down. Silence, then the sound of sandaled feet slapping across the portico.

"Lemnos," Xena whispered. Telemachus nodded—she could barely make out the movement, near as the boy was, even with the ruddy torchlight shining on his hair. "Douse that again—not all the way." He nodded once more, squatted down. The light flickered once brightly and then was gone. When he stood, only a bright ember the size of a small coin was visible, and of Telemachus only the least hint of pale face against the very gloomy night. "Go," she urged. "Palace steps."

An anxious Lemnos was waiting at the very foot of them, one hand braced against the lowermost column. He jumped and caught his breath in a faint squeak when she came up behind him. "Shhh!" she warned softly. "Keep it down, little man."

"I can't see—" he began in a hoarse whisper.

"So? No one can see you, either. And if you shut up, they can't hear you." He nodded, then jumped again as Telemachus stepped into the open. "That's the prince."

Lemnos didn't like it; she could tell. He kept his mouth shut, though, even when she asked, "Where do I find Polyces?" For answer, he took her shoulders and turned her toward the camp, then stepped in front of her and shoved one of his many loose leather ties into her left hand. Telemachus shifted his grip on the torch and followed close behind.

After a few dozen paces Lemnos stopped. Damp rocks rose on two sides of them, very close; the air reeked of dead fish and wet moss, and tiny airborne insects were everywhere. "All right," he whispered. "No one comes down *here* even during the day. I don't wanna go in completely blind." A brief, tense silence, which he again broke. "Draco's out cold; so's Rammis, I won't be missed. You

213

didn't mention the boy. Tell me what's up.''

It wasn't worth arguing. ''He's helping. This isn't going to be a real fight, Lemnos. Polyces is stupid; he'll believe what I tell him. Besides, when he and his men sneak down to the western shore by the swineherd's, they'll hear oars, they'll believe it's really Odysseus. You're gonna stick with me until we're done with the camp, and *then* you go back to the palace, wake Draco. You come back here—this place, close as you can. You can find it?''

He sighed faintly. ''I can find it.''

''Good. I'll be here, waiting for you.''

''Meronias ain't gonna believe you. Why the west shore?''

''So we can keep the fighting away from the palace and the village.''

''No—I mean, he's gonna ask why, you got an answer?''

''I don't owe Meronias an answer,'' she replied crossly. Silence. ''Once they're both in position, the fun part begins. I'll get to Polyces, tell him Odysseus outflanked him and he's about to get shoved back into the sea; you get to Meronias, tell him you just saw a beach full of ships and Greeks.''

''This is lunacy,'' he grumbled.

''You agreed to it earlier, Lemnos—we're wasting time out here! This is our best chance of taking on Draco and two hundred men and coming out alive. You got a better idea?''

''Idea—that ain't my job, ideas. Meronias'll suspect something and kill me.''

''He won't. Two things are on our side—drunk men just dragged awake and this fog. We keep both sides thinking the other's Odysseus and his army until it's too late.''

''Lunacy,'' Lemnos repeated. ''You meet up with Marcus before I do, down there, you tell him I tried.'' He gripped her fingers and forearm with both of his surprisingly well-muscled hands, then transferred his grip to her shoulders and turned her around. "Polyces sleeps near the hospital tent, and most of his fellas are grouped around him. Meronias—he's still near the east end; last I saw, his company was staying close to him, Metrikas been causing a split between the two."

"Good. Wait," she added, and shifted Metrikas' heavy swordbelt from her shoulder, then leaned toward Telemachus. "Give me your hand." She eased the sword and belt into it.

"What—?" he began, startled. She clapped her hand over his mouth, removed it as soon as he nodded faintly. "It's—the big man's, isn't it?"

"It's yours now. For defense *only* tonight, though—got that?"

His whisper sounded strained: "I understand."

"You won't need to blood it. Defense only—swear it."

"By my father," he murmured gravely, and shifted around so he could slide the enormous belt over his head.

She eased around and laid a hand on Lemnos' arm. He was sweating freely, despite the cool air. "Go," she murmured against his ear, and rose with him.

Except for an occasional ear-rattling snore, the camp was quiet; what few fires there were had burned low or gone out altogether. A few men lay sprawled around them; they'd have been hard to see on an ordinary night, and in the fog, they made walking particularly hazardous, but Lemnos moved quickly and surefootedly. He paused once, not far into the camp, pointed out a tent. She slowed, then stopped. Plain tent: no markings, no banners. Lemnos touched her arm and nodded—she could just make out that much by the faint light of a distant fire. Something pungent here—something burning—nothing else to tell this place from another. They continued on; the odor died. *He'd better be able to find it again,* she thought grimly.

Lemnos was practically trembling as they eased past the last of the tents on this side of camp; then a small open space, the faint warmth of a fire burned down to cinders. More tents. Someone lay across the entry to the plain little tent belonging to Polyces; guard perhaps, but he was breathing heavily and the air around him reeked of ale. She smiled faintly and stepped over him. Telemachus stood uncertainly where he was, sword clutched two-handed; she gestured broadly for both of them to back away, then slipped past the flap.

It wasn't quite as dark inside the tent; someone had left a torch stuck in the ground near the center and it still put out a faint light. Enough for her to find Polyces, who lay fully clothed on his back, arms and legs sprawled, mouth wide open. Her own mouth twisted; then she went to one knee and pinched his earlobe, her free hand ready to cover his mouth. The trick worked, though. His eyelids fluttered and he was awake.

"Polyces, Draco sent me to get you—shhhhh, keep it quiet," she added as he strove to sit up. "There was a boat late this afternoon, a spy—" His eyebrows came together. "Meronias didn't tell you? Wants all the credit with Draco for himself and his company, I guess. Odysseus is back; the boat was his, and his ships are on the way, they're gonna land while it's still dark and attack the camp as soon as it's barely light."

He was silent for a long moment, his mouth hanging open once more. "Odysseus! They said he was—"

"Dead? He's not. The little man in the boat said he found out on the mainland that Draco's here; he's out for blood, Polyces. Everyone's blood."

"We gotta—" He stopped, thought again, finally blinked up at her. "What *do* we gotta do, Xena?"

"Get your men—don't bother with Meronias' men, Polyces. When I heard the trick he'd pulled on you, I came to let you know so you could take out the Greeks yourself. There won't be that many of 'em and they won't expect you. Get down to the western shore, close to the swineherd's, and wait."

"Swineherd's—Greeks—yeah, right. Good idea. Ah—" His eyes followed her as she rose. "Where you going?"

"Back to Draco. There's any change in plans, I'll come tell you myself."

"Hey—that's good of you." He stumbled to his feet, felt around the bedding for his sword, then along the ground for bow, arrows, and three knives on a leather armband. "Some guys like Metrikas kept telling us all this stuff about you, but I never believed it for a minute, Xena."

"I knew you wouldn't," she purred, and ran a hand along his jaw. He blinked and turned a deep red. "Get your men out there fast as you can, get them settled in. It's not that much longer until the sun comes up."

The guard outside was still sleeping; Telemachus materialized at her left shoulder, Lemnos at her right. She took hold of the boy's sleeve, one of the little cook's loose straps; the fog seemed thicker than ever, and it was beginning to feel cold. Lemnos led them back the way they'd come. Twenty or so steps into the other side of the camp, he stopped, pointed. One plain, ordinary tent flanked by other ordinary tents—but she could smell the same acrid smoke as before. Not quite as strong as it had been.

There was a rough bench covered in old, tattered maps and a flickering oil lamp holding them down. Meronias had fallen asleep across the maps; the smell she'd noticed was a long hair or two that had fallen across the wick. *He's lucky that's all that burned.*

His luck wasn't going to hold. She stood very quietly for some moments, listening. Someone out beyond the tent was snoring in an irregular fashion, but under that she could hear distant, stealthy movement; the muted clink of armor, the creak of leather—someone grumbling, then falling silent as someone else violently shushed him. The collection of noises faded even more, moving downhill, toward the water. Xena remained where she was for another very long moment, then drew her dagger and grabbed the sleeping man's shoulder with her free hand.

"Meronias, wake up," she whispered against his ear. "And stay quiet!"

He was a better soldier than Polyces; he came awake with a violent start, but the order against his ear kept him silent. He blinked, rubbed his eyes, eyed the dagger in a fuddled fashion, then looked up to see who held it. The eyes narrowed. "Xena. Why're you here?"

"Draco sent me."

"You're lying," he said flatly; his eyes moved back to the dagger. "Where is he?"

"The palace—"

"Why'd he send you?" And before she could answer he said, "You're lying to me."

She shifted the dagger to her other hand and leaned back against the bench. "Fine—go ask him yourself. I'm sure he'll like being interrupted just now."

"Interrupted—" Meronias laughed sourly. "At what? You're *here*. Or maybe he finally made it into the queen's bed?" He smiled unpleasantly.

Her smile matched his; her eyes were chill. "I'll remember that, Meronias," she replied softly. "He's down in the cellar, interrogating a Greek who tried to sneak ashore to-

218

night.'' The captain blinked again, shook his head. ''Greek,'' she offered. ''He's Odysseus' man—his spy.''

''Odysseus—'' Meronias struggled to his feet. ''He's here?''

''Shut up, sit still, and listen,'' she snarled. He eyed the dagger, settled back onto his stool. ''Not here—yet. He's on his way. Draco says he's landing before it gets light after the tide slacks, down on the west shore.'' Silence; the captain drove a hand through his hair, looked around the tent, and scooped up his helm. ''He said for you to get your men together, get down there, and surprise them when they land.''

''Surprise,'' Meronias mumbled. He stalked over to the tent flap, looked out, let it fall with a mumbled oath. ''Man can't see two paces in that! It's a trick—''

''The Greek spy wasn't in a mood to play tricks when *I* left,'' Xena replied evenly. ''Odysseus knows the weather around here; his men know the waters. Easy for them to sneak ashore and attack the camp at first light.''

''Easy—'' He set the helm aside, picked up a wineskin, eyed it thoughtfully, then let it drop. ''Yeah. After a night like this, it'd be easy enough.'' He cast her a suspicious, sidelong glance as if to see how she took his reply. ''All right. Where you gonna be?''

''Back at the palace,'' she said. ''You don't need or want me here.''

His lips twisted. ''I don't much care. Draco wants you, fine. But my brother don't like you. Things'll work out better if you stay away from him.''

''Meronias, you have my word on that,'' she said very softly, and left before he could think of anything else to say. She paused just outside the flap; from the sounds within, he was fumbling for his weapons. Telemachus was at her elbow, sword in one hand, the belt trailing from the other. She caught hold of his shoulder and tugged, then turned to Lemnos and nodded once, sharply. The little man turned and ran. Telemachus eased around her and started for the shoreline and the wet rocks.

It shouldn't have been so easy, or worked so well, she thought sometime later. Polyces had been as gullible as ever, though; Lemnos had somehow managed Draco, and the orders the warlord shouted from the palace steps had only increased the confusion. Telemachus threw himself into things more than she wanted, but she had to admit it was effective; that high boy's voice couldn't have been anyone else but the prince, shouting, "Father! This way, they're trying to cut you off!" And later, from an entirely different angle, "This way, Father! Straight on to the palace!" Lemnos, some distance from her, "They're running for the boats, cut them off!"

She kept quiet most of the time, unless she could find Polyces. After a while, when the fighting sprawled all across the beach, two or three men battling another two or three and the shoreline and incoming tide littered with wounded and dead, she began moving from fight to fight, putting in a sword, a foot, or a fist and adding to the confusion.

It was still nearly impossible to make anyone out; in the dark and fog one armed man looked much like another. Telemachus' voice came in rapid succession from half a dozen different locations and she could only hope he was being careful about getting too close to any one group of men. He still sounded healthy, though. Lemnos came up beside her, and nearly got run through before she heard his voice. She pulled him away, back into the surf, as Draco went roaring past them, yelling for Polyces and then for Meronias. Someone shrieked in pain and fell, covering her

220

in spray. Lemnos was gone when she came ashore and she could hear him somewhere down the beach, yelling for Meronias to block the shore. "They're breaking through, heading for the palace! Get down here by the water, help us!" Meronias, west of her, cursed angrily, and moments later she could hear men storming down the beach.

It couldn't last forever—but her luck held for longer than she'd dared hope. The fog was still thick as the first gray light eased across the beach; one swordsman, his face unrecognizable under a layer of blood and sand, staggered forward to peer into the face of the spear-armed man he'd been fighting. "Amnius? Is that you?"

"Bezanian? What's going on?" Xena tugged at Lemnos' arm and dragged him back along the beach, toward the palace.

"Where's the boy?" the cook demanded in a whisper.

"Supposed to run for it," she muttered. "He should be—"

"Right here." Telemachus sounded a little winded, and his sword bumped on the ground behind him. "How—many—left?" he panted as they skirted the rocks.

"We'll find out. Fewer than there were earlier." Behind them, she could hear wounded men wailing, someone cursing in a high, furious voice; Draco's bellow over all. She couldn't make out what he was shouting. They gained the palace steps without incident, then the portico. Xena drew a deep breath, stopped to look back the way they'd come. The fog was still too thick to see anything beyond the lower steps and the farthest column, but it was noticeably lighter. "All right. You both did good. Go on up to the queen's quarters, make sure no one tries to get in there."

Telemachus hesitated; Lemnos nodded. "Sure. Where you gonna be, you mind my asking."

"Right here. Somebody's gotta talk to Draco and let him know it's over."

"I *knew* it." Rammis' reedy voice came from behind them, and when she turned, blade in hand, the little Egyptian was just inside the doorway, a long-bladed knife in each hand. "Lemnos, you rat, Draco's gonna reward me for spilling on you."

Lemnos tried to smile. "Hey—it ain't what you think, Rammis!"

"Back off, Lemnos," Xena said coolly. She drew her dagger and stalked forward. "You won't have to tell Draco a thing, little man. Even if you're able. But he's gonna be down that way awhile, counting dead men. *His* dead men." Rammis bit his lower lip, backed up a pace. His eyes shifted one way, back again. "He's lost the island, Rammis, even if he doesn't know it yet. You know what side that puts *you* on, little man?" Silence. He took another cautious step away from her. "You're on the losing side, little man."

"It's a lie—" he began, all bluster and narrowed, frightened eyes.

"You tell Draco that; he'll be in a good mood, glad to see his old friend Rammis. . . ." She was ready when he threw the knives; her dagger came up and deflected both. He was already sprinting down the hall when she snatched up her shakra and sent it spinning after him. The shakra, a razor-sharp circle of steel, ricocheted off one wall and sped straight for Rammis. Lemnos gasped, but the sharp edge of the weapon only grazed Rammis, hitting him instead with the heavy inner circle. He tripped, staggered two paces, flailing wildly for balance, and crashed headfirst into the wall. Lemnos cringed as the shakra sailed back toward them, but Xena stepped in front of him and easily took it down from the air.

Lemnos ran down the hall, Telemachus on his heels; Xena followed, stopping to pick up the Egyptian's neat, leaf-shaped blades.

"You didn't have to do that, Xena," the cook said as she came up behind him.

"He was your friend, Lemnos. And I told you before, he's not worth killing." Lemnos shook his head.

"I don't understand you. Man would think you didn't like killing."

"Maybe I don't. Maybe I'll explain it to you one of these days."

"We ever get the chance," he said. "Maybe I'd like that." He tugged at Telemachus' sleeve. "Come on, Prince; we got a lady to protect."

Telemachus cast Xena an abashed grin, eased the heavy strap over his shoulder, and settled the sword more comfortably before following.

Xena watched them go, then strode back toward the portico; there was more light now, perhaps a little more visibility. Plenty of noise well down the sand, but no one in sight. She settled her shoulders against the outside wall and leaned back to wait.

The sun was casting watery light all around her when Draco stormed up the steps; his right shoulder was bloody, the sword clutched in his left hand red to the hilt. Some distance behind him, Meronias came limping, one worn-looking man holding him up, another half dozen or so behind them.

Xena held her ground, waited. Draco stopped just short of her and glared for a very long moment, then pointed back the way he'd come. "That has your sign, all of it; it reeks of you."

She smiled faintly. "That all you could find on their feet?"

"Another fifteen who might make it—maybe." He was quiet for a moment, narrowed eyes studying her face. "Why?"

She shrugged. "Queen Penelope already has a husband, and I decided I don't want a kingdom. Good enough?" Silence. She broke it, finally. "You've lost most of your army; it's over, Draco. Even if you beat me, here and now, you haven't got enough men to hold this island." Another silence. His face was unreadable. "But you won't beat me. Best way for you is to pack up and take one of the boats out there, go. Back to the mainland. You can take your tents, all the stuff you brought over here, but go. Today." Her eyes moved beyond him, came back to his face. "That's your army? I can take that. And you."

He looked briefly murderous, but he let the sword drop. "Last time you'll ever pull a trick on me, Xena. I wouldn't trust your word for anything—not even if you said the sea is wet." He drew a breath, would've said something else, but Meronias came up behind him. His armor hung in tatters, and blood ran down his fingers.

"Where's my brother?"

She jerked her head to the right. "Up where the boats were last night."

He took a step forward; Draco's strong arm swept out and held him back. "I'll kill you for that."

She shook her head. "No, Meronias, you won't. Not today, not now. That's the kind of talk that got *him* dead."

Meronias' eyes were black with hatred. "Not today, no. Someday—someplace and time when you least expect it, I'll be there. You'll pay."

Not worth answering; her mouth twisted briefly as Draco

snarled at him and he backed down the stairs, then let his man lead him back toward the camp.

"I've got things inside," Draco said finally. He sheathed his sword, spread both hands wide. "All right if I get those?"

"All right," she said, and stepped aside to let him pass.

He was quiet all the way to Odysseus' private banquet hall. Once inside, Xena leaned against the table, arms folded, watching as he gathered up a shirt, several worked leather straps, a small shield, and piled them on the opposite end. One boot followed; he bent down to look under the table, retrieved the other. "You won't believe me," he said. "I'm gonna tell you anyway. Last night, I sat in here, thinking about things." He glanced at her, looked back down at the boot rather thoughtfully, then settled one hip on the edge of the table. "This ain't no kind of life for a man like me. Living in a palace is boring, there's nothing to do, and it's real bad for my men. You saw them, that camp: they drink and they fight each other, they bicker like old village women. Back on the mainland, that was a bunch to be proud of, Xena. You'd never have pulled off a trick like last night." He swung the boot, dropped it onto the table with the other. "So, sure, I'll take my men and go. You stay here and guard the queen, though. A season of that and you'll be an easy target yourself."

"Maybe I can find more to do with my time than eat nasty little bits of food and drink," she said.

"Yeah." He laughed shortly. "You keep Lemnos—don't bother to lie for him, I know that little rat was out there helping you. Besides, I'm going back to real food I can eat with my men." His lips twisted. "What you left me."

"You'll have fun putting together a new army," she told him. "Just keep it away from Ithaca."

"Or—? Never mind, save the threats." He grinned and gathered up his things. "I'll tell you, though; it's fate, you and me. One of these times, it's gonna work."

"Keep thinking that, Draco," she replied. "If it makes you happy, you just keep thinking that."

Rammis hadn't moved. She nudged him with her foot and said, "Take all your things. That includes him."

"I won't take him far," Draco replied; he cast the unconscious little Egyptian a chill glance, then stepped over him.

"That's your business and his problem. I told Lemnos I wouldn't kill him, and I meant that."

Sunshine reflected blindingly off fog; she could just make out the outlines of the nearest tents. A faint breeze lifted the hair from her forehead. "Nice day for a sail," she remarked. He nodded.

"Should be. You putting us all in one of those open fishing boats?"

"No. Leave the ship up on shore; they can retrieve it later."

"Maybe. If I'm still in a good mood when we make land." He took one step down, turned and looked up at her. "I'll see you around, Xena. And watch out for Meronias; you've made a bad enemy."

"I'll survive that," she said. He walked off; she watched him until he disappeared among the tents. Air shifted; fog drifted past in gray tatters, settled down again. Not before she'd seen bodies piled all along the sand, two men dragging another out of the water. Up the other way, movement caught her eye. Meronias and two men, working to build a pyre—probably wood from one of the ships they'd sunk when they first arrived. She remained where she was, watching the western shore and the northern one. When flame shot from Metrikas' pyre, she turned and went back inside.

Rammis still lay flat and insensible; she caught hold of his ankles and dragged him outside, down the steps, then took the main staircase to the second floor and the queen's apartments.

Epilogue

It was quiet and warm on the mainland, dusty among the aging and neglected olive trees. Gabrielle turned back to look at the southern road and the harvested field beyond it where skinny boys were grazing the village Isos' sheep. She stretched out to peer as far south as she could, but finally gave it up and hurried to catch up with Xena, who was leading her horse around the fallen trunk that still blocked the path. Someone had been hacking at it again, but they still had a long way to go. "I can't see Telemachus on the road, they must really be moving," she said.

"He wants to make Pylos in three days, he'll have to hurry," Xena replied.

"Well, I just hope King Nestor will *do* something to help."

"Maybe. If appearances count, old Nestor will be impressed enough to aid him. He looks downright heroic. Queen Penelope's proud of him. But she isn't counting on anyone's help."

"I know. Poor lady, you'd think that—well, at least you left her better protected than she was. Better fed, too."

"Hard to make overnight fighting men out of sailors and swineherds. They'll manage against any ordinary threat. And Lemnos swore to me he'd keep doing what he could to teach them."

"When he's not making funny little bits of food. Who'd have thought Queen Penelope would *like* that? I mean—raw *fish?* In fancy little—"

"Yeah. I know." Xena smiled at her friend, then turned her attention to the trail once more. "Anyway, Draco's men will spread the word of what happened out there; it'll be a while before any of that kind are fool enough to test their own fortune."

"Well, I hope so. You know, Telemachus is really *good* with a sword, isn't he?"

"He's quick; he should be good by the time he's grown."

Gabrielle sighed. "I hope his father gets to—well, you know."

"I know. There's a chance."

"And Penelope—but maybe her luck changed with this."

"It could have been worse," Xena said. They came out of the woods, into the open, skirted the midwife's shrine, and headed for the well.

"Worse—than *Draco?*"

"Sure. She's a queen, a whole kingdom to herself, the rumor of great wealth. Some nobleman might've shown up with his whole entourage, eaten her out of house and home."

"Or more than one nobleman—I've heard stories like that." Gabrielle splashed water on her face, then shook her head to scatter the drops. "Oh, that feels wonderful. I'm hot already, and it's gonna be a *long* afternoon. Sure—Penelope would be obligated to offer hospitality, and once you do *that,* especially if you're royal or noble, you can't get rid of the guest until he wants to go.''

"I'd wager Odysseus wouldn't let that bother *him.*"

"No—but Penelope." Gabrielle sighed and splashed her face again before they turned away to cross the meadow. "She's such a nice person. Still, if someone tried to marry her, she'd never give in to *that.*"

"She might not have a choice," Xena reminded her.

"Oh—sure she would. Remember the story I told her? About weaving all day and picking it out all night?"

Xena laughed shortly. "That's a *story,* Gabrielle. It's a nice story, but it would never work in real life."

"Well—maybe not." Gabrielle was quiet all the way down the ravine, but once they reached the road again, she clapped her hands together and said, "Well! So, what's next?"

"I should send a message to King Menelaus—"

"Who doesn't deserve it."

"No, but it might keep him and his men away from Ithaca."

"Oh. That's a good point," Gabrielle said promptly. "But you can send the message from just about anywhere."

"Yeah." They ambled down the road in companionable silence. Late-afternoon sun cast a golden glow across the cart tracks, and a bee droned around them twice before moving slowly off into the woods. "So, was there somewhere in particular you wanted to go?"

"Sure—Athens."

"Oh?" Xena looked at her companion across the horse's broad back and raised an eyebrow. "Why Athens? You want to see Orion?"

"Homer, remember? No—well, yes, actually, but that's not why. The autumn festival and the footraces, remember? I know I told you about the footraces."

Xena laughed. "Gabrielle. You can't go into the Olympic grounds unless you're male or a priestess."

"It's not Olympics—and I really don't understand," Gabrielle said, "why it's such a big deal. I mean, who hasn't seen naked men? But no, this is in honor of Artemis, some special thing, only every other year. And before we left Athens this last time, I heard *Atalanta* was gonna be there for the next races!"

Xena's mouth quirked sourly; Gabrielle, intent on her story, didn't notice. "Oh. How wonderful."

"Yeah! It's gonna be great! She can outrun just about anybody, and she's just this wonderful virgin-hero type— well, you know," she added confusedly but her eyes were shining.

Atalanta. I haven't seen her in over a year, Xena thought grimly. The last meeting hadn't been pleasant. But Gabrielle was so excited over the prospect. *It might have been my fault as much as Atalanta's that we parted on less than amicable terms.* "All right, Gabrielle. We'll go to Athens, see the races. I figure after that sea voyage out to Ithaca, I owe you at least that much."

"Oh—oh, boy!" Gabrielle tipped her head back and shouted; her voice echoed from the distant treetops. "Great golden apples, this is gonna be absolutely *terrific*!"

HERCULES

THE LEGENDARY JOURNEYS™

__BY THE SWORD 1-57297-198-3/$5.99

When a mighty sword is stolen by marauders, it is up to Hercules to recover it—though he may be in for more than just a fight with ambitious thieves.

A novel by Timothy Boggs based on the Universal television series created by Christian Williams

Coming in December '96 : SERPENT'S SHADOW

XENA

WARRIOR PRINCESS™

__THE EMPTY THRONE 1-57297-200-9/$5.99

In a small village, Xena and her protégé, Gabrielle, discover that all the men in town have disappeared without a trace. They must uncover the truth before they too disappear...

A novel by Ru Emerson based on the Universal television series created by John Schulian and Robert Tapert

Coming in January '97: THE HUNTRESS AND THE SPHINX

VISIT THE PUTNAM BERKLEY BOOKSTORE CAFÉ ON THE INTERNET:
http://www.berkley.com